PIP DRYSDALE

THE STRANGERS WE KNOW

Published by Simon & Schuster

New York   London   Toronto   Sydney   New Delhi

SIMON &
SCHUSTER
CANADA

A Division of Simon & Schuster, Inc.
166 King Street East, Suite 300
Toronto, Ontario M5A 1J3

Originally published in Australia in 2019 by Simon & Schuster (Australia) Pty Limited
Suite 19A, Level 1, Building C, 450 Miller Street, Cammeray, NSW 2062

This Simon & Schuster Canada edition November 2023

SIMON & SCHUSTER CANADA and colophon are trademarks of Simon & Schuster, Inc.

For information about special discounts for bulk purchases, please contact Simon & Schuster Special Sales at 1-800-268-3216 or CustomerService@simonandschuster.ca.

Manufactured in the United States of America

10 9 8 7 6 5 4 3 2 1

Library and Archives Canada Cataloguing in Publication
Title: The strangers we know / Pip Drysdale.
Names: Drysdale, Pip, author.
Description: Simon & Schuster Canada edition.
Identifiers: Canadiana (print) 20230175287 | Canadiana (ebook) 20230175333 |
    ISBN 9781668021491 (softcover) | ISBN 9781668021507 (EPUB)
Classification: LCC PR6104.R97 S73 2023 | DDC 823/.92—dc23

ISBN 978-1-6680-2149-1
ISBN 978-1-6680-2150-7 (ebook)

For you

We all have a wound so deep the air can't get to it,
a wound that explains everything.

Pilot

SATURDAY, 25 FEBRUARY 2017 (9.07 PM)

It was a Saturday night at Electric House and my life was about to change forever. I didn't know it yet, of course, just like how Julia Roberts in *Pretty Woman* didn't expect Richard Gere to pull up in that Lotus Esprit. Or, you know, how Marvin in *Pulp Fiction* didn't expect to get his face blown off. It can always go either way, right?

It was raining and cold that night, so the heating was on and the windows had misted up. I was supposed to be meeting my best friend Tess for a drink; I hadn't been out much since "The Breakup" and she'd said if I didn't practise doing my eye makeup and flirting with someone soon I'd probably forget how. So I'd strapped myself into my prettiest dress, highlighted the shit out of my cheekbones and forced myself to go. But now here I was, alone at the bar, staring down at her text message: *Work emergency. 20 mins. Sorry. xxxx*

I looked up and around, searching for my bartender: *My drink, I need my drink.*

That's when I first saw him: Oliver.

Watching me.

He had thick, dark hair, a chiselled face, broad shoulders and was wearing a white t-shirt under a dark dinner jacket. He was leaning on the bar. Alone. And I remember thinking: *Very James Dean.* Our eyes met and I thought he'd do what people usually do when you catch them looking at you: look away. Stare down at *his* phone. Pretend it hadn't happened. But he didn't. Instead he smiled this big, perfect smile. And, for a split second, I awkwardly smiled back.

But then insecurity hit: *Shit. He's probably smiling at someone behind me.*

My face grew hot, my blood raced—*How embarrassing*—and I quickly stared back down at my phone, frowning at the screen like something very important had just come in.

Ba-boom, ba-boom, ba-boom.

It's okay, Charlie. Just pretend it didn't happen. You're an actress—you can do this.

Calmly, I looked up again, my face set to neutral as I watched the slowest bartender in the world fiddle around with lemons and limes near the far wall. I refused to look back at Oliver—that would just make it worse—but there he was in my peripheral vision, right where I'd left him. He shifted his weight. Cocked his head. Instinctively the movement drew my eye. And do you know what he did next?

He poked his tongue out at me.

For real.

There, amid all the ripped-jean wannabes living on their credit cards and acting cool and superior, was this incredibly handsome man sticking his tongue out at me. You couldn't have scripted a better "meet-cute." I burst out laughing—it was ridiculous. But that was always the thing with Oliver. He was anything but predictable. No. He was the closest thing to magic I'd ever seen: it was as if he'd stepped straight out of a rom-com. Like the cast of *Friends* might be trailing close behind.

But *shit, shit, shit*—what was he doing? He was moving towards me now. I could see him weaving his way through the crowd.

I wasn't ready for this.

My head grew light.

"So," he said, appearing beside me for the first time. He was six foot two. I'm five foot seven so we matched well. And from the way he looked at me, it felt like maybe, just maybe, the pendulum was finally swinging back my way.

The bartender was back. He slid my drink across to me on a napkin and I took a sip. Chilled. Tart.

"So," I replied. I could smell his cologne: Ylang-ylang? Spice? And feel the warmth pulsing from his chest.

He grinned at me and leaned in to talk into my ear. The music was loud, it would have required shouting otherwise. "I'm Oliver," he said. His hair smelled clean and my heart was pumping hard.

"Charlie," I said into his ear, the warmth of his cheek against mine.

"Like the perfume?"

"Pretty sure that's what I was named after," I said, pulling back to look at him. Our eyes locked and all I could hear was static. We were standing close. So close. Grinning at each other. Neither of us breaking eye contact. I was proud of myself: if this wasn't flirting, nothing was. I couldn't wait to tell Tess. And for the first time since my breakup I wasn't thinking things like: *How will I hold it together when Josh asks for his key back?* That was his name. The one before Oliver: Josh.

Instead, I stood soaked in the present moment, my fingers wrapped around an icy glass, my eyes tracing the stubble on Oliver's jaw; his mouth, his eyes. His eyelashes were unjustly long. But there was something in his expression that told me he was mentally weighing things up: should he say it or shouldn't he?

"What?" I asked—*Say it*—and he smiled.

Then he leaned forward again. "Are you feeling brave?" he asked.

I squinted at him. "In what way?"

"Well, I realise this is forward but do you fancy going somewhere? Grabbing some supper?"

His eyes were clear, traffic-light green and full of promise.

"Ummm," I hesitated, taking another sip of my drink. *Ba-boom, ba-boom, ba-boom.* I needed something good to happen, something to make me believe in life again. In *me* again.

"It's just dinner, Charlie. Don't overthink it," he said. "Yes or no."

I liked the sound of him saying my name and, logically, he was right. What harm could dinner do? A little bit of spontaneity, a dash of recklessness, would be good for me.

He smiled at me again, his hands in a prayer position: "Pretty please?"

And I laughed. "Sure," I replied, reaching for my phone. "I just need to text my friend."

And as I typed out the message—*I think I met someone. He wants to go for dinner. Can we do drinks another time? x*—I thought: *Wow, I almost didn't come out tonight. I almost missed this.* It felt like fate, really it did.

It was only six weeks later that Oliver admitted to me what that movie-style meeting really was: a bet. Courtesy of Justin, his best friend and long-term work colleague.

Nothing is ever as it seems, is it?

So there you have it: how we met. Where it all started. How I ended up here, years later, still trying to figure out how something like *this* happens. Because things like this are not supposed to happen.

No, we like to believe we're in control of our lives; that if we buy insurance, think positive thoughts and pay our bills, we'll be safe. Everything will be okay. But the truth is: sometimes it's not okay. Sometimes all it takes is one plot twist to realise nobody is who you think they are and everything you know to be true is actually false.

Well, a plot twist *and* a dating app . . .

Let's fast-forward sixteen months: to Tess's thirty-second birth-day. The fifth of June. A Tuesday. We'd gone for drinks at one of Tess's favourite Mayfair bars: all amber lights, blue velvet furniture, expensive suits and the sociopaths who wore them. Oliver would have been there too except he was flying in from a business trip—Brazil—at 7.30 pm. He'd had dodgy internet access for the past ten days and all I'd received from him were a couple of garbled calls via WhatsApp, a handful of photos—some tourist shots, a selfie on a beach, a shot of his wet legs with Sugarloaf Mountain in the distance—and a few "I love you baby" texts between meetings.

I hated it when he went away: his absence gave my mind the opportunity to go to dark places, to replay his side of phone conver-sations I'd overheard between him and Justin that sounded stressful (they always sounded stressful), to question how safe he was when he went away to places like Nigeria, then came back with stories about how someone had an AK-47 in the meeting room, and to think of all sorts of improbable ways things could go wrong. That I could lose the happiness I'd finally found. I couldn't wait to see him; for the bad thoughts to stop. To feel his warmth around me, smell the ylang-ylang on his skin and his shampoo on the pillowcase in the morning. Our bed was too big for one person.

Tess was my oldest friend. We'd met in the loos at Tramp one night when we were both nineteen and new to London. We'd soon become each other's family here; each other's "in case of emergency" person. She was more a sister than a friend, really. And she was in good spirits that night, mainly complaining about the daytime heat and how hard it was to wear a jacket to meetings throughout the summer. By "summer" she meant the five consecutive days of sunshine we'd just had—a British heatwave, if you asked the papers. But she was a fledgling family lawyer at Legal Aid and had her ex's name (Marc) tattooed in cursive on one of her wrists, so jackets were compulsory. But that night she was jacket-free in a silver sequined cami and a pair of black jeans, her sparkly eye shadow just a little heavier than usual. That meant one thing and one thing only: she was, in her own words, "open to making new friends."

Now, you need to understand something about Tess: she wasn't like me. When Josh broke up with me it took weeks for me to ditch the dry shampoo and stretchy pants routine, returning to semi-normal function. Who knows how long I may have continued to wander through my life like a ghost if Oliver hadn't swept in and changed *everything*.

Because Oliver was like one of those brightly coloured dividers between sections of a school folder.

There was my life "before Oliver": where reality was such a far cry from what I'd thought life would be like. The overpriced rent, the panic attacks, the disappointments inherent in a career in the arts and the truth about relationships—that nobody runs through an airport for you and even when you're an "us" you can feel marrow-achingly alone. "Love" with Josh was confusing at best. There were moments where I was sure we loved each other, but ninety per cent of our relationship could be characterised by: Josh working long hours and refusing to communicate his emotions (if he had any) when I needed him most, me checking his horoscope or doing Myers-Briggs personality quizzes on his behalf to figure out why he was like that (INTJ?), then him frequently breaking up with me due to feeling like he, and I quote, "never did anything right." Which was fair: he didn't. There was always the sense that somehow, even though I'd chosen it, I was in the middle of the wrong life. That I must have taken a wrong turn somewhere because this was *not* how it was meant to turn out. It was meant to be bigger, brighter, more luminous. But I wasn't sure which way to turn to find the "right" life.

Then there was my life "after Oliver": where I was calmer. I felt, I don't know, healthy. It was all okay. Good even. It wasn't twenty-four-seven bliss, but when I was sitting beside him, watching a romantic scene in a movie, I wouldn't flinch, horribly aware of the fact that what I was feeling was far removed from the characters' feelings. With Oliver I felt all the *right* things. "Love" with him meant I was seen, I was safe. We weren't perfect, no, but together we were stronger than we were apart because we loved each other, accepted each other, and when I woke at 4 am, thinking about death or remembering things I didn't want to, even when he wasn't actually in my bed, I could feel him there with me. And that would calm me. It gave me strength. As though my love for him formed a secondary spine.

I had no idea how Tess pulled off life without an Oliver, but here's the thing: Tess didn't want one.

And there was a reason: Tess had suffered too.

Of course she'd suffered: we *all* have a wound so deep the air can't get to it, a wound that explains everything. It's there, whether we're aware of it or not.

Mine meant that when I walked into a room, I immediately scanned it for potential weapons and exit points. Salt and pepper shakers (or anything solid that fitted in a hand) could be used to at least buy me some time. Lamps were a strong choice, although they were usually plugged into the wall and that could cause problems with swing. Right now, I'd probably use the glass in my hand or the little metal vase of flowers in the centre of the table. It had a sharp, geometric edge that would at least stun an assailant. So yes, I could refuse to think about it. Refuse to talk about it. But there it was: living in my actions.

Tess's wound was different, but that's not to say it wasn't as deep—it still fractured her heart, rattled her faith: an affair with a director at the private law firm she'd worked at straight out of university. Marc. Yes, the tattoo. He'd told her he was "unhappily" married and on the verge of the divorce papers coming through, that his wife was cruel and cold. But after a few months, the feeling that something was "off" about Marc became so strong that Tess had launched a low-level investigation into him.

Of course, Marc wasn't on the verge of a divorce, was he? No, he was not. Instead, Marc was "happily" married to a woman with bouncy chestnut hair who, judging from her Twitter account, was not enjoying her last trimester of pregnancy. Tess confronted him immediately, desperately needing to be wrong.

It was the very next day that the office gossip began.

Within a week everyone had heard Tess was obsessed with Marc. In love with him. E-stalking him. That she was trying to break up his perfect family but he was fending her off. It was the sort of rumour offices love. And as their relationship had been a closely guarded secret—he'd insisted on phone calls instead of texts and no photos (these were the very things that had her embark on her investigation in the first place)—she had nothing to prove otherwise.

Besides, she was too tired and fractured by then to truly fight.

Those were dark days: lots of crying, blocking and unblocking his wife, vodka and googling tattoo removalists. But after the initial meltdown period, Tess had gathered her strength, quit her job and filled the cracks from within. It meant she recovered quickly, far quicker than I ever did, but her heart had hardened in the process. Now she treated dating like a life-sized chess game; men like recreational drugs.

"But don't you want to fall in love again?" I'd asked her more than once. And each time her answer had been short and clear: "No."

Like I said, Tess wasn't like me: she didn't fall apart over men and she wasn't looking for "true love"; she was looking for "fast love." Which is how the three of us—me, Tess and some dark-haired girl whose name I'd forgotten—ended up squished onto one of those velvet sofas, tipsy and swiping our way through a dating app. It was fun for the first five matches or so. Having gone straight from a six-year relationship with Josh to Oliver, I'd bypassed the entire Tinder revolution, so everything I knew about ghosting, slow fades, the tyranny of two-blue-ticks, gathering intel via Instagram comments and faking a butt shot (close-up of a closed inner elbow—try it) for sexting had been through Tess. And so it was interesting, informative, to hear her explain how she'd used two different filters for her photographs because it improved both her complexion and her matches. How she'd set her "radius" to three miles because she liked the catchment area. "Oh," I said, "clever." Then I sipped my wine, checked the time and issued silent gratitude for the fact that *I* wasn't single. That *I* didn't need to fake anything to get a date.

And I'm pretty sure that was it: the smug thought that irritated the gods.

Or maybe I'm giving myself too much credit and someone else too little.

But I wasn't really paying attention: just vaguely aware of her thumb swiping left, right, then left again, wondering inane things like: is my nail polish just a shade too dark? It was almost black; I'd had a manicure that day. And then, with no prior warning, there it was: *bam*.

The antidote to smugness.

Oliver.

My husband.

I only glimpsed the image for a splinter of a second. *Maybe it was just someone who looked like him.* But here's the thing: I recognised the picture. I'd *taken* that picture. It was him, at a distance, walking back to me from the swimming pool on our honeymoon. Lake Como. My chest grew tight. My breath caught in my throat. And a kickdrum flared up in my chest: *ba-boom, ba-boom, ba-boom.* But by the time I registered what was happening Tess had already swiped "No."

"Can we go back?" I asked through a Malbec haze as she continued to swipe.

"Huh?" the other girl asked, slurping her drink. "Why?"

"I just—" I started. "That looked a lot like Oliver."

Tess burst out laughing. "Charlie, don't be silly," she said, shaking her head. "Which one?"

"The one by the pool. Can we just check?" *Ba-boom. Ba-boom. Ba-boom.* My vision was white at the edges and adrenaline pulsed through my veins. What was happening? But Tess shook her head again, her short dark pixie cut catching the light as she moved in what seemed like slow motion. "There's no way to un-swipe, babes. Sorry."

I looked at her. Pleading.

"It's fine," she said slowly, drawing out the syllables. Her brow was tensed in a concerned frown and she was touching my arm with reassurance. "Charlie, it wasn't him. He's a good guy."

And she was right: he was.

But that didn't change the fact that the walls were swaying towards me and my breathing had all but stopped.

I needed to go home. I needed to talk to him. So I paid my part of the bill, said I was tired and, as I made my way out the doors into the cold night air, I remember feeling like my entire life was mid-implosion. Little did I know infidelity was the least of my problems.

—

10.29 PM

Twenty minutes later I was sitting in a cab, my stomach a tightly knit ball as we pulled away from the kerb and I stared out through the window: two friends hugged goodbye on the sidewalk, men in well-cut suits wandered down towards Piccadilly and a group of girls in high heels and short skirts made their way down the little alley I'd just come from.

My mind was a tangled mess. Tess had said it wasn't him and maybe she was right. Because there had been no other solid signs: no rogue hairs on sweaters, no perfume in his hair, no lipstick on his collar. *Surely I'd know if he were cheating?* I clenched my eyes shut as though to focus on the truth but then there it was again: that photograph. Branded onto my inner eyelids like I'd stared into the sun for too long.

What the hell was I going to do—ask him?

If it *was* true, wouldn't he just lie? *I'd* have lied back then, if it were me.

I'd learned the hard way that honesty was not always the best policy. Sometimes it just wasn't worth the cost.

But this was Oliver we were talking about: he was the best man I knew. Honourable. Strait-laced. And after seeing the pain his mother endured with his father before he left, he just wouldn't do that to me. Would he? Besides, the counter-argument was strong: I was the screensaver on his phone, I'd met his mother, I had a very expensive rock on my finger, our wedding photos were all over his Instagram wall; we had our own hashtag for fuck's sake: *#charlieandollieforever.*

No. Logically, it was extremely unlikely.

If he is on there, it's definitely Justin's fault.

I thought back to the night we met. To the bet. Justin had sworn that was simply a "one-time intervention"—that he needed to "save" Oliver from the clutches of his "miserable-psycho" girl-friend. Oh, yes, that's another thing: I didn't realise it at the time, but Oliver wasn't exactly single the night we met. He was still dating a girl named Alyssa, they'd been together for just over a year and she "had problems." I told myself, when I first found out, that if Oliver was really in love with her he wouldn't have taken the bait, agreed to the bet, no matter how unstable she might have been. No matter how much Justin pushed. I *needed* to believe that because that's the Oliver I was falling in love with. Noble. Kind. Protective. And he was falling in love with me too. I knew that because he'd won the bet the moment I agreed to dinner. He could have excused himself right then. Right there. I could have met Tess as planned, and he could have gone home to "her." But he didn't. Instead he waited for Tess's reply to come in—*Of course, woohoo*—took me by the hand and led me outside into the frosty winter air.

But after seeing that app, everything looked different. *What if Justin's turning on me now?* Then came a flash of memory: Justin, tipsy, bragging to us about his date the previous night with a "brunette so hot she must be bonkers" and his nocturnal rendezvous with a redhead later that night. Hadn't he met them both on an app? Yes, yes he had. But in my recollection, Oliver hadn't flinched. He hadn't seemed that interested. Still, there was no escaping that awful truth: we were only together because he'd cheated on Alyssa.

Was it my turn now?

No. No. No.

That was where my thoughts were by the time the cab pulled to a stop.

I passed a twenty-pound note to the driver and as he fiddled around for my change I looked out the window at our building: a red brick mansion block, white trim, facing Battersea Park. It was late for a work night, so only three lights were on: Natasha (our noisy upstairs neighbour who had a thing for Oliver), the flat to the upper far right of the building, and ours. Our flat was on the ground floor on the left-hand side and there was a gentle glow creeping through the crack of the curtains. Which meant he was probably still up.

We'd moved there just nine months before, straight after we got back from our honeymoon. Our old place was near Kensal Green, closer to my work, but we'd been broken into and Oliver's car keyed up. He got nervous after that and insisted we move.

This flat was our new start.

The advert had said: cosy, park-facing sanctuary. And "cosy" was right: it was teeny-weeny and overpriced, a two-bedroom where the second one was the size of a single bed. But Oliver used that as a study, so it was perfect for us. As the door closed behind me and I moved into the hallway, I thought of how happy we'd been to find it and my pulse sped up again: we had been happy, hadn't we? I wasn't one of those women blind to the latent misery of her husband, was I?

I moved past the lifts and caught sight of my reflection in the metal doors: blonde hair to my shoulders, amber eyes, slim build and a naturally red mouth. In every indie film, every play, every commercial I'd ever been in, I was always cast the same way: as the token-blonde wife. You know the type: supportive, pretty, un-blemished. I mean, sometimes they'd give me a quirk or flaw to make me more relatable, especially in more recent years, but that didn't change the fact that I was only there for two reasons: (a) so we could learn about the hero via intimate dialogue with some-thing other than a wall or a volleyball and (b) to keep the producers happy—"Romantic subplots win over female viewers" after all.

If this were a movie, the narrator would now say: *Charlie was not, in fact, unblemished.* And that narrator would be telling the truth. But in real life that didn't matter, I was always cast that way because that's what I looked like—on my headshot and in real life. I was the leading lady. The love interest. A sweet little ingénue life hadn't left its fingerprints on yet. Which was intentional: that was the "me" I'd re-created when I'd moved to London to start afresh at nineteen. I couldn't change my interior monologue, my fears, nor my wounds, and so instead I changed what I showed people. I created an illusion and I wore it like armour.

See: none of us are who we appear to be.

Not even me.

But here's the sticky bit: even though "the love interest" was my castable "type"—the only type of role I'd ever successfully secured—just before we got married, Oliver asked me to stop accepting auditions that required me to be intimate with other men. I think he was just jealous, but the official version was it was bad for his professional image to have his wife simulating sex scenes. And I'd agreed. I knew how hard he'd worked to get to where he was and how important his image was to him. And it wasn't like I was being cast in blockbusters anyway; the biggest role I'd ever landed was my most recent one, a Netflix series, but they'd cancelled it after filming the pilot. Acting was so unpredictable and Oliver was like a song I wanted to keep on repeat. Like free drugs. And so I'd told myself we all had to choose between "us" and "me" eventually. That, if anyone was worth the sacrifice, Oliver was.

But still, it *was* a sacrifice.

It meant Clarence (my agent) rarely called me anymore. And Oliver knew that. So surely he wouldn't have asked that of me if he were cheating. It would be hypocritical.

But as I moved down the brown-carpeted hallway towards our front door, I now wondered if I'd missed a red flag there. Weren't jealousy and a controlling nature the hallmark signs of a toxic relationship? Wasn't a preoccupation with image the calling card of a narcissist? I was pretty sure that yes, I remembered those things from one of the many online quizzes I'd done with Tess to diagnose Marc after it all went down. How had I missed this? What if Oliver wasn't who I thought he was? Or worse, what if he was—what if it wasn't even him on that app—and I was letting my baggage take the reins and ruin things? It wouldn't be the first time I'd jumped to conclusions.

You see, that's the problem with trust issues: eventually you find you can't trust yourself either.

I reached into my bag and pulled out my keys, imagining how the rest of the night would run. Would he be waiting for me, watching TV? I couldn't hear anything playing through the door. *Maybe I should just ask him?* But I'd asked him something similar before and so I knew how quickly his walls could go up. Trust was important to him too. I'd been so looking forward to seeing him and I didn't want to ruin things.

Fuck.

I slid the key into the lock, held my breath and twisted.

Episode 2

The flat was empty when I opened the door: just the whoosh of the washing machine, the smell of pizza and the amber glow of the kitchen light that had been left on. I looked to the fruit bowl—pale blue ceramic, full of ripening bananas and a couple of wrinkling oranges. His keys glinted from their usual spot beside it. He was definitely home. But our bedroom door was shut. He must have gone to bed. My chest panged: he usually waited up for me. I pulled the door gently closed behind me, slipped off my shoes and moved over to the pizza box sitting in the middle of the white marble countertop. I opened it—one slice left—and took a bite.

What the fuck was I going to do?

The last time I'd asked him about something like this had been four months after we met. It was spurred on by his ex—Alyssa—that time. The one he'd left for me. The one I knew nothing about.

I'd tried to gather intel about her. I suppose I wanted to reassure myself that they were wrong for each other, or she was at least mildly evil, to ease my guilt, but no matter how subtly I asked the question, Oliver never wanted to talk about her. It's supposed to be a post-coital rite of passage—sharing war stories from past loves—but every time I started to talk about Josh or ask about Alyssa, Oliver would say: "I don't want to know about your exes and I don't want you to know about mine. Let's pretend we're each other's first and last. Let's stay in our 'bubble.' "

I'd nod. Snuggle into him. Pretend I agreed and try to be

grateful that it let me keep my own secrets. But I'm not sure I'll ever be spiritually evolved enough for that kind of blind faith. I like data. Lots of it. That's how I feel safe.

But with Alyssa, I didn't even know what she looked like. I'd trawled through Oliver's Facebook photographs searching for her as soon as I'd learnt of her existence—of course I had—but there was nothing: he'd deleted all traces of her. There was nothing on his Instagram page either. And so it was only via true tenacity—a Google image search for "Oliver Buchanan" which, on page three, amid a lot of people who were definitely not *my* Oliver, offered up an old picture of the two of them together at an event—that I finally saw what she looked like and learned that her last name was Shaw. Now I could google.

Not that it did me much good.

She wasn't on Twitter. I couldn't find her on Instagram. She *was* on LinkedIn but I didn't want to e-stalk her there because you can see who views your profile on that platform (and that would have been embarrassing). But eventually: hooray! She *did* have a Facebook page.

Unfortunately, however, all her settings were super private. And so, while I'd found nothing to worry about on the internet, I'd found nothing to make me feel better about stealing her boyfriend either. And that, together with Oliver's flat refusal to talk about her, meant Alyssa remained a dark question mark buzzing around me like a mosquito I just couldn't swat.

And then one day fate stepped in.

Oliver and I were hand-in-hand, standing by the Sainsbury's till on a Sunday afternoon, when it happened. He was joking about my crappy choice of movie the night before and I'm not sure who clocked who first—him or her—but it definitely wasn't me. All I knew was one moment Oliver's eyes were watering with amusement, and the next they changed, his spine stiffened, his hand grew limp and, instinctively, I turned to see what he was looking at. She had the same dark hair and almond-shaped eyes from the photographs I'd seen, but she was thinner now and taller than I'd have expected. Her eyes were puffy and her face was pale as cigarette ash. She was about four steps away from us, holding a basket containing a packet of chocolate digestive biscuits and three big bottles of white wine. I thought she might make a scene; her eyes were welling with tears. But she didn't. Instead, she gracefully laid down her basket in the middle of the floor and, the moment before she turned to walk out of the shop, she shot him this look I will never forget.

It was harrowing.

I'd never seen Oliver properly rattled before that encounter. We sat there in the parked car, orange shopping bags in the back, his eyes on the windscreen for a good ten minutes before he told me a secret: he'd been terrified to leave Alyssa in case she hurt herself. I squeezed his hand: she *had* seemed a bit fragile. I hugged him. And I left it at that. What choice did I have? Our relationship was so new; far too new to start dissecting his ex's issues and demanding analysis.

But that didn't mean I could ignore it. I couldn't. Because I'd had my heart broken, and I'd seen it happen to Tess, I knew what it looked like and it wasn't Alyssa. She looked devastated. Which left me wondering: what had he done to her?

A thought like that will jar you back into reality; I was falling for this man, but how much did I really know about him? He'd been with Alyssa when he met me, he'd cheated on her with me. Was I the first? Would he cheat on me? Then: are they still in contact? Is that why she was so horrified to see us together?

I didn't want to ask him outright because I knew I'd come across as jealous and insecure and I hadn't wanted to have to explain all the reasons for my trust issues yet either. And so, I did the only thing available to me: I checked. One evening, when I was over at his apartment and he'd just nipped to the loo, I accessed his phone before it locked. The first thing I did was check his messages, but there was nothing suspect there, so I moved to his calendar, quickly flicking through the days, looking for god knows what.

And then, just as I heard the loo flush, there it was: *private meeting*.

It was to be held at the Mandarin Oriental hotel at 7 pm three days later. That sounded a lot like a rendezvous. Why else would it be "private"?

Thus, on the night in question, there I was from 6.45, sitting cross-legged with a dry mouth and a pounding pulse on a sofa near the entry of the Mandarin Oriental. Waiting for him.

All this might sound a bit bonkers to you but there's a limit to how many times one heart can be broken. It had already happened

26

to me a couple of times. I was keen to nip things in the bud before I got in any deeper.

So from just before 7 pm my eyes remained glued to the door. Would they arrive together? Would he arrive alone and head straight upstairs in an elevator to the room? Or would he do neither of those things? Would he instead head straight past me, eyes down, into the restaurant and sit at a table with a man of around fifty-five he'd later identify as "a big client from South America" whose last name was Machado?

Yes, the last one.

In the months that followed I'd hear the name Machado a few more times when I was curled up with Oliver on the sofa, a documentary on pause, while he spoke to Justin on an "urgent" call (all of Justin's calls were urgent). I came to realise Machado was a name that invariably left Oliver's expression in some sort of knot and I always wondered if that had something to do with the fact that he came with three big bodyguards (very much in evidence that first night I saw him).

So there I was, having trailed my new-and-perfect boyfriend to a hotel only to find it was clearly a business thing. But it was still salvageable. All I needed to do was scurry on home and pretend it'd never happened. That I didn't have next-level trust issues. And I would have done precisely that if Oliver hadn't looked up just before I was out of view and seen me.

It was horrible.

And so I was *forced* to explain myself—it was that or have him think I was a proper out-and-out psycho who was following him for no good reason. And given the whole episode at Sainsbury's with Alyssa, that didn't seem wise.

He denied it, of course, said there was no way he'd ever cheat on me, that it was "us," forever. That he didn't want anyone else. Machado was still waiting for him in the restaurant, and there was such pain in his eyes at my distrust; pain I'd caused.

Despite all my certainty: I'd been wrong.

So I made a choice: I chose to trust him.

I stopped googling Alyssa, stopped checking his phone and chose to be happy.

But it wasn't that simple. The damage, it seemed, had been done. Shortly after that accusation, a wall went up. It was transparent and flexible like plastic wrap, almost imperceptible. But it was there. I could sense it between us even when we made love. And there was a sadness that clung to him. I'd begun to think it would never get better; that I'd ruined things by being so fucking broken inside.

Then three months later, we were sitting in the back of a cab. I thought we were heading to see Justin at a new bar he'd "discovered" but I didn't recognise anything out the window and we were getting further and further away from the sorts of places Justin liked to claim as his own. I leaned in towards Oliver and whispered: "Where are we going?"

Oliver's face took on this very serious expression right then, his eyes went all odd, and I was sure he was about to bin me. That he'd been planning on us just driving around in the cab until he got up the nerve.

As he opened his mouth to speak, my vision blurred and I braced myself for a re-enactment of the night Josh ended things. Told myself I'd be strong. Fixed my expression to "fine." But he didn't bin me. Instead he took my cold hands in his warm ones and said: "Charlie, we have one life to live. One chance at this. Please would you live yours with me?" It was spontaneous and raw and it felt like a scene from *True Romance*. Oh, the fucking relief. So I said yes, of course I said yes.

A moment later he pulled out the ring and the cab continued to the airport.

Did it concern me that the proposal seemingly came out of nowhere? A little. But that was part of his allure.

I took another bite of pizza as I stared at the spot by the big bay window where we'd put the Christmas tree last December. Large, shiny red baubles and little wooden Harrods ornaments hanging from golden strings, silver tinsel wrapped around the base: our first Christmas as a married couple. How many hours had we spent together in this room, sitting on that big brown sofa, watching Netflix? A thousand? Five thousand? A wasted hour never felt wasted with him; we were so good together. I was his one "non-negotiable." So why on earth would he be on a dating app? It made no sense.

And then my throat grew tight and my heartbeat slowed as I realised what it *could* be.

I'd told Oliver something about myself just a couple of months before. We were having a deep and meaningful, boozed-up chat late one night and it just sort of came out. No, that's a lie: I'd *wanted* to tell him for a while but I was scared. I didn't tell him everything, just the basics: the first time I had sex it was a house party, I was drugged, I didn't remember much, it wasn't ideal, and I was sorry I hadn't told him earlier. It was one of those things I'd always felt like I *should* tell him before we got married but was terrified it might make him see me differently and change his mind. And since Oliver never liked talking about exes or past sexual experiences, it was an easy secret to keep. But when it did come out he was so loving, so protective. He didn't say any of the things that Josh did: "Why didn't you just report it?" And I'd thought that meant he didn't judge me for it.

But what if I'd been wrong?

I dropped the pizza crust back into the box, and as I did our bedroom door opened. And there he was. Still awake. My husband.

He was wearing an old white t-shirt and some green pyjama bottoms and, fuck, it was so great to see him.

"Do you ever stop eating?" he asked as he came over to me, a grin on his face.

"I thought you'd gone to bed without saying goodnight," I said as he wrapped me in his arms. He smelled like his cologne mixed with whatever laundry detergent the hotel had used while he was away.

"Like I'd dare," he said, pulling back to look at me. He had stubble and it glimmered in the low light. I loved him with stubble.

"How was tonight?" he asked.

And despite all my reasoning to the contrary, all I could think was: *velvet sofa, dating app, swimming pool, you.*

I looked down. "Fun," I said, hugging him again, my head pressing into his chest as I swallowed hard. *Don't say it, Charlie.*

No point causing a problem if it was nothing.

"Are you okay?" he asked, his voice three tones higher.

I nodded and said, "Yep," refusing to look up. I have one of those faces that is easy to read; according to my acting teachers that was what made me great on screen. The audience could see the thoughts dancing behind my eyes. They knew they could trust what I was feeling. But in real life it screwed me over sometimes. I was superb in small situations—I could fake "fine" with the best of them—but the deeper something cut, the more obvious it became. The only way around it was to believe a different truth, to think the opposite thought: *Oliver would never cheat on me, we're so happy together, he's the perfect husband.* Usually I could pull it off—but this was such a shock, so personal, and I'd had too much booze and too little time to prepare.

"Charlie?" he asked, taking me by the shoulders and pulling me gently away from him. He squinted as he looked into my eyes. "Oh my god, something is definitely wrong. Look at your face. What happened?"

"Nothing," I said, frowning. Jaw clenching.

"Oh please. You look like you're about to cry. Just tell me what it is and we can fix it."

I stared into his eyes—if a designer had a hand in it they'd be named something like cut-grass green—and all I could hear was *ba-boom, ba-boom, ba-boom*. What if I asked him and it turned out it *was* him? What if he admitted it? What would I do then?

"Charlie?"

My throat grew tight and my cheeks grew hot and he looked at me with raised eyebrows as if to say: "So?"

Shit. He was looking at me expectantly now and there was no getting out of this, he knew something was wrong. He wanted to know what. I was tipsy, I couldn't think of an excuse and, fuck it, I'd seen something that worried me—*Communication is important*—and I needed to hear a denial in his voice.

And so I said it. I took a deep breath and then: "Are you cheating on me?"

Except it sounded different than I thought it would. Different than the last time when it was sort of apologetic. This time it came out measured, calm and monotone. Like I'd just asked him if he'd remembered milk. And it lingered in the air as though nobody wanted to claim it. Not me. Not him. But *fuck, fuck, fuck*, now it'd been said.

"What?" he asked, stepping back from me.

Shit, shit, shit.

I was right. Holy fucking shit. I was right. "It's okay if you are," I said, swallowing hard, trying to fix things; why was I always trying to fix things? "I mean, no, of course it's not okay if you are." My eyes were prickling with tears. "I just need to know."

I watched his expression for clues. His jaw twitched. Was that a flicker of something behind his eyes? Guilt?

No.

It was something else.

Amusement.

He was trying not to laugh.

"Are you laughing at me?" I yelled, fake-hitting him on the arm. But my shoulders relaxed with his reaction. My cells contracted. It was okay. It was all okay. My life was not falling apart. And his walls weren't going up.

"Of course fucking not," he said. "But my sweet, sweet wife, have you thought this through?"

His face was pink from holding the laughter in. "When on earth would I have the time to cheat on you?"

"I don't know, busy people cheat all the time," I said, sheepish. I crossed my arms and he swiftly, gently, uncrossed them.

"Hey," he said, his forefinger under my chin and lifting my face to look at his. Our eyes met. A thousand volts, straight to the heart.

"Of course I'm not cheating on you, silly," his voice calm, his face kind. "I'd never do that to you," he said. I fell into his embrace again.

"I know why you feel this way though," he said.

I let out a big exhale. "So do I. You're always bloody away."

"True," he said, his hand stroking my hair. "But also I'm pretty fucking irresistible."

"Oh shut up," I said into his chest.

33

And we stood that way for a few moments, pure relief pulsing through me. Relief that I'd been wrong. Relief that I wouldn't have to start asking new men if they had any brothers and sisters and sitting at the singles table at weddings. "Did you bring me a present?" I asked eventually, puncturing the silence. I wanted to change the focus of the conversation and he usually brought me something— perfume, chocolate, nougat—from duty free.

"Oh right, so first you accuse me of cheating on you and now you want your present? Interesting." Then he led me by the hand through to the bedroom. The air smelled like *our* laundry detergent in there because I'd changed the sheets that morning. I sat on the bed and watched him rifle through his suitcase.

"Here we are," he said, pulling a lime-green ribbon into the light.

"What's that?" It looked like a shit present.

"A Bahia bracelet," he said, sitting next to me on the bed.

"Is it edible?" I asked, pouting as I mock-frowned down at it.

"They're good luck, silly. A business associate put me on to them."

He reached for my wrist, the inside facing up, then wrapped the ribbon around it. "Now, I make three knots and for each knot you make a wish. When it breaks off, the wishes will come true." He nodded towards his own wrist. "See? I've got one too." The ribbon around his wrist was orange. "Never going to guess what I wished for." He winked.

I knew exactly what he'd wished for—a baby. How had I

34

doubted him, this man who was more into our family unit than I was? He'd grown up with a struggling single mother and a younger brother and was keen to provide in the way his father never had.

"Ready?" He grinned at me, our faces only a few inches apart.

I nodded.

He tied the first knot and I made my first wish.

Now, I'm not sure that I wish like a normal person. I don't think about it logically. I don't articulate the wish in words. I see the thing I want and feel the feeling I might feel if it came true. What I wanted for that first wish was to get that film role I was up for. And so I visualised myself in the newspaper, and what I felt was a surge of adrenaline: there I was in black and white.

He paused for a moment, then he tied another knot. This time I saw the app from that night, the picture, and imagined being wrong, seeing it again and realising it was someone else altogether.

He tied the third and final knot, his fingers lingering on the edge of the ribbon as I thought: *God, I don't know . . . world peace?* But as horrible and selfish as it makes me sound, there was something I wanted so much more than world peace right then. And so, as I glanced up at him, I visualised him and me, and heard the words "Till death do us part."

He lifted my inner wrist to his mouth and, still looking me in the eye, kissed it. Electricity ran through my core.

"What did you wish for?"

"I can't tell you or they won't come true," I said.

Little did I know I wouldn't want them to come true.

"Oh really? I bet I can get it out of you." He grinned as his fingers came towards me. I squealed as he lay on top of me, tickling my ribs, my underarms. But then his face was right near mine, and I could smell toothpaste on his breath, and he leaned in and kissed me. Soft. Metallic. Warm.

And just like that, we were back to "us." Back to my rom-com reality. On the surface at least. But underneath? Well, that bomb had been armed, the timer set to just five days' time, and even though I couldn't hear it yet, somewhere deep inside I could already feel it: *tick-tock, tick-tock, tick-tock.*

I woke to a wet patch of dribble on my pillow, a mouth full of hair, and Oliver hard and pushing himself into my lower back as his warm hands moved beneath my t-shirt. "Morning," he said into my ear as he tugged at my underwear.

I reached my hand back into his hair. "Hey," I said, my voice croaky and eyes struggling against the muted glare coming in through the space between the curtains. We really should have made more of an effort to shut those fucking curtains. Though perhaps that would have done little to change how things turned out.

Who knows.

It was Wednesday, which meant I was supposed to be at Pilates, but instead my underwear was around my knees and Oliver was sitting up beneath the covers, the cool morning air on my skin as I rolled onto my back and watched him pull them from my ankles. He was brown and healthy looking. He looked like an advert for the Brazilian tourism commission, a firm tan line on his hips and upper thighs, and as he smiled down at me, deep laughter lines formed around his mouth. His eyes were a deep green as he pulled the crisp white covers over his back and lay down on top of me, his chest warm and his weight propped up by his elbows. He moved my legs apart with his knees. The window creaked with the breeze and as he stroked my hair with one hand he used the other to guide himself inside me. Our eyes were locked. A brief moment of mild pain. And then we were moving together. Slowly. Gently. Deeper. His lips—his

37

breath—never far from mine. Our hearts only separated by his rib-cage and mine. See, that was the thing with "us": we never fucked. Never-ever. Not even when we fought. Even at the most passionate of moments he was always holding my hand or stroking my hair. Those were the sorts of things that made it so hard to believe he might stray: he loved me.

—

Twenty minutes later we were lying there in the morning light, me facing the window and his arms around me. Big spoon. Little spoon. And Natasha upstairs was stomping across her floor: *ke-clunk, ke-clunk, ke-clunk.*

"The baby elephant is up," Oliver mumbled into my hair. Then he reached across me to my bedside table, picked up my phone and squinted at the time. It read: 7.43 am. "I have to get up," he announced with a big exhale and rolled over to his side of the bed.

His feet hit the floor—bam. There was no stealth mode with Oliver. If he was in a room he was *in a room.* Everybody noticed. A bit like Natasha upstairs really (she was loud, had a lot of dark hair and was five foot ten), though I'd never have said as much. Now Oliver was groaning, standing up and wandering through to make coffee, arms above his head as he stretched. The coffee machine whirred and he slammed a cupboard door as he pulled out cups and tried to find the pods—the black ones—he liked.

In went the pods, and the whirring started up again. I smiled down at the green ribbon around my wrist and thought of my wishes. Then I thought of my audition the following day. Of the pages Clarence, my agent, had sent through. It was a very serious scene in which the housewife gets arrested and is chatting to the policeman. Surely there was something interesting I could do with it? I wanted that part. I needed it. And then I thought of how Clarence said I needed to build my Instagram following. That I needed to post more.

You see, even though you wouldn't know it from my IMDb page, I'd had a tonne of callbacks. But nine out of ten times it went the same way: I'd be passed over for a bigger name, someone with a bigger Instagram following, someone with connections or a sex tape. And the second one of those was the only one I was willing, or able, to affect. So yes, Clarence was right, I needed to post more.

But posting on Instagram was a tricky business.

You see, Oliver was next-level security conscious. He got like that after the break-in at the old flat.

So his Instagram page was set to private and there were only a handful of us deemed worthy of being accepted as followers. He'd strongly encouraged me to do the same, but I didn't want to have a private account; the whole point was to up my public visibility. So we'd struck a compromise: I wasn't allowed to post anything easily recognisable in case someone figured out where we lived. That meant nothing where the park might be visible through the window for example. Nothing of a pizza box with the logo visible. There were *lots* of rules. Which meant my Instagram wall was a mishmash of random snaps, sporadic shots of brightly coloured cocktails, throwback wedding pictures, headshots, waiting-on-set shots, close-ups of flowers from the flower market, selfies against plain walls, snippets of poetry I'd stolen from other accounts, my feet in the straps at my Pilates studio—anything, so long as it didn't disclose our postcode. But being so careful all the time was stressful, so Clarence was right, I didn't post enough.

In fact, I hadn't posted in over two weeks; it was time.

And so, as the smell of coffee filled our small flat, I had an idea: I reached for my phone, pointed the lens at my Bahia bracelet with just the sheet as the backdrop, nothing recognisable, took a photo and uploaded it as an Instagram story with three hashtags: #charlieandollieforever #threewishes #allforyou. And then I tagged Oliver. How cute were we?

Yes, to anyone looking on, our bliss-bubble was entirely without puncture. We were a team.

A moment later he was wandering back through to me, his penis flopping around in its dark nest on the whiteness where his swimming trunks would have been as he sat down on the bed and handed me my cup. I put down my phone and took it from him.

"Got much on today?" I asked him as I took a sip.

"Just some meetings," he said. "What about you?"

"Nothing too exciting for me," I said, getting ready to drop the bomb. "I have an audition tomorrow, though."

"Do you just?" He kissed me on the forehead. "No kissing other men."

Oliver took his coffee through to the bathroom and pushed the door half closed. I could see him in the mirror as the pipes creaked and the faucet turned on, then he was stepping inside. And I was thinking about my audition: I really wanted that part. It was for a film; most of my auditions were for films. Which was probably because that's where my heart was.

I loved the theatre, of course I did, but I love-love-loved being in films. The lighting, the process, the freedom that was granted with the word "cut" and the second chance at perfection that always followed. It offered up something life rarely did: the chance to have a do-over. Besides, I had the sort of face that just looked better once it had gone in the lens, been reconfigured and spat out the other side.

My phone beeped. Tess. A screenshot.

It was from some guy I vaguely recognised from the app the night before. She'd matched with him soon after the whole "Is-that-my-husband?" debacle. Aside from a question mark, the message was written entirely in emoji: *Eggplant? Monkey with its hands over its eyes.*

Modern-day hieroglyphics for: *Hookup?*

The little texting bubbles started going so I waited for the next instalment.

Beep: *Oh good, an illiterate one. PS. I hate that fucking monkey.*

It was times like this when I was most grateful for Oliver. We'd completely bypassed those shitty first stages of dating: the indifferent text messages, the push-pull, the awkward what-are-we chats, the subtle decaying of each other's self-esteem in preservation of our own. With "us" it had always been simple.

A little while later the pipes creaked again as the water was turned off and the whirr of Oliver's electric toothbrush echoed off the red tiles of the bathroom. A flicker of that picture on the app: him wet and walking towards me from the hotel pool. I pushed the thought away. The whirring stopped and he emerged in his towel, the hair on his legs and chest sticking to him in dark streaks. "All yours," he said, his eyes smiling from behind waterlogged lashes.

"Thanks," I replied as my phone beeped again. I glanced down at the screen, smiling at Tess's most recent message: *I'm going to send back three knives, just to see what he does . . .*

I wrote back: *xx*

"Who on earth are you texting so early?" Oliver asked, watching me as he dried himself off. My mind moved once again to the night before. To the app and the picture, the accusation and the denial. I saw an opportunity to issue an itty-bitty test. Press a little button.

"My other boyfriend," I said, putting down my phone.

"Your other *boyfriend*," he said, lengthening out the syllables of boyfriend as he opened his underwear drawer and pulled on some boxer shorts. "Babe, look I don't want to freak you out, but remember that day last September in Vegas? White dress? Ring? You know what that was, right?"

"First communion?" I asked, smiling at him as he opened the wardrobe. "Something like that." He pulled out a light pink shirt and held it up to his chest. "How do you feel about this one?" he asked.

"Good. Works with your eyes."

He laid it on the bed and started unbuttoning it. Oliver worked for a small private equity firm; it paid less than the big firms might have, but it also meant he skipped the pushing-paper-around-a-desk stage and went straight to international-due-diligence trips. It was a very grown-up job that meant he had to spend a lot of time in places like Brazil and Nigeria, negotiating directly with boards of companies they wanted to invest in. I sound like I knew exactly what he did, but I didn't really: I'm just regurgitating what he'd told me. All I really knew was he earned good money, it was very serious, and every time he went away I was scared he'd never come back.

"Argh, I should get up," I groaned, pulling back the covers and standing up. I was just in my t-shirt now; my underwear was on the floor somewhere. He wolf-whistled as I moved past him into the bathroom and turned on the taps. I peeled off my t-shirt and stepped inside.

The smell of herbal shampoo filled the air and warm water cascaded over my face. I could hear Oliver in the other room, chatting to me, though I wasn't sure what he was saying for the sound of water hitting tiles. I rinsed off my hair and quickly wrapped myself in a towel.

"Are you saying something?" I asked, popping my head out through the door. My hair was dripping wet and he was fully dressed now: the pink shirt we'd decided on together and grey suit pants.

"I'm off," he said, leaning in for a kiss. His breath smelled like tooth-paste and his hair was still damp.

"Have a good day." I smiled at him, squeezing the water out of my hair with my towel, then slipping on my bathrobe. It was one of those white fluffy ones you get in hotels; Oliver had stolen it for me on one of his business trips. I could hear the front door click shut as he left and I picked up my phone and coffee cup and headed through to the living room. I sat down on the sofa and looked around me.

There, straight in front of me, was a big bay window with mauve curtains that looked out onto the park. Against the left hand wall sat our vast dark wood bookcase, my Stanislavski, Meisner and Kundera mingled haphazardly with his Lee Child, Terry Hayes and Le Carré, like we never expected to have to separate them. In the middle of the room sat a big chocolate-brown sofa, with a TV and ornamental fireplace on the opposite wall. Above that mantel-piece hung three polaroids set in resin and secured to the wall by nails Oliver had drilled in one Saturday evening while I drank gin, joking about them being crooked. They were from our wedding day: Vegas, last minute, a white boho seventies dress. A screen-worthy love story in the making if ever there was one. And beneath those pictures sat Oliver's big bronze Ganesha on full display. He was convinced that thing would bring us luck.

Beside all that, stuffed into the corner because it was the only place for it in our tiny flat, stood a dressmaker's mannequin I'd taken from the shop I worked in. It was a vintage clothing store in Notting

Hill, just off Portobello Road. It gave me flexibility for my auditions, when I got them. That was where I was due to be at 10 am that day.

My phone buzzed: another text from Tess.

A screenshot of a penis this time.

Typing bubbles then: *WTF?????*

I wrote back: *Haha. It's not even 8.30 am!* Then I clicked on my Instagram story. I wanted to see if Oliver had seen my post yet. Or Clarence. Or better yet, maybe my ex, Josh, had seen it. I'm not sure that it says anything good about me, but there had been a certain satisfaction in being the one to move on first from Josh, especially since he was the one who ended it. Like, by being loved by Oliver I could prove to the world (to myself) that it was Josh, not me, who had the problem. I know: petty. But being a human is complicated.

I scrolled through the faces: friends from school, Tess, a couple of directors I'd worked with who'd added me, my mother, people from acting classes I'd taken over the years . . . I didn't have that many followers (hence Clarence's suggestion) and most of them didn't bother watching my stories, so it didn't take that long. Josh wasn't there. Neither was Oliver. But there was one profile I didn't recognise at all. Perhaps it was the name that drew my eye: *@lover7*.

I frowned: I mean what was up with that handle, right?

So I clicked on it.

The profile picture was of a girl in a bikini staring off into the distance. Her face was covered by a big straw hat and no hair was visible, just a shoulder. And her profile was private.

My stomach clenched.

I wasn't following her and she wasn't following me.

This was back in the golden age when you could still see your Instagram story views for longer than twenty-four hours, and so those were what I checked next: my highlighted stories saved at the top of my page. And when I did, there she was: *@lover7*. She'd watched all those too.

My ears roared with blood and my mind yelled, *This is bad, this is very, very, very bad.* Because now I was thinking of that app and that picture, wasn't I? And as the room swirled around me I could only think of one reason *@lover7* would be watching all my stories. The same reason Tess had been trawling through Marc's wife's social media: she was looking for answers.

@lover7 was someone Oliver had met. Probably on the app. And she was scoping me out, trying to figure out if we were really on the verge of separating or whatever else he'd told her.

That might sound neurotic to you, but on the deepest of levels, it made perfect sense to me: despite all my efforts to rebrand as the kind of woman a man like Oliver might want, I'd never really understood how I managed to pull it off. So *of course* he'd grown bored, *of course* he wanted more. Especially now that he knew I was damaged.

I stared down at the phone, my heart hammering, goosebumps all over me as I tried to figure out what the hell to do.

There's probably a perfectly reasonable explanation. And maybe I could have talked myself off the ledge if I hadn't seen his picture on that

46

app just the night before. But now the doubt was there, stuck in my chest, and I couldn't dislodge it.

Shit. There was no point asking him. If it wasn't true those icy walls would definitely go back up again, and if it *was* true he'd already lied once, he'd just do it again.

There was only one thing I *could* do. And so I reached for my phone and texted Tess: *What was the name of that dating app from last night?*

Tess: *Why? Xx*

Me: *Will explain later.*

A moment later, in flew a screenshot.

And, thirty seconds after that, the app was downloading onto my phone.

9.13 am.

It was around then I started feeling watched again. The heat of eyes on my back. The little hairs on the back of my neck standing to attention like miniature soldiers. I hadn't felt that way since right after the break-in at the old flat. But I told myself I was just anxious because of what had happened the night before, because of those Instagram story views, because somewhere out there someone was watching what I was eating, how I took my coffee and what my sheets looked like behind my Bahia bracelet. That was unnerving. Creepy, even. But it was also the inherent nature of social media to be watched.

And what could I have done about it anyway? Put my Instagram on private? That may have slowed things down, but it wouldn't have stopped it. Looked over my shoulder every ten seconds, hoping to catch a glimpse of someone following me? Told the police I had "a funny feeling" and then watched their eyes glaze over when I pointed to my Instagram story views as my proof? Exactly.

—

I took a seat by the window—a smudge of fingerprints, dry shampoo and god knows what else—and stared at my reflection: pink silk shirt, black jeans, vintage Chanel belt and three thin gold bangles that jangled as I moved. I looked care-free. Nobody who looked at me would have guessed what I was planning that day. What I'd already started. What I'd been doing at the bus stop as the yellow-lit board counted down the minutes to the next bus (nine, seven, five) and the air swelled with dust, petrol fumes and impending rain.

Because I wasn't checking Instagram at that bus stop. Nor was I checking my messages. No, I was thinking of a Netflix documentary Oliver and I had watched together, curled up on that sofa. It was on catfishing—you know, strangers pretending to be other people on the internet. And I was sifting through my memory for tips.

You've probably noticed I do that a lot: think in movies and TV. Well, it's not just because I'm an actress, though it might be part of why I became an actress. No, movies get a bad rap for being unrealistic, and sometimes they are, but I really think movies saved me. They helped me find my faith in life again when I was sixteen and thought I never would.

48

It was a movie that taught me happy endings could happen for anyone no matter what your life story (*Pretty Woman*), a movie that told me I wasn't a prisoner to other people's opinions and could re-create myself at any moment (*Legally Blonde*), and a bunch of Netflix documentaries that taught me all about DNA, evidence collection, how to make your phone untraceable (take out the battery) and the rituals of serial killers. Some of those tidbits turned out to be more useful than others.

I mean, yes, to be honest movies also gave me next-level expectations around love but, you know, no life philosophy is perfect. And at least mine gave me some agency. But that's what they were: the lens through which I viewed the world.

Because everyone has a way they get through those impossibly dark nights when the phone won't ring and sleep won't come; those mediocre, greyscale days where time slows down and sticks to your lungs. Some of us hand it over to the gods, some of us blame a hyperactive butterfly on the other side of the planet, and some of us post inspirational quotes on Instagram. All fair choices. Me? I pretend I'm in a movie and I'm the main character. That if I just get through this one shitty scene, the next one will be better, because everybody knows the heroine wins out in the end, right?

So that's how I decided what to do whenever I was scared or stuck or didn't trust my own reactions: I just asked myself what I'd want the heroine in a movie to do if she were in my shoes. And then I did that. Simple. Which is how I came to be sitting at that bus stop, creating the email address: AnnabellaHarth98@gmail.com.

I'm not sure why I'd decided on that name, but somewhere between me seeing @*lover7* on all my Instagram story views, texting Tess for the name of the app, throwing back three shots of Nespresso and dressing myself, she'd been named: Annabella Harth. That would be the name of the identity I'd create. The one I'd use to check if Oliver was cheating.

I know it sounds sneaky, but fuck, if he was cheating on me I deserved to know. I *needed* to know. I was going to go crazy if that @*lover7* woman kept watching my Instagram stories and I didn't know why; I was already imagining them together, torturing myself with all sorts of scenarios. The sorts of scenarios only a creative mind can conjure. It was as if I'd ingested poison and swiping my way through that app was the sole antidote.

Which meant I needed to create a profile he couldn't swipe "No" to before I found him.

But I couldn't sign up to the app until I had a Facebook page. And to get a Facebook page I needed an email address.

It was a process.

The next thing my alter-ego needed was a face: a pretty one. A "swipe-yes" face. I knew Oliver liked blondes—I was blonde, after all—so "Annabella" would be blonde too. And so, as commuters gathered around me, all checking the board (seven minutes to go) and then staring down at their own phones, I googled: blonde girl.

All the pictures that came back were stock photographs, marred by watermarks in the corner. So I resorted to stealing some off Instagram. It was easy, really. Easier than it should be. I just went to the hashtag option and looked up #blondegirl.

The one I picked looked a tad like me. Just younger. Big blue eyes, slightly bigger boobs and shorter hair. All I had to do then was screenshot the photos of her, crop them to size and save them to my photo reel.

That took about four minutes.

I glanced up at the yellow-lit board: three minutes to go.

Next, I needed to create a Facebook profile. I was running out of time so I made her a Pisces like me, just five years younger. Female. Then I uploaded her pictures and *boom-bam-bang*: she was a real-life girl.

But it was getting quite crowded at the bus stop by that point and I was worried someone might look over my shoulder and see what I was doing, so I was careful to hide my screen as I joined the app. Allowed it access to my Facebook photos. And let out a deep exhale.

It was done.

A few moments later, the people around me started fiddling around in their bags, pulling out their Oyster cards and wallets, so I knew the bus must be coming. I stood up, looked down past the park, and there it was, the bus: a splash of lipstick red against a tin-grey sky.

We stood in line, swiped our cards in silence, then I went upstairs, and took my seat by the grimy window. There was only one thing left to do: write Annabella Harth's bio on the app. Which was intolerably hard: I had no idea what it should say.

I needed it to say something that was impossible to resist, otherwise my whole plan would fail.

What was Oliver looking for that he wasn't getting from me?

Sex. It had to be sex.

Shit, was I bad in bed?

I swallowed hard, stared down at my phone and typed in the same emojis Tess had received: *Eggplant? Monkey with its hands over its eyes.*

If Oliver was looking for sex, that should do it. Then, still thinking of Tess, I remembered how she'd explained the radius thing on the app. And so I went to my settings, changed my preferences to over six foot one and within a five-mile radius.

And then, my chest aching, I started to swipe.

Episode 3

Let me tell you something about looking for your husband on a dating app: it takes an unnaturally strong heart. And I'm not talking metaphorically either. I mean, your heart quite literally needs to be able to beat at double time, triple time, quadruple time, every time any man who even vaguely resembles your loved one fills the screen.

Which is why, forty minutes and ninety-seven swipes "No" later, as I made my way down Portobello Road, I was exhausted. Everything around me looked the same as it had yesterday: the red-velvet cupcakes of the Hummingbird Bakery, the vintage map sellers who were just opening up, the tables full of silver and brass trinkets reflecting the tin-grey sky. But everything was *not* the same. No, now I had a problem. A proper problem. And instead of making me feel better, swiping through that app had made me feel worse. Because now I knew what the singles market was like out there. Think: zombie apocalypse with dick pics. I turned left down a small side street and walked quickly towards the vintage clothing shop where I worked, Boulevard.

Nine steps later I was glancing at my reflection in the window that stood between me and the eclectic window display I'd put together just the week before: a fictional set-up of a desk, a black vintage typewriter, a chair with a light blue velvet cushion on its seat, a grey blanket on the floor, a pink hat box and a couple of mannequins mid-gesture. One was wearing the sort of pink-and-white Chanel suit everyone recognises and the other was naked aside from a faux fur leopard skin coat. I pulled my keys from my bag, pushed them into the door and twisted.

The buzzer on the door—installed to cut down on shoplifting when we were out the back—let out its loud and high-pitched *bzzzz*, I went inside, and the door banged closed behind me as I flicked on the lights.

Moving over to my desk, I dropped my bag on the floor and my keys on the desk by my computer. I flopped down into my chair, pushed off my trainers and slid my feet into the pair of black kitten heels I kept under my desk. Then, as I fired up my computer with one hand, I reached for my phone with the other. It was before ten. I was early. Maybe I could get through a few more swipes before Grace got there.

Bzzzz.

No such luck.

I looked up just as Grace walked in. She was sixty-five with snow-white hair to her shoulders she kept back in a chignon. She was wearing khaki pants, a white shirt and a vintage navy and red Hermès scarf. She owned the place, had a good heart, and enjoyed ordering me around.

"Morning," she said, all singsong and cheerful as she moved over to her desk and sat down, laying the newspaper she was carrying out in front of her.

"Morning," I said, flashing her a smile and opening up my emails.

"Have we heard back from the Oliver Goldsmith people?" Grace asked.

"Hmm?" I replied, her words taking a moment to register. When I heard the word "Oliver" I immediately thought of my husband and the app and how many times I'd logistically have to swipe "No" before I got a definite answer. But she wasn't talking about him. She was talking about "Oliver Goldsmith," an iconic sunglasses house in Notting Hill. They'd designed all the sunglasses for a load of movies in the sixties and seventies—think Audrey Hepburn in *Breakfast at Tiffany's*. And they were doing a new campaign.

Organising rentals to stylists and brands was one of the many hats I wore in that job. It was the one I liked most because (a) it was fun and (b) I got half the fee we charged them. My other hats included sorting out our Instagram page, keeping the website updated, hoovering and sending out orders as they came in.

"Yes," I said, opening an email from their marketing department and quickly scanning it. "They want to come in on Friday."

"Great," she replied, her blue eyes twinkling before she started flicking through the paper.

I glared at my phone. What was I going to do if I actually bloody found him?

"Right, I think we need a coffee," I said, standing up and grabbing my phone and bag. I didn't really feel like coffee at all; my mouth was still sour from the third cup of Nespresso I'd thrown back before leaving the house. But I needed to swipe my way through the rest of that app so I could prove to myself that Oliver was exactly who I thought he was and I was just crazy. Seriously, I *wanted* to be crazy right then.

"Please make sure mine's properly hot this time," Grace said. "Last time it was lukewarm."

"Sure," I replied, and headed out the door. The sky was close to charcoal now and the air smelled of soil. It would rain in a bit. I crossed the street to our local café. It was small and brown brick, with a blue neon "Open" sign hanging in the far left window that flickered as though it had some sort of electrical fault. It reminded me of a Tarantino movie. I pulled open the door and was hit by a gust of warm air and the sounds of a jazz record—brushes, brass—and coffee beans being poured into the grinder.

I was third in line: just me, a man with a shiny, balding head and a box of cigarettes poking out of his back pocket—I would have killed for a cigarette right then—and a woman in Louboutins at the front. As I waited, I took a deep breath, stared down at my phone, opened the app and started to swipe. No (ninety-eight). No (ninety-nine). No (one hundred). No (one hundred and one). No (one hundred and—

"What can I get you today, Charlie?" asked the girl behind the counter. I think her name might have been Meg; she'd told me ages ago and I'd promptly forgotten it but she made my coffee every damned morning so asking again seemed rude at this point. Especially since she remembered mine.

"Latte and a long black," I said with a smile. "Can we make them extra-hot?"

"Sure."

I paid with my card and moved over to the collection point,

staring back down at my phone: No (Where was I? One hundred and three?). No (One hundred and four).

There were so many men on there. So many half-naked mirror shots and should-you-be-advertising-that dick pics. So many questionable profile names like: @rodeoman, @bemyqueen898 and @lustyboy22.

I stood there frowning down at my screen. Surely Oliver wasn't there among them? He wasn't like that, was he?

"Charlie," came a voice. I glanced up and Meg smiled at me, placing our coffees on the counter. But seeing them sitting there gave me an idea.

Because what I needed was a clear sign.

One final chance for the gods to show me this was all in my mind.

"Thanks," I said, picking them up and moving over to the window; it had started to drizzle and small raindrops glistened from the glass. I placed them down, took out my phone, angled the lens towards them and snapped a pic. *Nothing special, just two coffee cups by a window. Nothing worth looking at, folks.* Then I uploaded it to my Instagram stories. Maybe @*lover7* wouldn't look. Maybe I could just relax and stop with this madness. Then I dropped my phone in my bag and ran back to the shop through a mist of light rain.

Grace, who'd watched me cross the road, opened the door for me. "Here she is," she said. "Which is mine?"

I nodded towards the cup on the left and she took it. "Your friend is here," she said. And my first thought was *Fuck.*

Have you ever noticed that? That people always pop by on the very days you want to be lying alone in a darkened room with only a spinning ceiling fan as company?

"Hey," came a voice from behind Grace.

I looked up and faked a smile. There were three people milling around in the shop by then, all browsing through things and it took a moment for me to figure out who was talking. But then I saw her: tall and slender, with curly hair the colour of 85% dark chocolate that rested on her shoulders and big brown eyes made bigger with winged, sixties-style black eyeliner. She was standing by my desk and my shoulders relaxed.

Thank god. It was just Brooke.

"Brooke," I said. "Aren't you working today?"

Like most creatives in London, Brooke had two jobs: her day job as a temp at a financial services firm in the city and her every-other-moment job as a personal stylist.

Making new friends as a grown-up is a complicated business. Most people seem to just give up in their early thirties, trading their dreams for a house they can't afford in a commuter town they hate, the sparkle slowly fading from their eyes until all that remains is a cadaver running through the routine aspects of living for another fifty years or so. That can make it hard to relate. But Brooke wasn't like that. She had sparkle-in-spades and similar interests, and she'd moved to London all alone at the age of thirty-one with hardly any money because she had a dream. I respected that. I understood it.

"They think I'm at a doctor's appointment." She winked, nodding down to her arm. There was a piece of cotton wool secured over a vein with a bit of that opaque white medical tape you get at hospitals (or chemists). "Blood tests. But *really* I have a client meeting." She smiled mischievously, the pair of black velvet pants she was wearing catching the light as she walked towards me. She smelled like Moroccan hair oil and vanilla perfume.

"Hilarious," I said. If you haven't caught on, the blood test thing was bullshit. "But you should have texted to say you were coming. I would have bought you a coffee."

"*Waaaay* too caffeinated already," she said in her soft Scottish accent, rolling her eyes on the word "way" for emphasis. "*Some* of us have been up since five-thirty, you know. *Some* of us are disciplined and turn up to our Pilates classes . . ."

That's how I'd met Brooke—at Pilates a couple of months before. Ironically, I hadn't liked her much at first. She seemed grumpy and a bit too earnest. The sort that paid a lot of attention to the teacher when they bleated on about pelvic floor instead of checking the clock to see how much time we had left. But then we'd struck up a conversation in the change room afterwards and I'd learnt that (a) she was new to London, (b) she was only there at that Battersea studio because she'd bought a Groupon and (being new to London) didn't realise it was so far from home (she lived in Bow, East London, a lengthy commute that explained her bad mood) and (c) she was a dreamer. She'd just started a small business, *Brooke Thompson Personal Styling*, which meant she was always either (a) taking pictures for Instagram or (b) complaining about having to take so many pictures for Instagram.

It was that last point, the personal styling, that had me tell her all about Boulevard and ask her to come and take a look around sometime. We'd become fast friends after that—coffees, a French movie, cocktails—but this was the first time she'd popped into the shop, so even though my insides ached and my mind was plagued by the swiping still to come, I needed to make a show of being happy to see her. Because I really liked Brooke.

She was the sort of friend you could have deep and meaningful chats with about almost everything. I could do that with Tess too, but Tess knew me too well. She'd been there for so much of my history. She'd remind me of things and I could never fake anything with Tess. With Brooke, it was different. I got to only show her what I wanted to and it was fun. Like playing a part. Being my best me.

But hang on, she was looking at me now, like she was expecting me to say something. What were we talking about? Oh yes, Pilates.

"Shit, sorry," I said. "I should have texted you to tell you I wouldn't be there. Oliver got home last night. He wouldn't let me get up."

This is what I meant when I said I only showed her what I wanted to.

The picture I'd painted of my marriage for Brooke was one of closeness, one where we told each other absolutely everything, where I was his go-to person when something went wrong at work, his sounding board, his problem solver. Where we knew everything about each other and he was so sure I was "The One" when we met that he'd left his girlfriend at the time—Alyssa—for me. Of course, the moment I said *that*, I realised I sounded like a man-stealing bitch, so I'd quickly backtracked, adding that Alyssa was highly unstable. Poor Oliver. That I'd met her once in a supermarket and it was quite scary. But then all I could see was Alyssa's ashen face as she gracefully laid down her shopping basket. Guilt. It spiralled quickly.

Tess knew about my insecurities, about that night I followed him to a hotel, and she'd been there last night when I thought I saw him on that dating app, but to Brooke we were just a big, movie-worthy love story. Partners in crime. And I know it makes me sound superficial (maybe I was) but I loved that Brooke saw me that way. Because that was the truth I wanted. That while she was relatively newly single and struggling to date in London, Oliver and I had these comfortable married-couple routines and inside jokes. It gave me a sense of wholeness being viewed like that by someone.

So no, I didn't want to have to admit the potential truth. What if I was wrong and it wasn't even him on the app? Then when she met Oliver she'd have that dodgy version of him etched into her mind, a version that would never truly be erased.

Because I *needed* to be wrong about this.

"Oh, right," she said. Wink. "No mind, my fucking Groupon has almost run out, so I can find a studio closer to home soon. Anyway, so where should I start?" she asked, looking around.

"Well, as you can see, everything is arranged by colour," I said. "Is there anything specific you're looking for?"

"I don't know," she said, moving over the reds and fiddling with a few of the sleeves. "It's one of those I'll-know-it-when-I-see-it sit-uations." I really liked her accent. It was soft and natural, and as she spoke I could feel my mouth forming in a way that I might mimic her. Actress-y occupational hazard.

"Oooohhhh," she said, holding out a short, brick-red, Mary Quant-style dress with a cream collar and matching cuffs.

"You should try it on," I said, taking a sip of coffee. Brooke was from a little town not far from Edinburgh—I couldn't remember the name—but as I watched her hold the dress up against herself in the mirror, I wondered whether (in the event that Oliver *was* cheating on me) we might be able to escape there for a girls' mini-break. Maybe we could find a castle on Airbnb to rent out. Maybe I'd just stay there.

"No, I'd better not," Brooke replied, fiddling around with her phone, then taking a picture of the dress. "Can't buy anything until I get more clients. London is so fucking expensive." She put it back on the rack. "Still, Instagram doesn't need to know that." She winked, posting the picture. I glanced over at my own phone, charging facedown on my desk, and thought again of that dating app. My heart flinched.

The door opened at that moment—*bzzzzz*—I glanced over at it and a man walked in. He had dark brown hair, was wearing a green t-shirt and looked uncomfortable, like he wasn't sure what to do in a dress shop but was there because someone he loved wanted him to be. Like maybe he was buying a gift.

If you're not paying attention right now, snap out of it. Because I know he seems extraneous, but I noticed him, and I need you to remember him later when I'm trying to figure out what the hell happened.

"So," Brooke said, drawing my attention back to her. "There's this new cocktail bar I read about. It's Shoreditch way. Keen?"

"Sure," I replied, still watching Grace and the man. "What about next week? Thursday or Friday when I'm all on my lonesome again?" Grace was happily chatting to the man, sipping her coffee and showing him to the scarves. I managed to pick up a couple of stray words: "timeless," "autumn colours." And then Brooke was speaking again. I looked back to her.

"Sounds good," she said, glancing down at her phone. "Shit, I'm late for that client meeting. This one better hire me or I'm going to become a dog-walker."

"Good luck," I said, secretly happy that she was leaving so I could get back to my covert operation of swiping through the app.

The man who'd been talking to Grace left without buying anything and Brooke followed him to the door, caught it before it shut and stared up at the bruised sky: "What happened to summer, hey? I swear it's greyer here than home."

A moment later she was gone and Grace was saying: "She seemed nice."

"Yep," I said. "She is. Stylist."

I sat down and stared at my computer. Scrolling through to the Oliver Goldsmith email I replied: *Wonderful, see you then.* Then I opened up Photoshop. That's how we edited all our pictures for

Instagram and the website. We needed to colour match them so the screen version of a garment matched the version in-store as closely as possible before uploading them to Instagram. Otherwise it just meant a load of returns.

My phone pinged: a message from Oliver.

Justin wants to do dinner tonight at the place downstairs? Keen? Xx

And all I could think was *Fuck*.

I'd never really liked hanging out with Justin, but now that I suspected he'd encouraged my husband to sign up to a dating app to oust me the way he had Alyssa, I liked him even less. You wouldn't have liked him either if you'd met him. He was around six foot three with light blue Weimaraner eyes, thinning strawberry-blond hair, pink cheeks and a signet ring he fiddled with whenever he wanted to feel special. He belonged to a few private members' clubs in London, always calling the ones he didn't frequent "arriviste" or other adjectives people then had to google. I'd tried to like him, really I had: I mean, he was the whole reason Oliver and I had met. I'd even naively hoped Tess and Justin would hit it off and we could do loads of double dates. But on the handful of occasions I'd put them in the same room (including a particularly awkward dinner at Tess's flat), it was as if they were identical ends of a battery that repelled each other in a way I hadn't expected. When I asked her about him later she crinkled her nose and said, "I don't trust him." And as time ticked on I found that I didn't trust him either. I could never tell if he was really on Oliver's side or not. But what I *did* know was Oliver changed when he was around.

I stared down at the message. He was acting so normal: he was probably doing nothing wrong. So I typed back: *Sure, what time? Xx*

Beep: *7?*

Me: *k*

So I was holding my phone—staring at it, actually—when it beeped a strange sound. It was a new sound. One I hadn't heard before. It wasn't a text, it wasn't a Facebook alert. I stared down at it and a line of text graced the screen: *@serialheartbreaker has sent you a gold coin.*

"You're popular today," Grace said from her computer.

"Just Tess," I lied. "Sorry." Then I turned my phone to silent.

It was from the dating app, but it made no sense. I hadn't swiped "Yes" even once, so how could *@serialheartbreaker* be sending me a message? That wasn't my understanding of how these things worked. I thought it had to be mutual. I clicked through to the app and tried to figure it out. It seemed a gold coin was not a message, it was just a feature that allowed one member to get another member's attention. Jump the queue, so to speak. Because I'd been given the choice of declining or accepting.

Decline.

But that was the first of many such notifications that day and so I turned them off before I went to meet with Oliver and Justin that night. The last thing I needed was for him to see a gold coin flash up on my screen and have to explain it. But the rest of the day passed calmly: the door buzzing when a customer came inside, me helping them find something to match their eyes or uploading things to Instagram when Grace was in the same room and swiping through the app whenever she went through to the back room to make a call or go to the loo. And then, when she left at around three like she always did, me running through lines for my audition the following day, putting a reminder in my phone to take a spare headshot and a pencil, pulling the door closed after me as I left, and hearing a heavy click as it locked.

So no, as you can see: still no neon signs flashing at me, warning me of what was to come.

—

6.56 PM

The restaurant-slash-bar we were meeting in was a basement underneath Oliver's building. We'd been there a few times before; it was one of those black walls, black ceilings, menus on chalkboards sort of establishments that finance guys always liked because it made them feel edgy. He and Justin were already at the table, already on their second drink—Scotch—by the time I got there.

"Charlie," oozed Justin as they both stood up to meet me. Yes, for all his being a knob, he certainly didn't lack manners and superficial charm when he wasn't having a hissy fit. He grabbed me by the upper arms to keep me in place and then kissed me on each cheek. His grip released and I looked to Oliver.

"Hi." Oliver smiled at me, kissing me on the mouth.

"Okay, enough of that, you two," Justin said as we all sat down. There was a small bowl of mixed olives in the middle of the table. The bowl itself was small, black glazed ceramic. It looked hard. *I could hit someone over the head with that. Knock them out. Get away.* The easiest way out would be the front door through which I had entered, but I was pretty sure there would be an emergency exit out by the loos and kitchen too. Maybe a window in the loos themselves, though that might have bars . . .

I reached for an olive as Oliver and Justin picked up whatever conversation they were having when I walked in. It was loud in there, the combined sounds of music and chatter and glasses clinking.

Oliver put his hand on my leg. "Justin and I are just talking about a Brazilian company," he said, dumbing it down for me nicely. He always did that when Justin was there, as though by talking down to me he could prove his own masculinity. Dominance. That side of Oliver had come as a surprise; he'd seemed so very confident when we first met. But there was another side to him. A side that needed approval. And so I let it slide because I loved him and I knew he didn't mean anything by it. He just idolised Justin and his smooth, privileged, gelled-hair ways. Justin was everything Oliver aspired to be. Because everything Oliver had achieved was a result of clenched-jaw determination. He'd paid his own way through university, found his own job as a junior at an investment firm, worked while he did his MBA and secured his present job, with no help from family money or connections pulling strings. Which, frankly, was more admirable in my eyes.

But not to Oliver. He worshipped the idea of old money. Of ease. Of belonging to that certain set of people. And so whenever Justin was around, it was pure bravado.

But in private he told me at least a little bit more. "Told" might be a bit strong, actually—it was more that he shared his fears via osmosis. I knew, for instance, from the way he'd wake up breathless in the night, that some of the individuals Oliver and Justin worked with were dangerous. He'd never said as much but I got the sense that Machado was one of them, that if this were a film, he'd be one of "the bad guys." But then, in real life we're all bad guys sometimes. Still, *these* bad guys were the reason I'd spent much of the lead-up to Christmas liaising with our lawyer, sorting out Oliver's life insurance policy and our wills. Oliver had insisted after the break-in. He said he needed to know I'd be okay if the worst thing happened. And he *did* seem calmer after it was sorted.

I smiled back at Oliver, putting my hand onto one of his legs and squeezing it under the table.

A few moments later their conversation stopped and the topic moved to me. "So, Charlie, what's new with you?" Justin asked, leaning towards me with a grin.

That was one of Justin's classic arsehole lines. Because it sounded like he actually gave a toss on the surface, but he always asked those sorts of things with narrowed eyes and always followed up my answers with some sort of backhanded compliment or slight.

"Not much," I said, reaching for another olive, my fingers slick with oil. "I have an audition tomorrow, so that's exciting." That's when I glanced across at Oliver, looking for moral support. But he wasn't listening anymore, he was staring at the waitress: pretty, young, dark hair. It's not like I'd never seen him look at another woman before—women loved Oliver and he was only human—but now it felt different. Now it *meant* something.

He felt me watching him and turned to me with a smile. "Let's get you a drink." Then he motioned to the pretty brunette.

"Oh, you're *still* acting?" Justin said. I turned back to him.

Here we go.

You see, by "still" Justin was referring to the fact that I was over thirty. And I'm not just being hypersensitive (as my mother might have suggested). I knew that for a fact because he'd pulled me aside one evening and solemnly told me that if I hadn't made it by now I probably never would and it would be so much better for my psyche not to keep, and I quote, "flogging a dead horse." When I told Oliver, he said I'd probably misunderstood. But I hadn't. And I never forgot it. Fucker.

"Yes, Justin, I am," I said with a tight smile. But I couldn't help it, my tone said: *Fuck you.*

"Charlie," Oliver said with a tense smile as he put his hand on my shoulder and squeezed it. That was his secret signal to "not be a bitch." I hated how he always sided with Justin.

"Good for you," Justin said, pure condescension.

And my reaction was the same as the one I'd had when he'd told me Oliver's ex had been batshit crazy, "not like you"; my cells instinctively contracted.

Because yes, she hadn't been in top form when I met her. Yes, she clearly needed a shower. But I wasn't sure I'd have coped any better if the roles were reversed: if I'd run into Josh (happy with someone else) while looking like shit. Breakups are hard at the best of times. I knew what it was to watch someone fall out of love with you a little more each day. For there to be not a damned thing you could do about it. For you to resort to checking their horoscope for clues as to when this shitty "phase" would be done. It's humiliating, even when they don't leave you for someone else. And Oliver had left her for *me*.

So even though I put on a strong act and pushed it down inside, overcompensating with my he-and-I-are-soulmates bravado, deep down I still felt guilty about that—when I let my mind go there. And so whenever Justin-the-knob called her crazy, my first instinct was to stand up for her. A bit like I wished other women had stood up for me . . . We'll get there.

Besides, let's be fair, if Oliver and I hadn't married, Justin would have happily confided to the next girl that I, too, was "batshit crazy." Oh how lovely life might have been without Justin. But no, they came as a package deal, so I had to play nice. Still, I didn't really know where to take the conversation from there and Justin was looking at me like it was my turn to say something. Oliver's mouth was smiling at me, expectant, but the expression in his eyes was pure: *Please don't make a problem for me.* So I did the only thing I could think of.

I escaped.

"I'm just going to nip to the loo," I said, just before the waitress arrived. I could hear Oliver ordering me a gin and tonic as I moved to the far side of the room.

The restaurant was full now, all the tables taken, and I had to weave through chairs that screeched across the floor—fingernails on a chalkboard—as they moved for me to pass. Eventually I was there, pushing my way through the big door and then locking myself in a cubicle. I didn't really need to pee. I just needed space. I needed to check the app again. It was becoming a compulsion: Would he be there? Would I be right? Or was I the sneaky one, not him?

I sat down and pulled my phone from my bag, navigating to the dating app. I'd received a couple of new gold coins by then, but my phone was on silent so I hadn't heard them come in. I clicked through and looked at their profiles: more mirror shots, highly filtered shots, or those double chin oops-is-the-camera-on shots that should be immediately deleted. But none of Oliver.

Relief flooded my veins.

Then I remembered my Instagram test. I'd checked it a couple of times since posting that morning, and each time *@lover7* hadn't been there. It was starting to look like she was nothing to worry about after all. But I was in no rush to get back to that table and Justin's judgmental glance, and so I said a quick prayer that she wasn't there—I'm not really religious, but fuck it—and went to the app.

I tapped on my story and scrolled through the views, holding my breath.

But the prayer hadn't worked: there she was.

Halfway down.

Again.

@lover7.

It was three days from the moment that would change everything forever, change *me* forever, and I was still wandering through life oblivious to the danger all around me. My focus was on things like a potential cheating husband who'd left his washing strewn all over the sitting room instead of putting it away. And the fact that I was fifteen minutes late by the time I got to my audition, my hair damp with sweat and the thin green maxi dress I'd finally decided on sticking to the middle of my back.

I'd woken up angry with Oliver that morning even though I obviously couldn't tell him why—how could I say it was because a strange girl was looking through my Instagram stories and my instinct was screaming at me that it had something to do with him? It sounded paranoid, even to me. And he'd just laugh it off the way he did when I was angry with him for something he'd done in one of my dreams. So instead, when he tried to have sex with me I pushed him away. He'd huffed and puffed a bit, then went to have a shower and left. And I'd been left alone with only a burgeoning panic attack and my imagination to keep me company.

Who was she?

But I'd told myself I was fine, just fine. I'd done my makeup, narrowed my outfit down to that green dress, and even paid attention to my phone reminder: *Take a headshot and a pencil.* The pencil was for marking down notes they gave me, action points. It looked professional. And I was a fan of scripts, of notes, of things going to plan. Not like in the real world where I had seemingly zero control.

But I couldn't find a pencil, could I?

And it was my reaction to that—tears, gritted teeth, slamming of drawers—that told me how far from "fine" I really was. Because it was *just* a pencil. And so, calmly, I took a red pen instead and then dropped an eyeliner, some highlighting powder and a small can of hairspray for touch-ups into my bag.

And then I realised I couldn't find my keys.

Yes.

My first instinct was to blame Oliver. He must have picked them up by mistake. But when I called him in a huff, he said he hadn't. And twenty minutes later I *still* couldn't find them and I was going to be late, so I had no choice but to leave without them.

I got to the studio just in time, dutifully following the printed A4 signs stuck to the walls to try to find the right room. But I somehow ended up in the wrong place anyway. I knew it was the wrong room as soon as I walked in and saw hordes of twenty-year-old tanned brunettes. And now, finally, here I was, rushing into the right room fifteen minutes late. It was filled with twelve (I counted) blondes, but I could tell from the other women in the room there was no way I'd get the role. I could already hear the feedback Clarence would get: "She's too soft, not serious enough."

I took a seat near the door, crossed my legs, then reached into my bag for the printout Clarence had sent me. The script was pretty average really, despite a fun premise—a bored, neglected housewife takes to shoplifting instead of, you know, fucking—but I'd done a lit-tle bit of googling on the way over in the cab and the producers and director were going places. This could be good for me. Certainly better than the student films I'd need to start doing again soon if I didn't get the role, just to keep my hand in. But I couldn't focus. My mind was too bound up in what was going on in my life. It didn't matter how many times I told myself that Instagram stalker was probably nothing, I just didn't believe myself.

Fair really, all things considered.

Still, at least I hadn't found Oliver on the app yet: that much was good.

I stared back down at the script and tried to focus.

And then they called my name: "Charlie Carter."

Carter. That was my maiden name and I'd kept it for acting purposes; it sounds like an actress name, right? But it didn't even feel like me anymore. And in that moment it seemed an echo of what life without Oliver might be like. I didn't want that. I just wanted him and "us" and the life we'd planned.

I looked up. Smiled. And followed the blond man who was waiting for me into the audition room.

—

An hour later I was walking into the shop, the door buzzing as it shut behind me. The audition had not gone well. They kept asking me to do things, I'd note them down, and then when I did them, they changed their minds. But, on a positive, at least they didn't take my spare headshot, which meant I wouldn't have to go and have more reprinted quickly. And I remember thinking that perhaps Justin (and my mother, but we'll get to her) was right—perhaps I should just let it go.

"Thank god you're here," Grace said as she stood up from her desk, the legs of her chair screeching along the floorboards. Grace had been sending me texts—*How much longer??*—for the past twenty minutes, but I was stuck on a Tube platform waiting for the train that wouldn't come. "How did it go?"

"Badly," I said, moving over to my desk. I dropped my bag on the floor and sat down heavily, going to turn on my computer. But something beneath the screen caught my eye, sparkling in the white light coming in through the window.

My keys.

I picked them up—cool, hard and uneven in my hand—and relief pulsed through me. I wouldn't need to tell the tenants' board now, something we were contractually obliged to do. *All that fuss for nothing.* I dropped them into my bag and glanced over at Grace. She was still standing, picking up her things. It was just after lunch but she looked like she was getting ready to leave for the day.

"Oh, I'm sorry—Charlie, maybe the next one will be better," she said, slinging her bag over her shoulder. "Anyway, I really need to go, I'm going to be late."

"Where are you going?" I asked, watching her move towards the door.

"Dentist. They had a cancellation, so they can fit me in." She opened the door. *Bzzzz.* "There are a few orders that need to be sorted out ASAP, and we need to pull some pieces for the Oliver Goldsmith people. They're coming tomorrow, remember?"

"Sure," I said, the glare coming from behind her making me squint. By "we" she meant "me."

My phone was sitting on the desk beside me on silent. I'd turned the app notifications on again and now that Grace was leaving, I switched the sound back on too. But she saw me do it.

"Just make sure you get those things done before you leave," she said.

"Will do," I said, then the door closed and she was gone.

I glanced through my emails, clicking on each new order and sending it to print. Then, once they were all in the print queue, once the printer beside me was purring like an electronic cat, I pulled up Google.

My first search was: *Why is she watching my Instagram stories?*

It turned out lots of people had asked Google that very question: approximately 269,000,000. But *usually* it was about an ex or a ghoster. The answers ranged from: *She still loves you* and *She is too shy to get back in touch*, to *She is a narcissist who doesn't want to let you move on*. None of those fitted my situation because I didn't even know who "she" was. But the one common thread was that it probably wasn't a mistake.

If someone kept watching your stories, there *was* a reason.

So what could the reason be with *@lover7* if not Oliver?

A big lump settled in my throat.

Because nobody wants to be the girl trying to catfish their husband on a dating app. Nobody wants to be the girl who's being cheated on. Nobody wants to be the girl who has the courage to ask him outright and then have him lie to her face. And if he was cheating, then that was what he'd done.

That was the girl I'd become.

The printing had finished, so the shop was silent aside from my breathing and the muffled hum of life leaking in from outside. But then came the click of my keyboard: *How to know if your husband is cheating.*

Up came a helpful box listing the top signs: *improved appearance, secretive phone or computer use, periods where your significant other is unreachable, changes in sex drive, an altered schedule, friends seem uncomfortable around you, when you ask your partner if they're cheating they deflect and avoid.*

Oliver *did* go away a lot for work—he was away as much as he was in London—and when he did, I often went days without being able to reach him. When I'd asked him if he was cheating, he'd laughed. Was that deflection?

My throat grew tight and my chest ached. I reached to the printer and pulled out the orders, flicking through them. There were five. I did all the parcel post stuff online, so I went to my search history to pull up the right part of Royal Mail's website. I'd used it only a couple of days before. My eyes scanned through the list: my recent Google searches, a couple of designer information pages, and nestled between them, something else.

Where to buy a taser in London.

79

Boom.

What the fuck was that?

Was it Grace? She had a thing for security (hence the loud buzzer on the door that sung out every time someone came in) and wouldn't have wanted something illegal in her own search history. So . . . maybe.

You see, that's what's so tricky about real life. Warnings don't come in the form of a menacing soundtrack or ominous lighting; they come shrouded in things like a search history.

And often, by the time we know what they mean, it's too late.

I stood up and went through to the back room. It smelled of dust and contained an old green velvet sofa, a heap of boxes and a series of moveable rails. I grabbed one of the rails and pulled it out front, then went over to the navies and blacks. There was a long navy lace overlay Biba dress I thought might be perfect for the Oliver Goldsmith shoot. Square neckline. Formed almost a full circle when you swirled. I pulled it out and put it on the rail. It was the only piece I could think of off the top of my head so I wanted it off the rack before someone bought it.

Next, I was onto the orders, looking for a burned velvet dress in orange-red. That was being sent out to Dublin. I moved over to the reds, my forehead frozen in a frown as my mind grappled with that Google search: *Why would Grace need a taser?*

I found the dress and pulled it out, putting it onto the other side of the rack. It was as I hooked the hanger over the bar that a ping rang out across the shop.

That ping from the app.

The gold coin ping.

I moved over to it and stared down at the screen.

It took a moment for the letters to register in my mind. For a word to form. For understanding to take hold.

But when it did, the walls became liquid and I had to grab onto the desk for stability.

@Oliver1982 has sent you a gold coin.

My skin prickled and my heartbeat sped up as I clicked through to the app, to the profile. There was still a chance I was wrong.

But then there it was.

The proof I feared. The proof I'd gone seeking.

The photograph of Oliver wandering back from that pool I'd seen just two days before in that yellow-lit Mayfair bar.

I hadn't been imagining things, I wasn't crazy, and I wasn't wrong.

And as I stared down at his profile I knew that my life, or rather "our" life, was officially over.

I just didn't realise *how* over.

—

7.12 PM

Rain gushed down in streams, blurring my view from the window: umbrellas, a charcoal sky and a tangle of traffic lights turning emerald to tangerine to fire-engine red. I was in a semi-trance, sitting still as a statue at a small square table in the corner of an Italian restaurant, drinking the water they'd put on my table when I came in. The glass smelled like a dirty rag and my eyes kept darting between the pale yellow, plastic-covered tablecloth, my phone screen (Tess had just texted to say she was almost there) and the green ribbon tied around my wrist. I swallowed hard and fought back tears as the last forty-eight hours presented themselves in a repeating loop of flashcards: the app, the accusation, the denial—*I'd never do that to you*—the wishes, the Instagram story, *@lover7* and finally the gold coin from *@Oliver1982*.

My phone screen flashed white in the low light. It was Tess: *2 mins xx*

I'd called her immediately, of course. Standing there alone in the shop, a locked door now between me and any potential customers and a thin layer of sweat on my forehead. She'd answered on the second ring.

"Hello?" she said, her voice low like it always was when she answered at work. I paused—I couldn't find my words—and so she spoke again: "Charlie?"

"Hey," I said. My voice had a flat, foreign timbre to it.

"Are you okay?" she asked. "You sound weird."

I swallowed hard and my stomach contracted. I was about to say the words out loud. And that would make it real.

"It *was* him. On the app. It was *him*," I said. Short. Sharp. Staccato. There. It was done.

Silence rang out over the line. A car alarm screeched outside.

"Huh?" she'd asked. "What app? Oh, you mean from the other night?"

"Yeah," I said.

"I really don't think it was, hon," she said, her voice distracted, as if she was multi-tasking.

"No, I mean it *was* him. I know for certain."

Beat.

"*How* do you know?" she asked. I could almost hear the cogs of her mind speeding up, trying to piece it together.

"I signed up and found him," I explained, clenching my jaw as I recalled the moment I clicked through to his profile.

Oliver.

38

Private equity

About Oliver:

Hi, Oliver here, looking for dates for Torture Garden, Subversion, Killing Kittens, Le Boudoir etc. Message me.

That was when the nausea hit.

"Shit," she said. Swallow. "Where are you?"

"Still at the shop," I squeaked through a tight throat as I looked around. What was I going to do? My heart was beating so fast. "I don't know how to deal with this. What am I going to say when I see him?" My voice was shaking.

"You can't see him," Tess said, her voice calm and firm. "Not yet. Hang on," she said, her voice lowering to a proper whisper now. "I can meet you at the Italian place in Marylebone at seven. Is that okay?"

"Sure," I said. "I'll leave now."

I was numb as I locked up the shop. Then, as I wandered down Portobello Road to the Tube, I texted Oliver to say I'd be late because Tess was mid-emergency. The air smelled of French fries and the soft mist of drizzle turned into light rain, so I put up my umbrella and listened as the droplets pitter-pattered on the fabric. Everything was a daze. Colours brighter, somehow. Everything so surreal. Was this what it felt like then? To find out your husband was cheating? *Interesting.*

And now I was here, at the restaurant, sitting beneath the red glow of a heater. Struggling to make sense of everything. The door opened—a creak and a blast of cold air—and I looked up. It was Tess. Finally. I watched as she dropped her wet umbrella in the basket then rushed over to me.

"Honey," she said, her grey eyes full of empathy as she slipped off her black coat and draped it over the back of the chair opposite me.

"Hi," I said as she sat down. It was such a relief to see her.

"Shit, haven't you even got a drink?" she asked, motioning to the waitress, who came straight over. "Could we please get two big glasses of Malbec?" she said, demonstrating that when she said "big" she meant "huge" with her hands. "And some gluten-free garlic bread."

She looked to me: "You must be starving." Then back to the

waitress: "I said gluten-free, right?" That was her way of saying, "Were you listening?"

The waitress nodded and left and Tess reached across the table for my hand. A cold squeeze. Her eyes on mine. A crack in her hard-boiled veneer.

We sat there for one, two, three seconds, then: "Can I see?" she asked, her face crumpling in sympathy.

I nodded, let go of her hand, found his profile and handed it to her. Calm. I think I was in some sort of shock.

She swiped through his photographs, one by one, taking a moment to linger on each. I could see them in my mind's eye. That first one: him at a distance, walking back to me from the swimming pool on our honeymoon. The second: a shot of his face, tanned and grinning. The third: the tuxedo shot in front of the mirror, my dark red nails and bangles visible around his waist even though I'd been cropped out.

"Shit," she said, looking up at me.

"Read his profile," I said, my voice flat.

"*Hi, Oliver here, looking for dates for Torture Gar—*" She started reading out loud and then stopped. Dead. "Wow." She looked up at me. "I'm so sorry, hon. Do you know what these are?"

"Well, I do *now*," I said. "I googled."

They were sex parties. FYI. Lots of them. My perfect husband wasn't just on a dating app—he was looking for women to take to sex parties. And I couldn't figure out whether that was better than him looking for a romantic connection, or worse.

It was at that moment, while mentally revisiting the images from various party websites—low lights, smiles, skin—I'd clicked on after reading his bio that the waitress chose to deliver our wine.

"Thanks," Tess said to the waitress with a smile.

I gave a flicker of a smile, waited for her to leave, then reached for my glass. "I asked him, you know. The night of your birthday. And he looked me in the eye and swore he wasn't cheating," I said, my voice cracking. "How could he lie like that? How could I have believed him?"

"I'm . . . I'm so sorry, hon," she said, reaching for her glass.

"Though, it does explain a few things," I said. I was thinking of how @*lover7* could easily have found Oliver via a quick Google search of the info in that profile. And if that hadn't yielded conclusive results, all she had to do was take a screenshot of one of his photographs and upload it to Tineye.com, the way I'd done many times when trying to figure out the source of a photo I wanted to use for the shop's website or an Instagram promotion. Once she found him, I was just a short jump away.

That's how I would have found me.

Tess was looking at me again, her eyes narrowed. "Explain things like what?" I could tell from her expression she thought I was going to reveal something kinky. Some sort of strange sexual preference Oliver had that was now all making sense.

"No, nothing like that," I said in answer to her silent question, thinking of how he'd never been like that with me—why had he never been like that with me? Didn't he trust me? "There's just this woman who's been looking at all my stories. Here," I continued, going to my Instagram and handing her my phone again. "@*lover7*."

I watched her expression as she went through my stories. I wondered if Oliver had given @*lover7* a Bahia bracelet too. My stomach clenched: which parts of our relationship were sacred—were any?

"Oh," Tess said, her mouth contorted into a yikes expression.

"I know," I said, gulping back wine. "It's suspect, right?"

"Do you want me to follow her?" Tess asked. "So we can see who she is?"

"No," I said, shaking my head. "She might look at your page and see me in the pictures. I don't want the extra layer of drama." I exhaled loudly. "Shit. I bet they've had sex already. She wouldn't be bothering if they hadn't, would she?" I took another sip of wine. "I really thought we were happy," I said, tears prickling behind my eyes. My mind was working double speed, trying to figure out what to do next.

Tess let out a long hard exhale. "Maybe he *is* happy with you. I *know* he loves you, it's obvious. I mean, maybe it's not about that. Maybe he just didn't think you'd be into it or—I don't know— maybe he's got a sex addiction or something?"

"Do you think so?" I said, my voice verging on hopeful. That would be so much better. A nice little sex addiction we could go to couples counselling for was better than him cheating for real. Bad yes, but we could work through that. And Justin had been dragged to counselling by one of his exes, so I knew Oliver might be open to it.

"I don't know," she said slowly. "But he had both of us fooled, hon. That means he's a really fucking good liar. Scary good." She looked up at me. "And *that* means he does it a lot."

All I could do was nod. Because I knew she was right, but I was scared if I tried to speak I'd break down properly. My heart was banging around in my chest. The reality of the situation was settling heavily on my soul.

And then I asked her the real question on my mind, the one I'd been muffling with all the others. "Why aren't I enough, Tess?" My voice was small and childlike.

She leaned forward and took my hand. "Oh, hon," she said, taking a deep breath. "It's not about you."

As I nodded, the hot tears I'd been trying to hold in streamed down my face. My mind was struggling to find answers. A way out of this. A way everything could be okay again. A way to make the pain stop.

"Maybe I should ask him about the parties?" I said, swallowing the tears. "I mean, maybe I'd get into it. I've never really thought about it, but I'm open-minded, and I've done loads of sex scenes, I even did that threesome one, remember? Maybe . . ." I shrugged. And I wanted to believe that—that we could be like Nicole Kidman and Tom Cruise in *Eyes Wide Shut*. But even then, as I thought it, I realised I couldn't remember how that movie ended and I was pretty sure it was badly.

"Hon," she said, measuring her words. "You shouldn't be doing things just to please him. And—" She cut herself off.

"And what?" I asked, wiping my cheeks with my hands.

"If he wanted to talk to you about it he would have. He out-and-out lied to you when you asked, remember? And you don't want to corner him and have some shame-bomb go off on you."

She was right. I knew too well how shame could erupt. I didn't *think* Oliver would hurt me, but I should probably play it safe.

"I'm not saying *don't* talk to him. I'm just saying you need to be careful here. Oliver's a clever guy and clearly good at hiding things. So you're going to need to be a bit strategic. Protect yourself in case it gets uglier." She paused, taking a sip of her wine. "You just need to know exactly where everything is and what's going on before you confront him. Try to get a copy of all your accounts and whatnot. Otherwise he might totally screw you in the divorce."

Even the sound of that "d" word made me wince.

"Oh god, do you think we'll get divorced?" I asked, the tears starting up again as I glanced down at my rings.

"I have no bloody idea," she said, shaking her head. "Two hours ago I would never have thought Oliver was on a dating app, never mind going to sex parties. He always seemed so Mr. Perfect to me. So strait-laced and into his reputation and work and what have you. I'm just saying be careful."

And I knew she was right. I had no idea what was going on with our finances. Which might sound naive in hindsight, but he was in investments; he had an MBA from London Business School. It made sense for him to deal with it. And if I'm really honest I hate numbers and budgets and tax time. It was a relief to have him take it off my hands. So yes, maybe if I had it all to do again I'd do things differently, but blah blah blah.

"How am I supposed to act normal?" I said.

"You're an actress, Charlie, a good one, just pretend it's a role."

I shook my head, clenching my jaw. "I don't think I can, Tess. You don't get how this feels." But then I wanted to rescind that last statement, because she did know.

"You *can*," she said, reaching for my hand. "Think of it this way, there are only two rules you have to follow: (1) Don't tell him you know about the app and (2) Get copies of everything you can find. That's it. You can do that."

"Like *Fight Club*," I said with a small smile.

"Yes, just like *Fight Club*," she replied.

Episode 4

I stared at the swirling grain of our dark wood front door, the murmur of the TV floating through it as I tried to calm my breath. Things are always so different in reality to how you plan them out in your head. I'd spent the cab drive home amping myself up, telling myself that if he wanted to screw with me he'd better bring his "A" game and practising my nonchalant "Hi, honey, I'm home" face. But now that I was standing here, keys in my hand, only inches away from having to face him, I could all but taste my heartbeat. I closed my eyes.

You can do this, Charlie.

I slid the key into the lock, turned it and the door swung open.

He was lying on the sofa, I could see his feet—grey socks, socks I'd washed and balled up many times—on the arm rest and some sort of cooking show on the screen.

"Hey," he said, popping his head up to smile at me. The shine of his dark hair caught the light and his eyes met mine. My pulse sped up. *Fuck.* I looked away immediately, turning back to the door as I slipped off my shoes.

"Hey," I said, closing my eyes to centre myself, then shutting the door behind me as my pulse thumped in my ears. "What are you watching?" I asked, dropping my bag on the kitchen counter. There was a pot still on the stove and the colander was in the drying rack by the sink: spaghetti. He must have made spaghetti. I moved over to him. He was wearing a pair of grey tracksuit pants and a white polo shirt.

"Something shit," he said, pressing pause on the remote control. The room was silent now apart from the muffled gunfire from whatever Natasha upstairs was watching on TV.

"Oh my god," he said, looking up to the noise. "I'm going to take up the trumpet one of these days just to even the score."

Then his eyes were back on me. "I missed you tonight," he said, wriggling towards the back of the sofa. From where I stood I could smell ylang ylang and the spice of his cologne. He patted the space in front of him and as I lay down he wrapped me in his arms, warm and tight, his breath in my hair. He was acting the same way he'd always done, but instead of comforting me, it filled me with nausea; that meant this wasn't new. It meant he'd been living a double life for as long as we'd known each other. Nothing had changed in his world.

But I was left wondering how many sex parties he'd already been to, what sorts of things he did there, whether Alyssa—his ex— had ever gone to them with him.

"What's going on with Tess that you deserted me like that?" he croaked, his nose nuzzling into the space behind my ear.

"Man troubles," I said through a tight throat, regurgitating the cover story Tess and I had formulated over garlic bread. "This guy she likes. He's being a knob." Our wedding photos were in my line of vision and my chest ached as I ran the memories through the filter of this new information. Searching for signs. Signals I might have missed. But there hadn't been any.

"Wow, Tess never likes anyone. Is she okay?" he asked and my lower lip wobbled as I nodded.

"Yep."

He took a deep breath. "So I have some bad news," he said. "I have to go away again."

"What?" He was supposed to be home for another week and my chest panged. And all I could think was: *One of the first signs of cheating is an altered schedule.*

Had the signs been there all along and I'd just been oblivious?

And where was he really going—was it really for work?

"Just for a couple of days," he said. "I have to go and smooth things over with a couple of investors in Nigeria."

"But you just got back," I said, clenching my jaw to stop the tears. Because I knew that was the last time we'd lie there on that sofa like this. I knew I'd ask the hard questions soon, and he would eventually have to tell the truth. And no matter what happened, everything would be different. We would never be this couple again. And what if we couldn't figure it out, what if we went our separate ways? Fuck, that would hurt. It was hurting already; a hot tear rolled down my cheek.

"Hey," he said, his voice soft and gentle as he propped himself up to look at me. "Don't cry. I promise it won't always be like this," he said, wriggling his fingers between mine and staring into my eyes. I nodded, but I couldn't hold his gaze. And my eyes landed on my Bahia bracelet. On the knots. On my wishes. And my lower lip trembled more.

"God, I hate seeing you sad," he said. "I'll be back before you know it. But you seem upset a lot at the moment—are you sure you're not pregnant?"

"Pregnancy doesn't make you upset," I said, wiping the tears away with my sleeve. How had this happened? How had we gone from "true love" to two strangers lying on the sofa, both with their dating app notifications off, in the space of a few days?

"The hormones might," he said. But all that did was make me cry more, because now we'd never have a baby together. The entire life I'd taken for granted with him was gone. But I needed to hold it together.

"When do you go?" I asked, steadying my breath and rolling back onto my side, my eyes scanning the room, our bookshelf, the coffee table, the curtains we'd picked out together, the life we'd been building. He hugged me tight and I closed my eyes. What would he do if I asked him again now? Lie? What if I showed him my app, if I presented him with proof? Would he explode? Find an excuse and then secretly move whatever money we had to a place I wouldn't find it?

I'd seen firsthand how everyone has a side of them you can't predict, a side you don't know is there until it's too late. And I was only just meeting Oliver's.

And so, as I lay there, not saying the things I needed to say most, I was filled with the kind of loneliness you can only feel when you're not alone. It stabs you far deeper than solitude. It slows your pulse and fills your lungs with darkness.

"Tomorrow night," he said, pressing play and kissing me on the head.

And I just lay there silent, watching the cheerful man on the TV chop things up and then drop them into a big pot of hot water.

It was one of the hardest things I'd ever had to do: lie in his arms and say nothing, pretend I didn't know. It took every ounce of self-control I had to hold it inside. But I knew deep down Tess was right, and so I reminded myself that there were only two rules and the first rule was: *Don't tell him you know about the app.* Imagining that rule in Brad Pitt's voice definitely helped.

It was then that Oliver's phone buzzed. He pulled it from his pocket and I looked up at him. I could see the white light from the screen reflecting as two little rectangles in his eyes as he moved through to his emails. His jaw tensed. His eyes changed. Hardened.

"Fuck," he said, sitting up, roughly pushing me aside.

"What's wrong?" I asked.

He let out a big exhale. "Fuck," he repeated, getting up. "Work emergency." And then he stomped through to his study. Said "Fuck" one more time. And then slammed the door.

And I was left alone, listening to the cheerful man on the telly tell me to leave things simmering on a low heat, like that wasn't the state of my entire life, wondering what had happened to piss Oliver off like that and whether this counted as *secretive phone or computer use.*

It was only the next evening that I realised what "work emergency" was code for.

I woke to pink-white sunshine streaming in through the window: the mauve curtains had been pulled open, my mouth was dry and full of hair and Oliver was in the shower. I could smell his shampoo on the pillowcase and hear the pipes creaking. The water hitting the tiles. And I lay there, drinking in every detail, wondering what it would feel like to have someone else sleeping on his side of the bed.

I clenched my eyes shut and hugged onto a pillow as I recalled the night before. The gold coin. The call to Tess. Our chat. Coming home. Oliver. The email. He'd shut himself in his study to work after that email came in and I hadn't seen him for the rest of the night. As for me, I'd sobbed in the shower. I'd prayed that I was wrong. I'd texted Tess for support. And then I'd tossed and turned, finally falling asleep at around 4 am. It was just after 7.30 now and my eyelids were made of cement, but something had changed in the night.

Gone was shock. Gone was denial. I was now well and truly into "rage."

And the thing I've learnt about rage is: it has to go somewhere. You can either let it eat you up inside until one day you explode, or you can use it. So, as I lay there, I consciously chose to use it. There would be no more moping. No more crying. And no more making excuses for him.

As soon as I got home that night and had access to his computer, I'd do exactly as Tess had instructed.

But he was still here right now, and so I needed to hold it together a little longer. Needed to keep pretending. I pried my eyes open against the sunlight coming through the window and reached for my phone. A message from Grace saying she wouldn't be in until that afternoon because of "dental issues" and an Instagram notification: *@JoshHammersley* added to their story for the first time in a while.

Perfect.

Josh was the ex I told you about. The one who broke up with me just before I met Oliver. He was tall and Scandinavian-looking, with high cheekbones, white-blond hair and blue eyes. To say our relationship had been painful, confusing and downright lonely at times wouldn't quite do it justice. But it wasn't all bad, and for all his faults, I'd never found Josh on a dating app.

So right then, seeing his name on my phone screen, I missed him.

Tess had told me to block Josh when we broke up that last time, her exact words: "Babe, block him, this is a cycle, enough is enough." But I didn't want to block him because it seemed childish. Or, rather, that's what I'd said. The real reason was I wanted him to see how "fine" I was without him; that usually made him want me back. And I needed him to want me back. And then, when he *hadn't* wanted me back, I met Oliver, and frankly at that point I wanted Josh to see how happy I was with someone else. To see how lovable I really was.

Yep, I was complicated. Messy.

Sometimes I suspected I might actually be crazy: but then

maybe everyone else would seem crazy too if their inner dialogue was audible.

In any case, no, I hadn't blocked him, had I?

And until now, what with his hectic work schedule and infrequent social media habits, that hadn't been a problem. Because until now, he'd always been the single one (hooray!).

But when I clicked through to his profile to see what he'd posted, I realised that had changed.

It was a picture. With a girl. A blonde one. A long-limbed, bronzed, fake-lashed, pretty one. They were on a plane, faces squished together. He had stubble; he was on holiday with her. Of course he was: it was summer, that's what normal people do with their summers, right? Post things like #nevergoinghome #holidayspam #Biarritz? Not like me with all my dark revelations. But life is always like that: it's as though it sets an egg timer and the moment your love life falls apart, *brrriiiiinnnnggg*: everyone else's seems to flourish.

My phone beeped. A text message.

Tess: *Are you okay?*

The pipes squeaked as Oliver turned off the shower. I could see him through the crack of the bathroom door reaching for a towel— one of the white fluffy ones we bought together at Peter Jones before I suspected he was the devil—as I typed back.

Me: *No. Want to die. Chat later on?*

Tess: *Don't crack babe. This is too important.*

But I had no intention of cracking. The bathroom door opened and Oliver emerged, a towel around his waist, his jaw tight as he moved through to the kitchen.

I was sitting there, watching him, watching the water droplets sparkle on his shoulders, and he didn't even say good morning. Whatever had happened at work the night before, whatever that email was, had really upset him. Normally I would have pushed to talk about it, tried to fix things, but I didn't have the energy this morning. We were no longer on the same team.

The coffee machine started whizzing from the kitchen as it turned on; the cupboard doors opened and banged closed again.

"*Charlie!*" Oliver yelled. "Where are the black pods? We're out!"

"Oh," I said. "I'll get more." That sounded normal, right? Like the sort of thing I might say if I wasn't planning my exit strategy? Far better than all the unsaid words bubbling on a low heat inside me. The unsaid words I wasn't allowed to say yet like: *Fuck you, I trusted you—well, sort of.*

I glanced over at his suitcase—he'd start packing in a bit. I didn't know how long I could pretend. I needed to get out of there as soon as I could. Or I would, indeed, crack. I'd show him the app and ask him outright. I could feel it. I might throw something at him. Drop his phone in the loo. And that might feel good in the moment, but I'd be screwing myself over in the long run. Because Tess was right, if he could lie to me so well about cheating, who knew what else he was lying about? What he was capable of? I needed to protect myself. Which right now meant getting out of there before I fucked it up. So, before he came back into the bedroom I got up, went through to the bathroom, shut the door and turned on the shower. That way I *couldn't* say anything.

—

An hour and a bit later I was in the shop early, sipping coffee at my desk and feeling very sorry for myself, as I stared down at Josh's Instagram feed. He'd posted a couple more holiday snaps since that morning with hashtags like #bliss and #summerlove (Was she helping him with these? He wasn't really a hashtagger) and he looked so happy. So uncharacteristically brown. I wanted to be a good person and be glad for him, but all I could think was why wasn't he that happy with me? And in that moment, it felt like maybe everything was my fault. Josh wasn't happy with me so he left. Oliver wasn't happy with me so he signed up to a dating app. I was the common thread here.

It was then that Mum started ringing. I stared down at my phone. *I should answer.* But I really didn't want to; if there was one person in the world who could crystallise the thought that it was, indeed, my fault, it was my mother.

I stared at her name flashing back from my phone screen, fragments of memory from the last time I saw her, this past Easter, flickering in my mind: Oliver and I, standing outside, about to knock on the door, him squeezing my hand and telling me it'd be okay. Mum fawning over him and ordering me around: "Darling, put on the kettle"; the self-satisfied look on her face when he pulled out an orange envelope and asked if he could leave a copy of his will and whatnot in their safe. Like I'd finally done something right in my life—maybe I wouldn't end up on a park bench after all—but it had nothing to do with my own efforts.

No. I couldn't risk feeling any worse right now, and so I let it ring out.

I'd always wanted to be one of those people with a great relationship with their parents, but I just wasn't. There was nothing bad about them per se: they were still together, still living in the same two-story, red brick house I grew up in out in Surrey; Mum still played bridge and tennis with her old friends and Dad was still loving but silent. But I hated visiting them for two reasons.

One: it reminded me of things I didn't want to remember, a version of myself I no longer wanted to be. And I'd moved to London to be different. To re-create myself. To make something of myself.

And two: Mum was always saying things like "Are you sure you want to be an actress? Don't you want to do something easier, something you can succeed in?" Or telling me how beautiful and brilliant all her friends' kids were, how much they earned in their safer careers as teachers and lawyers and secretaries. She didn't understand why acting was so important to me: that it was the one place I could be totally raw and emotionally truthful, and have it applauded as opposed to shunned. She didn't think in those terms: everything was practical with my mother. It'd always felt like she'd have been prouder of me if I'd become a prostitute—at least then I would have earned well.

So me marrying Oliver and his healthy salary prospects had improved our lukewarm relationship considerably and I wasn't looking forward to telling her it was over. That he was cheating. She'd somehow make it my fault. Blame my "hyper-sensitivity" or "mercurial nature." I'd heard those terms a lot growing up. Though, to be fair to her, she didn't have all the information.

A little ping sounded from my computer—an email—so I looked up. The Oliver Goldsmith marketing team wouldn't be able to make it that day. Relief flooded my veins. I'd totally forgotten they were coming and I wasn't prepared. My mind had been mush—an ashtray left out in the rain—from the moment I received that "gold coin" the afternoon before. I hadn't sent out any of the orders as I'd promised Grace I would (today, I'd do that today) and I still only had that one navy dress sitting on the rail out back for them. But I was pretty sure I'd seen something come in from an Italian shipment that hadn't been put out on the floor yet. It was a blue-and-white-checked Givenchy dress with a full knee-length skirt and thick black lace running down the front, around the neckline and at the sleeves. It might just be perfect.

I grabbed my coffee and headed back into the storage room. I wasn't sure where exactly I'd seen it. Running through the last few days in my mind, I tried to isolate which shipment it was in so I could figure out which box to open because they all looked the same. Eventually I chose one against the far wall. Kneeling down beside it, I pried back the cardboard lid: the contents smelled like a dry cleaner's. Lying on the top was a lime-green beaded dress. I pulled it out and hung it on one of our moveable hangers. I might as well get them ready for the floor while I searched.

A few minutes later I was pulling out a shoulder-padded Yves Saint Laurent power suit in a dusty grey pinstripe. I was feeling the lining, checking for any holes, when I heard something. A *bzzzz*? The door. A customer was here. *Shit.*

I stood up, my legs all pins and needles as I hobbled to the door and plastered a fake smile on my face. But before I made it out into the main room, I heard that buzz sing out again. They'd left.

Paranoia flooded my veins. Something was wrong. A shiver ran through me and I instinctively glanced over to my bag. It was still there, thank god—someone could have taken it—and pulled out my phone: 4.09. I'd be able to go home soon. There was a little shop on the corner that sold flip-phones, suitcases and gadgets I'd walked past many times; I was pretty sure they'd have a USB stick for me to buy. Then I'd go home and sift through Oliver's computer files, copy whatever I could find, and put an end to the pain.

But what then? I'd have to confront him at some point. He'd want to know why it was over, and how would he react then? He'd gone to such lengths to create the illusion of being the perfect man—would he become dangerous when he realised I knew his darkest secret?

I'd never been scared of Oliver before that, but once you learn someone has such a big secret, you begin to wonder what else you might have missed.

You begin to wonder if you know them at all.

—

8.11 PM

I stared at his blue-white screen, the walls around me glowing tangerine from the setting sun sitting just above the windowsill, my fingers poised over the keyboard. The window was partially open, creaking with a gentle breeze, and I could hear the wall-muffled sounds of children shrieking with laughter from Battersea Park across the road. I was in Oliver's study, his computer was whirring and I was trying to guess his password. Slowly, I typed in *@-l-o-v-e-r-7*. But I was grasping. I knew that.

I pressed "Enter."

Nothing.

How was this so hard? Was I right, did I not know him at all? Had I been sleeping beside a stranger all this time? Because I'd seen enough movies to know that people always use the things that mean the most to them in their passwords: people, pets, birthdays, memories. And I'd already tried: *C-h-a-r-l-i-e*, *O-l-i-v-e-r*, *K-a-t-h-e-r-i-n-e* (that was his mother's name), *0-6-0-3-1-9-8-5* (my birthday), *V-e-g-a-s* and *o-l-i-v-e-r-a-n-d-c-h-a-r-l-i-e-f-o-r-e-v-e-r* (that was my password, FYI, good wifey that I was). I'd tried variations with numbers, brackets and dashes too. I'd tried everything I could think of. Frankly, I was surprised his computer hadn't locked me out yet. I couldn't even take it to the Genius Bar and get them to crack it for me because Oliver had a desktop computer, the heavy sort you can't steal—a choice he made after we were broken into and his laptop was taken. I winced when I thought about that laptop: it was me who'd insisted he not take it on our honeymoon. That we have three days just for "us." Wow, he was pissed when we got home and found the house ransacked and the computer gone. I'd joked that maybe they'd return it when they found the "W" key was missing (it was) and that certainly didn't help matters.

And even though he'd managed to remote wipe it, he'd remained anxious for months about what sensitive information might have been accessed before he managed to do that.

Sensitive information like the sort I was seeking.

Sensitive information that had me wondering whether what I was trying to do was illegal or simply "frowned upon." But I reasoned that we were married, what was his was mine, so I was really breaking into my own computer, right? Besides, I was hardly the first wife to break into her husband's files. What were they going to do—lock us all up?

But as I stared at his login screen my jaw grew tight: I was all out of ideas.

Now, please do your best not to judge me here. I know I should have considered the whole password issue before now but I was new to this. I'd never had to break into a computer before. I had a lot on my mind. And I'd blanked it.

But I had to figure it out. I knew I wouldn't be able to keep up the charade for too much longer, so it had to all happen before he got home. And I was starting to worry about my mental state: when I got home that night it'd felt like something was different. A faint whiff of something I couldn't quite put my finger on lingered in the air. Like someone had been there.

I needed this whole thing to be over.

And I was so close. The small USB stick I'd bought that evening was already plugged into a port at the back.

There has to be a way in.

Somebody out there must have encountered this problem before.

And so I reached for my phone, pulled up a browser window and consulted our electronic collective unconscious. Yes, I asked Google, desperately typing in: *MacBook Pro forgot password reset.*

Enter.

The screen filled with links: computer magazine pages, advertisements and forums. A siren flared up from outside and my pulse quickened as I imagined Oliver finding me here. But he was safely on another continent right now, or perhaps still in the air. I hadn't even checked in with him. That was a sure sign it was over.

I scrolled down through the links.

The second one looked promising, so I tapped on it: *A step-by-step guide to resetting your Mac password.*

Perfect.

The instructions themselves looked pretty easy and they were numbered one to seven. So I reached for the keyboard and followed step one: *Hold down command and R at the same time.* The screen went black. I kept my fingers on those buttons, just like the instructions said, refusing to slip, and a moment later the little white Apple sign appeared in the middle of the screen.

My phone had dimmed and so I touched the screen to bring it back to life and went to step two: *Go to "Utilities."*

Step three: *Click on "Terminal."*

Step four: *Type in resetpassword.*

Oliver's new password would be 1234567$. That was step five.

Step six: *Save.*

Seven: *Restart.*

Eight: *Re-enter 1234567$.*

The window banged.

I jumped.

Turned to stare at it.

My pulse beat double time.

And as I turned back to his desktop, so bright in that darkened room, I realised I was in. There were files and folders everywhere. Any one of them could contain the things Tess said I needed. But I had to check something else first: his iMessage. I mean, wouldn't you? That little blue bubble on the bar at the bottom of the screen was all but singing a siren song.

There were messages in there from me, Justin, a junk message from a gym asking him to re-join and one from his phone provider telling him the cost of calls and texts in Brazil. Nothing incriminating. His inbox was far neater than mine. Though it did occur to me that might be incriminating in itself.

The external hard drive icon was showing up as a little orange rectangle on the right-hand side of his desktop. I dragged everything on the desktop into it.

As it started to copy across, I went to his "Documents" folder. It was filled with subfolders and random files with names that meant nothing to me. I needed to know exactly what I was looking for to make sure I got what I needed. And so, as I added the whole lot to the copy queue, I pulled out my phone and called Tess, chewing on my inner cheek as it rang.

My eyes moved to the time: 8.23 pm on a Friday. She'd have left the office by now, but she might be out.

"Charlie," she said, a low hum in the background, like she was in a bar or on a street.

"Hey," I replied.

"Are you okay?"

"Yeah, I'm on his computer right now, copying things. What *exactly* am I looking for? There's so much stuff on here."

"Everything. Accounts, spreadsheets—just take whatever you can find, and we can go through it together later," she said, pausing. I could all but hear her mind whirring. "Hang on, so you have his password then?"

"Not exactly," I said. "I reset it."

I thought she might tell me that was a mistake, that now he'd know I'd been in there. But she didn't.

"Perfect," she said. "Where is he now? He's not going to come home and find you or anything, right?"

"No, he's gone away. Probably to a sex retreat."

"Okay, good," she said, not even humouring me. "What browser does he use?"

"Ummm, I'm not sure," I replied, glancing down at the bar at the bottom of the screen. I clicked on the icon for Firefox first. Clicked on "History" and saw it was empty. So then I tried Safari—not much there either. Finally I went to Chrome. "Just a sec, I think he uses Chrome."

"Okay," she said. "Go up to where it says 'Chrome' and choose 'Preferences.' "

I followed her instructions and up came a screen I'd never seen before: Settings. "Done."

"Now in around the middle of the screen it should say 'Passwords.' "

"Okay," I said, "so I click on that?"

"Yep."

The click of my mouse echoed in the small, red-orange-lit room.

Up came a list of websites, his username for each and a dot-dot-dot below the heading: Password.

"There should be a button that looks like a little eye beside each one. Click on one of those."

I chose the one beside his Gmail account and up popped a window asking me to enter his password information. I slowly entered: *1234567$.*

Up came his password: *Onelife11.*

My throat grew tight and something twisted inside me. His voice echoed in my mind: *"Charlie, we have one life to live. One chance at this. Please would you live yours with me?"*

"Wow," I said, my voice almost a whisper.

"Now click on any others you might need and then take a picture."

"How do you know this stuff?" I asked, frowning.

"I have skills," she replied, her tone dry. But I knew "how." Her investigation into Marc had clearly run deeper than even I knew.

I clicked on some of the others: Facebook, Amazon, his banking site. Two out of three were the same password: *Onelife11*.

"Are you okay? Do you want to come over? I have to do some work but it might be better not to be all alone."

"I'll be okay," I said. I wanted to be alone. "Love you."

"Love you too. What about tomorrow evening? Catch up then?"

"Perfect," I said.

And then we hung up and I took that picture.

So there I was, staring down at his passwords on my phone. I now had full access to everything and I just couldn't help myself, could I?

I opened another tab and pulled up Facebook first. Then I entered his login information, and carefully typed in his password: *O-n-e-l-i-f-e-1-1.*

A moment later his circular profile picture was staring back at me beside his name: *Oliver Buchanan.*

Now, the most obvious place to look was his messages, so I

went straight there. But there was nothing suspicious in his inbox. A couple of messages from people I didn't immediately recognise—perhaps he'd gone to school or university with them—but nothing jarring.

Not until I looked up at the top. Beside "Recent" was the greyed-out text: *Message requests (39).*

Oliver always was a stickler for privacy. Whatever settings he had on his Facebook account would have filtered messages from unknown people into that folder.

My throat grew tight as I clicked on it.

I could read the first line of each as I scanned down through them: *Yes please . . . Torture Garden for me . . . Message me back, handsome . . .*

On the left-hand side of each was the profile picture of the woman who had sent it. And to the right was the date. Thirty-nine requests in less than a month. My stomach filled with cement as I imagined him trawling through them while he was in Brazil, while he was telling me he had no wifi.

My heart was racing by now, my mind out of control; I felt like I'd just run a red light. I did the only thing I could: I took a deep breath, shut down the page, pulled up Gmail and logged in.

Might as well be thorough.

The screen flashed white, a red and white envelope appeared, and then there were messages: junk mail, a couple of Facebook notification emails and halfway down that first screen was a message with the subject line: *!!!*. It was from Justin.

My eyes darted to the right: it had come in the night before.

My mind flicked back to us lying on the sofa, him saying there was a work emergency and then lapsing into the foulest of moods. Exclamation marks looked urgent, it had been read, and he worked with Justin. *That must be it: the emergency.* So I clicked on it.

The body of the email read:

Man—what the fuck are you doing? My sister just sent this through. Nobody cares what you do on your own time, but have a look at your LinkedIn profile! People are starting to figure out where you work and leave cute messages. We can't afford any more attention. Not after those emails. Fix it.

What did he mean by "any more attention"? What emails?

And *Wow: so Justin didn't know Oliver was on that app. Oliver had done that all on his own . . .*

I clicked on the attachment, waiting for it to open.

And I have to say, I didn't expect any more surprises by then; I was pretty sure I already knew what it was. Something to do with that dating app. The one I'd already seen. The one I'd presumed the women in his message request basket had seen too. The one they were keen to respond to.

Turns out I was half right.

But it was just a tad worse than that.

Because it *was* of a dating app profile for Oliver. It *did* say the exact same thing I'd seen before. It did list all the same parties. But this was from a different app.

How many of these things is he on?

And in that moment, my life seemed like one of those tapestries

114

Mum used to do when I was little: beautiful and neat on the front, but a knotted, tangled mess on the back.

I took a deep breath, logged out of his Gmail, cleared the browser history and turned off his computer just as a wave of nausea rolled through me.

I had no idea how everything had fallen apart so disastrously and so fast, but I knew I needed him out of the house. *Now.*

A muffled bang of a door rang through the house: Natasha was home upstairs. Then came the *clip-clippety-clip-clip* of her heels before she took them off, just above me. She used her second mini-bedroom as a walk-in closet—I knew that because I'd watered her plants a couple of times when she was away and had taken the opportunity to snoop. A few moments later, the TV was on in the adjacent room: a blur of news or something with one strong, low male voice.

I stood up and moved through to the kitchen, opened the drawer below the cutlery and pulled out a roll of black plastic bin liners.

I thought I finally had a clear answer to my question—yes, he was cheating. Which meant it was time for Oliver to pack. But how could I possibly have the right answer when I didn't even know what question to ask yet?

SATURDAY, 9 JUNE 2018 (8.02 AM)

Maybe it's the romantic in me, the part that yearns for meaning, but I will always remember that next day as a single sound: a little bird tweeting. Because when adrenaline woke me at 4 am, the sky a pre-dawn indigo and my pillowcase dampened with tears, the only sound that rang through the flat was a bird chirping outside the window. And I latched onto it. It was simultaneously a symbol of hope—the sound of a new day piercing through the darkness—and a witty, poetic juxtaposition.

A little cosmic meme that would never find its way to Instagram.

After I woke up, I lay there for a good two hours, just crying it all out, torturing myself with our highlight reel, pressing on the bruise. There were the big things, of course, like our wedding day: getting our marriage licence on the way to the most kitsch chapel ever built, the gel-haired, half-drunk witness they provided, the blurred, irreplaceable polaroids he took. Our wedding night: big windows overlooking the neon lights of Vegas, room service, me winning five hundred dollars on the roulette wheel and those pay-to-view movies. Then there were the seemingly insignificant things like how stressed Oliver always got buying my tampons. How no matter how many times I told him which ones I wanted, he always came back with the wrong ones, a sheepish look and "Sorry, I panicked." Or the health kick we'd embarked on in January. The organic box of fruit and obscure, unrecognisable vegetables we'd signed up for. The jokes about being slaves to "the box" after forty-eight hours

116

and the making of a large ratatouille. And Oliver's triumphant face when he arrived home the next day with two orange shopping bags full of Lindt chocolate, cheese, bread and wine.

What was I going to do with all those rusting memories now?

And how had they been replaced by things like the red lace garter belt I'd found in one of his jacket pockets?

Yes, packing him up had been illuminating.

By the time 6 am rolled around, I realised I definitely wasn't going back to sleep and the sad reel of memories wasn't going to cease, so I did the only thing I could think of: I got up, boiled a couple of eggs (beginning a keto diet seemed like a good way to handle things in the moment) and started sipping gin out of the bottle.

Do you remember that scene in *Bridget Jones's Diary* where she's super depressed and realises she can either lie down and die of sadness or fight? Where she takes to the exercise bike, quits her job and totally re-creates herself? Well that was my inspiration right at that moment.

All I kept thinking was *Channel Bridget.*

Even then, I was clinging to the idea that I was in the middle of some lighthearted rom-com where everything would be okay in the end.

And if that seems naive to you—fine, I get it. But right then I *needed* to believe life was like that in order to get through it.

Because this was not the first thing I'd had to get through.

Oliver had sent a couple of texts the night before, somewhere between me closing down his computer and stuffing all his things into black bags, and I hadn't answered. That was very un-me. He could clearly sense something was wrong, so by 7 am he was calling.

My phone was lying on the bed and I winced as his beautiful face, his name, flashed back at me. Part of me ached to reach for it, to somehow make amends, but a larger part knew I *couldn't* talk to him. If I talked to him I'd soften, and if I softened I'd stay, and if I stayed it would continue, and if it continued my cracks would deepen, and if my cracks deepened any more I might disintegrate altogether.

So leaving, or having him leave, was a matter of survival.

I stared at the phone, tight-jawed, until it stopped ringing.

And then I stuffed one more of his jackets into black bag number three and dragged it to the front door. I glanced through the window on my way back to the bedroom. The sky was a muted blue by then, slashed up like eighties denim with long lines of cloud, and a ball of white sun. It was a beautiful day to end a marriage.

I stared back at the other two bags.

One was full of soft things like clothing, and the other one was books and shoes and other random things with sharp edges that pierced the plastic and meant I had to double bag it. They didn't contain *all* his things, but they held the immediate visual traces of him. Anything that might stab me to look at it—body wash, razor, books. The problems I now faced were (a) they were heavy and (b) I didn't know where to leave them.

His mother was all the way over in Norfolk and I wouldn't have wanted to make that call even if she was closer, his brother was over in the States somewhere, probably getting high or arrested, and Justin was his only real friend (and frankly, back then I thought there was nothing that would make me call Justin). So I'd settled on his car. I'd put his things in his car. And I'd force myself not to key it like someone had done during our honeymoon, though now I understood the impetus.

I never told you about our honeymoon, did I? Well, it was magic. We spent it in Lake Como and it was a mini-moon really. Just three days. Three perfect days during which I'd taken the photograph he'd used as his profile picture on that dating app. So there you go: you just never know how things will turn out. But those three days were going to be etched in my memory forever, even long after he was gone. I knew that already. And as I stood there, considering how to get the bags out to his car, images flickered through my mind: the warm sunshine on my face as I woke up that first morning, my rings twinkling from my hand, my legs tangled in expensive white sheets, the blue and glassy lake lapping up against the window, a burnt-orange damask chair in the corner of the room, Oliver, still asleep behind me, hugging me, then breakfast and laughing and dinners and wine and sex and lots of tongue-in-cheek "my husband" and "my wife" talk. Then the three days were up and it was London's lights twinkling through the plane window, welcoming us home. Welcoming us to our new life together. As a couple. As Mr and Mrs Buchanan.

It was during those three days that the whole break-in thing happened.

And that's what our flat reminded me of right now: the time we'd been broken into. A big bloody mess, things strewn everywhere. Our bookshelf was half bare. Big, gaping holes where his books had been. An empty wall where our wedding photos had hung. And in the emptiness, Oliver's bronze Ganesha, the one that was supposed to bring us luck, seemed to loom on that mantelpiece.

I stared at it. He loved that thing. I knew I should pack it, but the mean-spirited part of me decided not to. Fuck him. Let him suffer. Maybe I'd take months to give it back.

In came a message from him: *Where are you, baby?*

I stared down at the screen, tears burning in my eyes, what could I even text back? And then my phone beeped. It was a message from *Brooke Pilates*.

It read *R u home? Emergency.*

I looked around the room, at the black bags and Oliver's things everywhere. I was quite clearly mid-catastrophe—I couldn't have her come over. And so I was about to text back *No, sorry*. But then my phone started ringing. *Shit.* It felt wrong not to answer. She'd said it was an emergency. What if she was hurt? She was alone in London, I couldn't just ignore her.

"Hello," I said, smiling in the hopes that it might imbue my voice with more positivity than I felt.

"Hey—sorry, babe, are you home? You live near Battersea Park right?"

"Ummm, yes," I said. Why was she asking? *Please dear god don't want to pop past.*

"Can I come over super quick? I'm having a bit of an issue. Actually a big fucking issue."

Shit. Shit. Shit.

"Ummm, sure," I said, "but I'm heading to work in a sec." I couldn't very well say no outright, could I?

"I'll come right now. What's your address?"

And so I gave it to her, hung up and rushed through to the bathroom to splash water on my face and brush my teeth. My hairbrush was sitting right there on the countertop so I pulled it through my locks. Then it was eyeliner, bronzer, mascara and lip gloss. I looked almost normal by the end, if somewhat puffy.

Brooke arrived just as I was done and I buzzed her in and opened the door.

"Hey," she said, apology in her voice and her eyes wide as she strode purposefully towards me. "Having a fucking nightmare situation as you can see." She was pointing at her white t-shirt: a big brown coffee stain covered the front and had the fabric sticking to her black bra.

She came inside and I closed the door after her.

"What's going on here?" she asked, looking around. I didn't want to tell her about Oliver and the app, not now, so I fibbed. "We're moving." And as I said it my throat grew tight because even though I meant it as a lie, I realised it would soon be the truth. One of us *would* be moving. "There's this great place nearby and it looks like we're going to get it, it's so exciting really. Such a great entertaining space."

Shut up, Charlie. I always do that: babble when I'm anxious.

"Oh, cool. Sorry, where's the loo?"

I pointed towards the bathroom.

"Thanks so much," she said as she rushed towards it and inside. The door was left ajar and I could hear the basin taps going wild. I imagined her in there, rinsing and wringing and cursing black coffee.

"Do you want to borrow something?" I stared down at my phone: 8.02 am. I still had a couple of hours before the shop opened, but I just wanted to get out of that flat. Away from memories of "us."

"No, I'm a Londoner now, I always carry a spare," she said, popping her head around to look at me as she pulled a plain black t-shirt over her head. "I have a client meeting in half an hour if you can believe my luck."

A moment later she emerged, stain-free.

"You're a lifesaver," she said, smiling as she looked around the room again, her eyes lingering on the gin bottle sitting on the countertop. "I owe you one."

And I'd soon be collecting on that "I owe you."

"Where's your hubby? Why isn't he helping with all this?"

I swallowed hard. "He's away on business, he's back tomorrow." *Do not cry, do not cry, do not cry.* I forced a smile but my lower lip wobbled.

"Oh, hon, are you okay?" she asked, moving towards me, hands reaching out to take mine. And I shook my head.

"It's nothing," I said, searching for a reason I might be crying that didn't involve the horrible truth. And, other than boys, there was only one other reason I used to cry. "I just found out I didn't get a part. It's silly."

"Argh. Life in the Arts, right?" And then her eyes moved to the mannequin in the corner.

"Oh wow, I love this," she said, moving over to it and pulling out her phone to take a picture.

Snap. Snap. Snap.

"Ooooohhhhh," she said, turning to our near-empty mantelpiece. "And this. Where did you get it?"

She was talking about Oliver's bronze statue. I watched as she moved over to it, leaning in to inspect the detailing.

And all I was thinking was: *Please fucking leave so I can get these bags out of the house and start rebuilding my life.* But you can't say things like that in real life, you have to say things like "I'm not sure. It's Oliver's."

She angled the phone towards it and took a photograph while I tried to make small talk so she wouldn't realise my whole life was falling apart.

"Stroking its trunk is supposed to be good luck," I said. But it was Oliver who told me that and so as I heard my voice mimic his words something twisted inside me.

"Wow. I have the best idea." She grinned. Brown eyes wide. "Can I get a pic of it with you? For my Instagram?"

The last thing I wanted was to touch it—to be reminded of him. And then I thought of Oliver and how careful I was supposed to be with posting things on social media. But seriously, why was I still trying to please him? Brooke was looking at me now, waiting for an answer. But I just wanted her to leave. And so I said, "Ummm, not sure, I'm a bit of a mess. Can we do it on a day I'm not crying?"

"What about if you hold the statue over your face, kind of like Bookface? It'll look cool. *Pleeeaaaase*," she said. "I need shit for my profile and I know exactly how I want it to look. I won't even tag you."

How the hell could I say "no" without explaining my crap mood? And so I picked it up and held it in front of my face and she took the picture. Anything to get her to leave.

"Hon, I'm so sorry I can't offer you a cup of tea or something," I said. "But I'm going to be so late." Lies, lies, lies.

"Totally cool," Brooke replied as we headed towards the door. "I'm going to be late too. But Pilates on Wednesday?"

"Absolutely."

"Text me if you change your mind. It's such a trek for me and I hate it when I'm there alone. Amy gangs up on me."

I smiled. Amy was one of the instructors and she was all about arm work.

"I promise," I said. "I'll put a reminder in my phone right now." And so I did, for two days prior to our next class. I was going to need my friends now, more than ever. I couldn't keep letting them down.

A few minutes later Brooke was gone and it was just me—me and those black bags and the wreckage of my life. But there was only one way to do it, and that was to do it, and so I grabbed my keys, Oliver's spare car keys, and my bag, opened the front door, pushed the bags outside and then let it bang shut behind me. I was halfway down the hall, pulling two of them and kicking the third when I realised I wasn't alone.

"What on earth have you got there?" came an uppity voice from the stairs. *Oh good—Natasha.* All five foot ten of her. She had long dark hair and was wearing aubergine and white Lululemon and trainers. But even so, even on her way to brunch or the gym or wherever she was going, she looked better groomed than me with my dry-shampooed hair, cheeks pink from gin, ballet flats, blue jeans, thin olive-green metallic top and the black leather jacket I was struggling to balance over my arm.

"Hey. Just have some things I'm . . . taking into the shop later. Need to put them in Oliver's car." *Good thinking.*

"Do you want some help getting them there?" she asked. Natasha didn't like me very much but she was as fantastic at faking "nice" as I was at faking "fine." She leaned in close to pick one up. "Big night?" she asked. Great, I still smelled like booze. Even through the toothpaste.

I could see her biceps clenching beneath her perfectly white, paper-thin top as she picked up one of the bags, then dropped it again. "Wow, this is heavy," she said. So we both awkwardly pushed our respective bags—her one, my two—down the hallway, past the letterboxes and towards the front door.

"Where's Oliver?" she asked, looking back at me when we got there, then glancing beyond my shoulder. "Why isn't he helping?"

You see, that's why Natasha was always so sweet to me: I was pretty sure she fancied Oliver and making friends with me was a good way to get close to him. She went all pouty-pouty and baby-talky when he was around, tossed her hair a bit too much for comfort and laughed a couple of decibels louder than was strictly necessary.

"He's away," I said, my voice flat.

A thin film of sweat was forming in my hairline—the bags were heavy—and I was out of breath. She pushed open the front door and kicked her bag outside, then held it for me.

"It's over there," I said, pointing to Oliver's dark green Range Rover and clicking the button on his keys so it beeped and unlocked. I opened the back door and Natasha stood there behind me.

"That was a workout." She laughed. "Don't need the gym now. So, when's lovely Oliver back?"

And I'm not sure whether it was just all the pent-up frustration, the gin, the fact that I'd had to put on such a good act with Brooke or the fact that I just didn't like Natasha (so how *dare* she ask me that?), but I didn't even think; the words just spewed out of me.

"He'll be back when he's finished fucking whoever he's fucking," I said. And then I flashed her a fake smile.

One, two, three seconds passed before she spoke again. I could see her swallow. "What?" she asked. Her neck was red, but her face—covered in foundation—stayed a nice tanned colour.

"Nothing," I said, my own face flushing hot. I hate losing control. "Thanks for your help."

"Okay," she said, her voice coming out strained. She seemed as shocked as I was. But a moment later she walked away, and I lifted the bags onto the back seat. Slammed the doors shut. Took a photograph. And sent it to Oliver with the following message:

I know all of it. Don't come home. All your stuff is in your car. Charlie.

—

10.07 AM

"Morning," Grace said as she came inside. *Bzzzz.* She was wearing a pair of white trousers, a silk shirt and a pair of golden sandals.

I was hunched over my desk sipping a cup of coffee I'd bought on my way in, nibbling on its white plastic lid. But it was cold by then. I'd been there for an hour—busying myself with staring at the coloured lines moving on my screensaver and thinking about the black bags that had been shoved into Oliver's car and the fact that soon he was going to get that message telling him not to bother coming home, if he hadn't already.

"Are you okay? You don't look well at all." Grace was looking at me. Frowning. She wasn't being mean—she was genuinely concerned. She had that same look Mum used to give me when she was about to take my temperature.

"I'm okay," I said, still staring at my screen. Remembering Natasha—*Big night?*—and that my breath probably still smelled of booze so it was best I didn't do anything silly like cry; that might make her come closer. Last thing I needed was to find myself unemployed. Especially now that I was going to be paying all the rent.

I winced at the thought. And as if by telepathy, my phone beeped. I stared at it. Reached for it.

Oliver: *What the hell are you talking about?????*

My eyes burned with tears and I clenched them shut. All I could see on my inner lids were those messages in his Facebook account and that attachment Justin had sent through to his email. I don't know whether I was angrier with Oliver for lying to me or myself for trusting him.

Because now it seemed so obvious. *How had I been stupid enough to believe he'd cheat on Alyssa and not on me? What else was he hiding?*

"Charlie, you really need to put that away and focus," Grace said, nodding at my phone. "It's work time."

"I'm so sorry, Grace," I said, looking up at her and then back at my phone, "it's just something's happened." I was still staring at the screen, my voice wobbly. It was happening. It was all ending. I bit my lip. *Do not cry. Do not cry. Do not cry.*

"Oh?" she said, a wariness in her voice now. "What?"

My throat tightened. "Oliver's cheating on me," I blurted.

Beat.

Silence.

"What? Charlie, that's terrible," she said, her voice gentle. "I'm so sorry." The room rang with silence. I could hear her swallow. The sounds of traffic floated in from the little street outside. My face grew hot.

"Can I make you some tea?" she asked, puncturing the silence.

The British Band-Aid for everything: tea.

I shook my head. "No, I'm okay, thanks."

More silence. Thick silence. Loud silence. People walked past on the street and I willed them not to come into the shop. *Not now. Please not now.*

"Do you want to go home?" she asked, her voice a little higher.

I shook my head again. "I'll either be sad there or sad here. I might as well be sad here," I said. And I didn't want to have to deal with all the memories.

She nodded and I listened as her computer fired up. I could hear myself swallow. Everything was awkward now. Grace and I didn't have that kind of relationship. I'd known her for a long time, but we didn't really talk about feelings.

"But if he calls here can you just say I'm out?" I said, forcing a smile.

"Of course."

Tap-tap-tap of the keyboard.

Silence.

I swallowed loudly.

"My husband cheated on me too," she said out of nowhere. *Tap-tap-tap.* That was the most personal information I'd learned about Grace in the five years I'd worked there.

"Do you mind me asking how you found out?" she asked. "It's okay if you don't want to talk about it."

"I found him on an app."

"One of those dating apps?"

"Yep." I nodded.

More silence.

"I found letters," Grace confided. She let out a sigh. "I'm sorry about Oliver. I really didn't think he was the type." Grace knew about our wedding before I did. She was the one who gave him the dress. She knew my taste, my size. And she kept the secret well—I didn't get a congratulations text until we were already in Vegas.

"Thanks," I said, staring back at my emails, "neither did I."

And then we both sat tapping on our keyboards. I went to some recent images of pieces we'd acquired and then found them on the racks to compare the colour balances. Then I sat down, adjusting them, uploading them to Instagram, just like I had a few days before when none of this was on my radar.

And all I kept thinking of was that night in the cab. How I'd thought we were going to see Justin and we were really heading to the airport. Of the quiver in his voice as he said, "We can still make the last flight to Vegas."

And the warmth of his breath after I'd said yes when he hugged me so tight and said into my hair, "Thank fucking god."

Then my phone buzzed again and we both stared at it. I could see the message on the screen: *Charlie?????????*

But then the door buzzed and a woman walked in. She was short, with a blunt, dark bob to her shoulders and she was wearing a pair of jeans with a black chiffon shirt. I could see her bra through it. The door banged behind her and I put on a smile.

"Hi," she oozed as she came over to me. "Charlie, is it?"

I nodded.

"I'm so sorry about yesterday. It all got too frantic, but here I am. What have you got for me?"

It took a moment for me to twig.

"I'm Mimi, from Oliver Goldsmith," she said.

"Oh hi, right. Just a sec." I left my phone on the desk and got up, rushing through to the back room. I returned with the two dresses I'd picked out, draped over my forearm.

"These are the two I think you'll love," I said, reaching for the Biba navy lace overlay dress first. It swept the floor and had a beige satin slip beneath it. "It almost forms a full circle when you twirl so it'll look fab in photographs."

She inspected the square cut neckline. "Great," she replied, glancing at the other one as I put dress one down over the back of my chair.

"And then there was this one," I said, showing her the blue-and-white-checked Givenchy dress I'd finally found the day before.

"Oh yes, I love this." I could hear my phone ringing from my desk. I assumed it would be Oliver so I let it ring out, cursing the fact that I hadn't put it on silent.

But ten minutes later when I got back to my phone I realised it wasn't Oliver calling at all. It was Clarence. He'd left a voicemail. My heart was pounding as I dialled. I needed some good news.

The automated voice started: "You have one new message. First message received on Saturday, June ninth at 10.21 am."

Then came Clarence's voice: "I'm sorry, Charlie, you didn't get a callback."

And that should have been it: rock bottom. A cheating husband and broken dreams. Fair is fair. But no. Life was just getting warmed up.

—

9.47 PM

Bubbles fizzed on the tip of my tongue and the back edges recoiled. The champagne was dry, almost too dry, but it was also free. I was almost finished with my fourth glass and the world had only just shifted into soft focus so I was looking around the room for a fifth. One of the girls in white shirts carrying silver trays was over by the far wall and I stared at her, trying to catch her eye. But fuck, no, she was heading in the other direction now. I turned back to the wall, back to the painting Tess and I were looking at: a black canvas full of texture.

We were at an art gallery in Shoreditch. It had been Tess's idea—she was on an app that matched people based on crossed paths and she wanted to cast her dating net a bit wider. So my choices were: an art gallery for intellectuals or a hospital for doctors. A hospital made me think of my ex, Josh, and the happy holiday snaps he'd been taking with someone else, so I chose the gallery. Besides, it was good to get out of my own head. Good to not have to go home. What with finding Oliver on that app, realising why he was there, breaking into his computer and kicking him out of the house, it had been a big week for me. The last thing I wanted was to sit between those four walls, staring at our empty bookcase and his fucking Ganesha, thinking of how it hadn't protected us at all. Nothing was as it was supposed to be. In that moment I never wanted to go back to that flat again.

No, I just wanted it all over.

And even more than that, I wanted to stop feeling like I was lapsing into paranoia. To stop feeling like I was being watched. I kept self-soothing, telling myself that it was my imagination. I was just anxious because of everything that was going on.

But our instincts are there for a reason. They are there to help us survive.

And so when mine told me I was still being watched, I really should have listened.

There was a guy standing near a set of black canvases—hand-stitched grey suit, salt and pepper hair, tall. Tess had noticed him when we first walked in and nudged me to take a better look. She was wearing a short faux leather skirt and a sheer pirate frill shirt, and right now she was toying with the neck of it, glancing over in his direction, then quickly looking away. Flirting 101. I was still wearing the same olive-green, metallic-thread top and jeans I had on when I left the house that morning.

"In his car?" Tess was laughing a little too loud, slight arch of the back, head tilted. She was doing it for attention. But it was nice to feel hilarious even if what I'd really said wasn't that funny: I'd just told her where I'd left all of Oliver's things.

"Yep," I replied, finishing my champagne. "Anyway, how's everything with you?" I asked, horribly aware that the last few days had been all about me. That I was becoming "that" friend.

"Ask me in ten minutes," she smiled, eyes quickly darting to the guy by the black paintings.

There was a part of me that had always been suspicious of Tess's shallow relationships with men, secretly thinking she was hiding behind bravado when she talked about them being free drugs, about breaking the oxytocin-bond by sleeping with someone else, secretly thinking she was just scared. I'd seen her after Marc. I knew how fractured she'd been. But right now I'd have given anything to be just like her. It was as though she didn't form scar tissue like I did. While I was moping around like a sack of potatoes, she just moved on into the endless possibilities of dating in London. I wanted to be like that too.

"What you need is a bit of a chemical distraction. What about him?" she asked, nodding at a man three paintings away from us.

I glanced up at him—he was dark-haired, well-dressed, nice-enough-looking. But he wasn't Oliver. "I don't want to just pick up a man in an art gallery," I replied.

"Why not?"

"It's too soon," I said. The champagne girl was coming in my direction now and I smiled at her. I almost bloody waved. *Oh yay, she's coming.*

"Thanks," I said when she arrived, taking a glass and putting my empty one down on her tray. The bubbles looked silver under the lights above us. I took a sip.

"Okay, but hon, don't let him hold you still for too long. Promise me," Tess said.

"I promise," I replied as we moved on to the next painting. This one was a deep burnt orange, lots of cracked texture and flecks of gold through it. I let out a sigh as I stared at it. My cheeks were warm from the booze now and I felt blissfully numb. "I just want to stop being so angry with him," I said to Tess.

"No, angry is good. First you get angry. Then you start hoping his head explodes. Then you start e-stalking. Then you get over it. It's a process, just ride it out. In three months you'll be fine."

It was around then that the guy she'd been making eyes at all night made his way over to us.

"Here we go," she whispered as he approached.

Then they both stood there side by side, gazing at the painting for what felt like an age. Silent. Their bodies abnormally close for strangers.

"Do you like it?" he asked, finally.

"Hmmm, I do, but I wouldn't want it on my wall," she said, smiling at him.

"Agreed," he said, sipping his champagne. "I'm Zach." He offered Tess his hand.

"Tess. And this is Charlie."

"Hi," I said, feeling totally like the third wheel. *I should be taking notes. This will be me soon.*

But as I watched her there with him, my insides panged: I didn't want to take notes, I wanted my husband back. Because you can always tell when two people are going to end up in bed. It might be that night, it might be in a week, it might be in a month, but it was going to happen. There was something in the electricity that passed between their eyes. Something in the way their bodies yielded to each other. They were two pieces of a puzzle yearning to fit.

That was what Oliver and I had been like the first night we met.

I ached for what we had been like before I'd seen him on that app. For how in love we'd been, or I thought we'd been.

I could hear Tess and Zach chatting beside me, but that just made me feel even more alone, and so I did what I always do when I feel awkward: I reached for my phone. And I'm not sure whether it was the champagne or just the deep yearning for Oliver, for "us," but something had me scrolling through to that dating app, finding Oliver's profile and sending him a message: *Hi, I'd really like to chat if you're available.*

If he wouldn't be honest with me as his wife, maybe he'd be honest with me as the other woman.

Ba-boom, ba-boom, ba-boom. What would he reply?

But the clock kept ticking and no response came. And even then, I still held out hope that I was somehow wrong, that it would somehow be okay. My mind was a whirlpool of all the positive reasons he might not be replying, reasons that didn't involve being in bed with someone else—maybe he was feeling guilty and was going to get off the app soon, maybe he loved me after all and it had just been an experimental phase. Maybe now that he'd had a taste of what it would be like to lose me he'd be mine again. We'd be "us" again.

Or maybe it really was all over.

Now I didn't want to be there anymore. I just wanted to be home. With the doors locked. I wanted to feel safe. And so I downed the rest of my champagne quickly—one gulp, two gulps, three—and as the walls started to sway towards me I touched Tess's arm. "I'm going to go," I said.

"What? Why?" she asked.

"Just want to sleep. Loads of love and see you soon." As I kissed her goodbye on the cheek, she whispered in my ear: "Are you okay?" I nodded, and then, as she said "Love you," I left her with Zach and made my way outside.

The cool night air hit my cheeks and tears prickled behind my eyes. Staring down at my phone I pulled up the TfL app, scanned through the list of Tubes currently delayed and tried to figure out how to get home. The air was filled with the sounds of chatter and footsteps and traffic. Fuck it, I should just get an Uber. So I went to that app instead.

But there, as I held it, my phone beeped. A message had come in.

From *@Oliver1982*.

I held my breath and clenched my jaw and clicked through to it, not knowing what to expect. And then I just read it: *Hey sexy. Great, let's chat. xx*

Episode 5

I sat up in bed, the grey-lit room spinning and damp sheets twisted around my legs. The sky had been treacle black by the time I got home the night before, so I'd forgotten to draw the curtains. I reached beside the bed for a glass of water and took a sip, looking down. I was wearing underwear and the metallic top I'd worn out the night before. Beside the glass of water was what was left of that bottle of gin I'd started the morning before. *Uh-oh.*

The expanse of time that stretched between me leaving the art gallery and finally going to bed was hazy at best. But I remembered there had been messages. Lots of messages.

Hang on, had there been sexting too?

I couldn't be sure, but my heart was speeding up. I moaned and reached for my phone on the table beside the bed. It was 8.33, my alarm hadn't even gone off yet—the shop opened at noon on Sundays—and so I had plenty of time to scroll through the app. To assess the damage.

I punched in my passcode, held my breath and went to the app.

Shit. I was right.

I'd been messaging with *@Oliver1982* for a good two hours after I got home. What had I said? Had I told him it was me? That I knew? And if I *had* told him, was that even a bad thing? I had all his files now, after all. I was safe, wasn't I? My eyes scanned through the messages, piecing it together, memories flickering in my consciousness.

@Oliver1982: *So tell me what you like.*

141

the strangers we know

I bit down on my lower lip as I read through our conversation. There were slightly suggestive emoji texts, a request for photographs, then my nipple, my lower back, and one of my inner elbow masquerading as my bum. I knew that trick would come in useful one day. That had gone on for about twenty minutes. And then Oliver, noble man that he was, had dropped a bomb.

@Oliver1982: I like you Annabella. So there's something you should know.

Me: *What's that?*

@Oliver1982: I'm married.

Me (straight away): *What??????*

@Oliver1982: Let me explain. I'm very unhappy. That's why I'm here.

My reply was almost instant. Drunk-Charlie needed to know.

Me: *Aren't you worried someone will tell her?*

He took two minutes to pen his reply to that.

@Oliver1982: No, the truth is I want someone to tell her. I want her to know, I want it over but I don't have the heart to let her down.

Whatever pain I'd felt the night before when those words first flew in hit me afresh as I read them again in the brittle morning light. And all I could think was *@lover7*. It seemed like that must be why she'd been watching me. She was planning on telling me. Yet she hadn't—why? Had she lost the nerve? Would I be able to tell a woman, a stranger, something like that? But as I stared down at those words, any latent hopes I'd been harbouring that maybe we could somehow work things out vanished.

I dropped my phone on his side of the bed and wandered through to the kitchen, pressing the button on the Nespresso machine and putting a little cup underneath the nozzle simultaneously. And from beyond its warming-up hum I could hear my phone beep from the bedroom, so I went back to check the screen.

Oliver: *Charlie, I love you. Be reasonable.*

I stared at the screen. It wasn't even anger I was feeling anymore. It was defeat.

And so I typed back the only thing I could: *I hate you. I never want to see you again.*

And then I did something very, very grown-up. The thing I'd always refused to do with Josh, the thing I should have done, the only thing I could think of in that moment to stop any more pain. To get back my power.

Yes, I blocked his number.

Then I spent the next couple of hours crying before eventually forcing myself to get ready for work.

—

Grace was squinting at the pages of a newspaper when the door buzzed and I walked in. It was just before noon by then.

"That's a pretty dress," she said as the door shut behind me and I moved over to my desk. I was wearing a hot pink woollen number and a pair of knee-high leather boots. That sounds like an odd choice for summer, but the weather was strange that day: air thick with moisture and low charcoal clouds.

"Thanks," I replied, sitting down and firing up my computer. "How's your tooth?"

"Fine. But I need new health insurance. Do you know I had to pay for the whole lot out of pocket?"

I watched the Apple logo glow white on the screen and started shifting things around my desk the way I always did when I was anxious. Because soon I was going to need my own private health cover—could I even afford that? Would the NHS be enough? There were all these things I now needed to think about. Like I was going to need to move eventually, find a flatmate, file divorce papers. But at least I still had my job. What if I'd quit? What would I have done then? What if I was pregnant like Oliver always wanted me to be? But no, I had an income of my own, a life of my own, I could make it on my own. But *fuck*, Oliver was due home today and soon I'd have to face him. How would that play out?

Maybe I could avoid it.

But probably the most confusing thing was I knew I didn't *want* to avoid it. As much as I hated him for everything, I was discovering that at the crux of it all I still loved him. I still found myself playing versions of how things might have been in my mind; I had to actively stop myself from constructing excuses for him. From living out conversations with him in my mind. It was illogical. It was like being ripped apart. It was love.

But all of that turbulence was internal. On the outside, the rest of that day passed in a state of relative calm. And soon it was time to go home.

—

6.46 PM

His car was still there, parked in its same spot, when I got home from work that day. My first thought was: *Maybe he just went straight to a hotel.* But as I walked past it I noticed that the black bags were gone. That was weird. Why had he taken his bags and not his car? I moved towards our building, a deep rust red in the evening light, and glanced towards our window. *Shit*: the curtains were closed, a thin ribbon of light peeking through the middle, and I'd left them open when I left that morning.

He was in there.

Fumbling with my keys, I made my way through the security door and hurried down the hallway to our front door. I slid my key in the lock, turned it and, as I flung the door open, heat rose from my solar plexus.

The sitting room was still a bit of a mess, but all his things were back in their places and the bookshelf was no longer empty.

It looked like last night had never happened.

Like I'd never packed him up.

What was he playing at?

My heart sped up as I slammed the door behind me.

"Oliver?" I called.

Silence.

I went to the bedroom, pushing open the door, my pulse wild: nope, not there. I moved through to his study. And there he was, wearing a thin navy cardigan over a white t-shirt, sitting at his computer, his fore-head creased, his phone in his hand and a Peroni beside him.

"Charlie, I'm on the phone," he said, his hand covering the mouthpiece. "I can't get into my fucking computer." He was talking through his teeth like he did when he was frustrated.

"*What?* Why are you even here? Hang up the phone, Oliver," I said, my voice strangled by frustration. I'd found the strength to kick him out, to do the hard thing, and yet here he was. Still. Like what I wanted didn't matter.

His eyes were wide in a "Can we do this later?" look. Like I was being unreasonable. But I wasn't being unreasonable, I knew that, and no, no we bloody could not.

"Look, I know you're upset and we can talk about it later, but I've only just got to the front of the wait queue. I need them to help me."

I couldn't quite understand what was going on. Why wasn't he pleading for forgiveness? Why was he being like this?

"Are you *serious*? Oliver, hang up the fucking phone!" I yelled.

"Charlie," he said slowly through gritted teeth, like he was talking to a child and didn't want to scream. "I need to get onto my computer right now and I can't." His face was getting pink and a vein was now visible on his left temple. "You have no idea what I am up against. So please, just calm the fuck down for a second and wait. We can talk about anything you want to when this is done." He was hissing by the time he finished and then he started talking to whoever was on the other end of the phone. Like I was being the unreasonable one.

For a split second I almost did what he asked. That's me: the people-pleaser. But then I remembered all those messages via the app—*I want someone to tell her. I want it over*—I remembered the red lace garter belt in his jacket pocket, I remembered his lies—"I'd never do that to you"—and something deep within me erupted. Because I'd trusted him. And trust didn't come easily to me.

It started with nausea.

Then came: *ba-boom, ba-boom, ba-boom.*

I stood there watching him chat politely to someone on the other end of the phone, but as I looked down at my hands I realised I was shaking. The heat of salty tears was on my cheeks. I was thinking of all those women in his Facebook message request box now.

I didn't know what to do, say, or feel. How was this man the same man I'd married? All I could manage was "Oliver?" Tears burnt in my eyes now, frustration and anger and hurt bubbling up inside me. But still, he ignored me, focusing on the person on the phone. Talking to them calmly about resetting things.

And so I decided to force his hand.

"You know what," I said, "fine. You want this over, I'll make it over. Properly over. But I'm not going to be made into the bad guy who walked away. I'm going to send a screenshot of your dating app profile to your mother. Then she can google all those sex parties just like I did. Help her understand who her son really is."

And then I stormed out of the room, slamming the door after me.

A moment later his footsteps were loud and following me.

"Charlie!" he called after me. I was in the kitchen by then, my

cheeks hot and my vision blurring as I scrolled through my phone to the app, my hands shaking with adrenaline as I took a screenshot of his profile. I knew I was playing with fire but I didn't care. How could he be like that? And I think I was actually going to do it, you know. I think I was *that* angry. That horrified. But I didn't get the chance. He got to me before I could find his mother's contact info and hit the phone out of my hand.

"Don't you dare!" he yelled.

"Don't *I* dare?" I yelled back, truth splintering around me. I leaned down to pick up my phone and he kicked it aside, I stood up, opened my mouth—a scream of frustration, betrayal, rage—and he pushed me against the wall. My head hit the plaster. A sunburst of white. My eyelids felt heavy. *Oww.*

A veil of fear fell over me as I looked into his eyes. What was happening?

"Shut up," he said, his eyes wide. "The neighbours will hear you." His hand was over my mouth and his jaw was clenched. His eyes were just an inch from mine and I could smell his cologne. But I couldn't breathe. I tried to pull away but he was too strong, and the more I struggled the tighter he held. A blind panic flew through me.

A memory.

A need to escape took over.

Adrenaline—*zing.*

My hands were flailing, scratching, I swiped him on the side of the face. He stepped backwards, his hands away from me now as he held his cheek.

148

"What the fuck, Charlie!" he yelled.

We stood there for one, two, three seconds just staring at each other. I thought maybe he'd try to explain now, but he didn't. Instead, he just stomped off back to his study and slammed the door. It boomed through the flat.

And I was left there in the kitchen, my lungs burning with oxygen like I'd been running. It was then that the sobbing started.

I needed to get out of there. Now.

My phone was lying on the floor by the kitchen counter. I reached down and picked it up—there was a long, horizontal crack across the screen. My bag was just above it and I took that too. I imagined Oliver in his study, still trying to get into his computer, as I grabbed my laptop from the bedroom. Who knew when I'd be back. He was still in there as I rushed to the front door. My hands were trembling as I pulled the door open.

All I could think of was Alyssa in that supermarket with her unwashed hair and basket of booze. Was this what had happened to her?

I slammed that door behind me. I needed him to hear. To know how I felt.

And then I ran towards the building's exit.

What just happened?

My mind was frantically trying to make sense of everything: our perfect love affair had deteriorated so quickly that I could almost smell the sweet stench of dead roses in the air as I pushed through the door and the chill night air hit my face. I rushed towards the road, looking back over my shoulder.

Surely he'd come after me; try to make it better?

But he wasn't coming. And so I started walking. Quickly. I wasn't really sure where I was going, I didn't have a plan, but I needed some time to cool down, to get my head straight. My arms were covered in goosebumps and my bag heavy on my shoulder as I strode towards the bridge that led to Chelsea. Cars drove past me. And I kept checking my phone for a call from him. Surely he'd get worried. Call me? Come and find me?

Shit. He was still blocked.

I scrolled through to his contact, unblocked him and waited a little longer for a call to come in. Maybe he could somehow explain . . .

Because that fight: it wasn't us.

But then none of this was us—the app, the sex parties, the fight, the lies, none of it.

And then, there I was: At the river. Crossing. But Oliver still wasn't calling.

I didn't want to go too far so I stood on the bridge, staring out at the Thames, joggers moving through streetlights behind me, my arms crossed over my chest and tears streaming down my face. I was shaking.

And I was thinking about all the things I'd tried so hard to forget.

Because there was more to the story of that night when I was sixteen. It didn't *end* with date-rape, that's just how it began. But before I tell you, I need to ask you a favour—please don't pity me. I've worked very hard not to play the victim in my own life.

I didn't tell the police what happened that night and I was

too ashamed to tell my mother, but a couple of weeks later I *did* tell a couple of friends at school. That's what you're supposed to do, right: tell someone? But when I did, all they said was: "But he was your boyfriend, right?" and "Are you *sure* you don't just regret it?"

Then one of them asked the boy in question, and he said: "She wanted it. She's just upset now because we broke up."

And they believed him over me.

From then on, I was branded a liar.

And I think that did almost as much damage as the night itself: it taught me that it was safer to stay silent.

So that's what I did. I pushed it down, pretended it hadn't happened, and spent my weekends watching movies, telling myself that just like the heroines in them, my life was going to get better soon too. I just needed to hold on. On the outside it looked like I was okay. I turned up to school, did well in my exams, laughed at people's jokes. It was only on the inside that I was a carbonated drink just waiting for one more shake before I exploded.

And that shake came about seven months later.

I was with a new friend, we were walking into a house party and "he" was there. Halfway up the set of stairs. Standing with a couple of other guys. We needed to walk past them to get inside. All I could hear was *ba-boom, ba-boom, ba-boom*. So I held my breath and told myself it would be okay.

But, just as we passed him, he gave this little snigger, and the air rang with his voice—"Slut."

My ears roared. Everyone looked at me. My face grew hot and my vision white. That was the moment my lid finally bounced free.

And I attacked him.

Right there—flailing fists, my vocal cords shredding from screaming—with all those witnesses.

Nobody could see the cause, of course. All they perceived was the effect. The crazy girl who'd lied about him was now attacking him.

Which meant I was the one who ended up having to explain myself to the police. That night, my behaviour, is probably still on record somewhere. But it was almost a relief, having a reason to finally tell them the truth: now I had no choice. But because I'd taken so long, because of what had happened, it looked to them like I was just trying to get myself out of a mess.

And once again, nobody believed me.

But I know what you're thinking. You're thinking the same thing Josh did: that I should have just told the police on the night it happened. You're probably right, but life is rarely that simple. To start with, I felt sick. Really sick. The world was blurred when I woke the next morning, wrapped in a white rug I'd crawled into at some point in the night. I only got home at 10 am, just in time for the vomiting of bile to begin, the porcelain of the toilet bowel cold beneath my arms as images from the night before flickered through my mind each time I heaved. And I was confused in a way I don't expect you to understand but need you to try. Because I knew I'd said "no" consistently before that party and into the palm of his hand in the fragments of memory I had of that night—that I'd struggled and he'd forced me and he'd hurt me, but I'd never had sex before and I told myself that maybe that was normal. The pain. The swelling. It was as though my mind was trying to protect me by saying things like *It's just sex, who cares?* Like if I could minimise it, if I could tell myself it was no big deal, I could somehow quash the pain. But the problem was that it wasn't just about the sex. It was about the helplessness. And no matter how much I tried not to think about it, I couldn't make it un-happen. Nor could I shake the shame because he was a "good" guy, so something must have been deeply wrong with me for him to do that to me, right?

And so, as soon as I'd finished school and saved a little money, I did what any good movie heroine would do: I left it all behind me. I drew a line in the sand, moved to London where nobody could remind me, and re-created myself. Yes. The token-blonde wife.

But as it turns out, nobody can outrun their past forever.

Nobody.

So that's why that night, my reaction to Oliver's hand over my mouth, the scratch and everything that followed happened.

I stared down at my phone. I needed Oliver to text. Call. Something. To make it okay. But nothing came. The wind whipped my hair around my face and it was getting stuck in my tears. I wiped my cheeks with the back of my hand. It had been fifteen minutes: he wasn't coming. He wasn't going to check on me. He was too busy with whatever was going wrong with his business stuff. He was probably on the phone to Justin right now.

I always had been number two.

And so I kept walking. As I got to Chelsea Embankment, I looked around. There was a black cab coming towards me. Its orange light was on. And so I reached out my hand, it pulled over and when the driver wound down the window I said, "Crouch End, please."

Then I got in, sank back into the seat and, as the car started to move, stared at my reflection in the window, telling myself that at least now it was over.

—

8.11 PM

Tess lived in a one-bed flat in Crouch End; a big, dishevelled, brown brick building on the outside—the functional, artless sort with the odd Legoland tree planted between slabs of concrete outside and staircase bannisters inside that you didn't want to touch for fear of picking up a bug. But her flat itself was lovely. She'd been in it since I met her thirteen years before.

When her grandmother died (and left her some money), Tess had the good sense to put down a deposit on a flat. So she was the only person I knew, aside from Justin, who owned their own place in London. Oliver and I had been planning on buying soon too, but that wouldn't be happening now.

Nothing I thought was going to happen would be happening.

She was on the fifth floor and when the lift opened there she was, waiting for me, the door open. She reached out and gave me a hug. Her hair was wet and smelled of coconut, like she'd just washed it, her face shiny from night cream, and she was wearing a pair of pink pyjama bottoms with a frayed grey t-shirt. "Shit, are you okay?" she asked, ushering me inside.

I nodded.

But we both knew that was a big fat lie. So did the cab driver who'd picked me up—I'd sobbed the whole way over, my eyes becoming more and more puffy, dazed and mascara-smeared as a darkening London whizzed by. By the time I got out, I'd stopped crying but looked like a very sad, heroin-chic cabbage patch doll.

"Fuck him," she said, closing the door behind me, heading to the kitchenette and opening the cupboard above the sink. "What can I get you, hon? Gin? Tea? Gun?"

I gave a small laugh. "Do you have any cigarettes?" I asked. I'm not a smoker per se, but I do smoke when I'm stressed or sad. It's like I'm trying to fill the cracks in my heart with tar before the whole thing falls apart.

"I may do . . ." She grinned, opening a drawer and rifling around. I moved over to the big denim-covered sofa that stood against a wall that was half window. I could see lights in the neighbouring building switching on and off as I sat down. There was a mirror to my left with a set of fairy lights twisted around the frame, an enormous desk-slash-bookshelf to my right that I'd helped her assemble and the door to her bedroom just beyond it.

"Here we are," she said, holding up a box of Marlboro Lights and some matches.

There was only a small sliver of window that opened. As

she unlatched it, I reached for a cigarette. I lit a match, the end of my cigarette glowed amber and I knelt on the sofa, dangling it outside to avoid setting off the smoke alarm again. That had happened once before. We got in trouble. And as I did all that, I caught sight of my reflection: I looked so fragile. *You'll be okay, Charlie.*

"So what did he say when you asked him?" Tess asked gently. She was kneeling beside me now, lighting her own cigarette and hanging it out the window.

"He didn't say anything really. He was on the phone and fucking around on his computer. Saying he had been locked out and had to get into it. It was awful." My forehead creased but I felt strangely calm now.

"Wow. Not even an excuse?"

I shook my head. "He wanted out. He was probably relieved."

"What makes you say that?"

I sighed. "I messaged him on the app, as Annabella." I reached for my phone, scrolling through to the app and finding the messages for Tess. I handed it to her.

Her eyes narrowed just a little as she read them—a wince.

"What a fucker. Did you tell him this was you? That you'd found him on the app?"

"No," I said, taking a drag of my cigarette. Blessed nicotine. "But I did tell him I was going to send a screenshot of his profile to his mum. So he knows I've seen it."

Tess started to laugh. "Good for you. Did you send it?"

My chest contracted as I remembered everything that had happened.

"No. It was horrible, Tess. I've never seen him like that. We had a fight and he got so angry." I took a drag, exhaled a cloud of smoke outside. "He banged my head against the wall. I mean, I don't think he meant it, but it happened."

Beat.

"It was so bad," I said, taking another drag. "But it was me too. I scratched him." My throat grew tight as I said the words.

She reached out and squeezed my hand. "It's over now."

I nodded and she let go of my hand. "And on a positive note at least you've still got the ring," she said, nodding to the yellow stone I loved so much, glittering from my finger. It was small and tasteful: a cushion-cut, natural yellow canary diamond surrounded by lots of little white diamonds sparkling in a halo around it. He'd said it was just like me. Unique. Unforgettable. And now look.

"Why don't you hock it and we can go on a holiday?" She stubbed out her cigarette on the windowsill and let it fall into the garden bed below.

I laughed. "God, can you imagine how pissed he'd be?"

"Would be so worth it to see his face when you told him."

Stubbing out my own cigarette, I reached for my finger and slipped my rings off—engagement ring, then thin gold wedding band—putting them in the inner pocket of my bag. "There, now I'm single."

Tess shot me a small, sad smile. Because she knew as well as I did that it wasn't that simple.

"I have an idea—let's go through his files. Where's the USB?"

I reached into my bag while Tess went over to her desk and returned with her laptop.

I handed her the USB stick and she plugged it into the side of her computer. I watched her face light up with the screen. She was frowning. Scrolling. Opening things.

"Shit, there's a lot here," she said. *Click. Click. Click.* "Okay, you have some fucking high credit card bills. But you have more than enough money to pay them all off. And now that you have these, any major purchases or withdrawals from now on will be his problem not yours. So good work, hon."

"I'm starving," I said as she kept clicking.

"There's bread for toast and cheese in the fridge. I think there might be half an avocado in there too," Tess said, not looking up. *Tap. Scroll. Tap. Scroll.*

So I left her to it and opened the fridge: nail polish, cheese, half a loaf of gluten-free bread, cottage cheese, some baby spinach, a browning half avocado on a side plate and an open can of pineapple. That was what my fridge would look like soon. Single girl food. Maybe I'd sign up for one of those food delivery services that count your calories for you.

"Do you want some?" I asked, pulling out the bread and cheese.

"Yes please."

I dropped four pieces into the toaster and the smell of toast filled the room. I reached for the red plastic cutting board and started slicing cheese with the smallest knife in the rack while Tess clicked away on her computer.

"God, I can't believe I'm going to need a flatmate again," I said, thinking of Tania, the girl I was living with when I met Oliver. She left dish soap in all our glasses and always used my razor. I wasn't looking forward to going back to that.

"Well, you can stay here as long as you need," Tess said, smiling up at me briefly.

The toaster popped up. "Thanks," I said, buttering it with the same knife I'd used for the cheese, then laying pieces of cheese down on top. I'd just picked up the plate to take it to Tess when she spoke.

"Well, hello," she said to her screen.

"What?" I asked, rushing over. I expected the worst: love letters to someone else, naked pictures, proof of polygamy.

"Did you know Oliver had a company in the Cayman Islands?"

"No," I replied, relief pulsing through me.

"Lucamore Enterprises," Tess said, frowning down at her screen.

"He's never mentioned it," I said, sitting down on the sofa and offering her a piece of toast. "Are you sure it's not just one of the companies they were looking at investing in?"

"Hmmm," Tess said, taking a bite.

"No, there's stuff here addressed to him. But this is good, babe, offshore means proper money. Maybe you can fleece him in the divorce." She looked up at me with a naughty grin.

"Maybe," I said, chewing my toast. "Might make up for the worst week ever." I left the plate by her legs and sunk into the sofa.

"At least now you know. At least this way you're still young and pretty and you can get out there and act again."

Tess hadn't approved of Oliver's no-more-romantic-leads terms and conditions. She said I shouldn't have to sacrifice part of myself—such a big part—for him.

"Yeah," I replied. I was wondering whether I ever would have discovered all of this if I'd gone home to Oliver just half an hour earlier on Tess's birthday. If that had happened, we wouldn't have been looking through that app. If I hadn't seen Oliver's profile I probably wouldn't have been so suspicious of *@lover7*. And I never-ever-ever would have been on that app as Annabella or breaking into Oliver's computer. It might have all just gone on for years behind my back.

I glanced down at the green ribbon around my wrist. The Bahia bracelet he'd tied three knots on. There was one final thing I had to do in order to be free. And so I sat up, let out a sigh and went back to the kitchenette. I opened the cutlery drawer and pulled out a pair of red-handled kitchen scissors.

Tess looked up as I handed them to her, offering my wrist.

"Can you cut this off?"

"Sure."

And as the blades hugged the fabric, in the very instant before she snipped, I thought of my wishes: being wrong about the app, the newspaper article, till death do us part.

And then *snip*.

It looked like I wasn't going to get any of my wishes. But it turns out, I was going to get all three.

"Okay, you know how to lock up, right?" Tess called from the kitchenette as she dropped her teacup in the sink with a ceramic-on-metal clang. I was still in bed, staring up at a crack in the ceiling. My tongue tasted of last night's cigarettes and my head throbbed.

"Yes, lock from the inside then pull," I said, repeating the instructions she'd given me twice in the last three minutes. I craned my neck and squinted out the window behind me. The sky was baby blue and flawless, and the sunshine coming in through the window was warm and the colour of daffodils. How was everything so fucked up? It was summer, when the air smells of sunscreen, jasmine and cut grass. Nothing bad is supposed to happen in summer.

"And don't forget the spare key if you go out," Tess said, popping her head back into the bedroom as she slipped on a lightweight trench coat.

I turned to her and nodded. With her pixie cut and taupe beige trench she looked like a brunette, tanned version of that American girl in *À Bout de Souffle*, the one who sells the *New York Herald Tribune*.

"Okay, remember coffee is in the freezer. Good luck today. Text me." She picked up her briefcase and with a bang of the door she was gone. The flat was cold and silent without her there, but it still smelled like her perfume: rose incense. I reached for my phone and turned it off airplane mode. I expected an apology to be waiting for me. A voicemail. Something to make me feel less sick.

But nothing.

161

And so I scrolled through to the app to see when Oliver had last been online.

I went to my messages, searching for his photo on the left-hand side to click through to his profile. But his messages were gone.

His profile had been deleted.

Which made sense after that fight and my threat of sending a screenshot to his mother. But my insides ached as the night before came tumbling back. I let out a small moan, rolling over and closing my eyes.

I lay there, trying to avoid thoughts, dozing fitfully for a good hour or so. I imagined him doing all the things he always did in the mornings: turning on the Nespresso machine, having a shower, picking out a shirt. Did he even miss me? Why hadn't he called?

It was just before nine that a need for caffeine finally got me out of bed and I trudged to Tess's kitchenette, big sulky footsteps. *Stomp. Stomp. Stomp.* I reached for the cupboard above the sink and pulled out a mug, then flicked on the kettle while the night before ran in a loop through my mind: his Peroni, me threatening to text his mother, my head hitting the plaster, his hand over my mouth, the scratch on his face. That would have left a mark. *How will he explain that at work?* My face grew hot. Shame.

Shame at still being triggered after all this time.

Shame that he would have banged my head like that. He'd always been so gentle with me.

I opened the freezer, pulled out the coffee and spooned some into the cafetière she'd left out for me. There was a bag of black liquorice on the table and I chewed on a piece while the kettle hummed to a boil. Breakfast of champions. The smell of coffee filled the air as I poured boiling water over the grounds, then took myself back to bed. That was a Monday and the shop was closed on Mondays and Tuesdays. So I thought I had a full forty-eight hours to spend in bed feeling sorry for myself.

Let's just say I was wrong.

It was then that my phone started ringing from beside the bed. I rolled over to look at it, expecting it to be Oliver. But it wasn't—it was *Natasha Neighbour.* That was weird. She'd never called me before, and the only time she'd ever texted was to check I'd remembered to water her plants—basil, orchid—because she was away (and a control freak).

The phone stopped ringing. It went to voicemail. But something was off, I could feel it. I sat up, picked up my phone and stared down at the screen. What did she want?

My phone beeped. A text. *Natasha Neighbour*. I frowned at it: what was going on?

It read: *Just checking you're okay hon. I heard the yelling last night. Where are you?*

Oh right, well that made sense then. Natasha was thinking of my outburst yesterday, coupled with the fight she'd overheard, and was hoping my relationship with Oliver was on its last legs so she could swoop in. *Well, Natasha, you are welcome to him. You, and every other woman in London.* I imagined her knocking on our door with a plate of cookies to "check on him." Seeing his face. What would he tell her about the scratch?

I picked up my coffee, letting the heat seep into my hands, and took a sip.

Tess had left a hot pink towel for me on the end of the bed. I needed a shower so I took my coffee, picked up the towel and went through to the bathroom.

I turned on the faucets, dropped the t-shirt I'd slept in onto the floor and stepped inside. The water was hot, too hot, on my scalp as it flowed over me, but it was good to have that kind of sensation to draw me into the present. I used Tess's shampoo and conditioner to wash my hair. Now I smelled like coconut too. I turned off the taps and reached for my towel, dried myself off, then wrapped it around me before wandering back through to the bedroom, sipping my coffee. We were on the fifth floor so nobody could see me, but I pulled closed the pale blue curtains anyway, then sat on the edge of the bed.

My phone beeped again. Another message from Natasha. *You need to come home right now. It's about Oliver. The police really need to talk to you.*

I put down my cup. What the fuck was going on?

I typed back straight away: *What? Why? What happened?*

But there was no reply.

And in hindsight I think it was her silence that first warned me. But then a final beep: *Just come.*

—

9.58 AM

By the time I got a clear view of our flat it was obvious something really, really bad had happened. The Uber had dropped me two blocks away—I had it stop the moment I saw the yellow, blue and white of a police car—and I went straight to the park across from our flat to get a better (sheltered) view. Our building had been sectioned off by do-not-cross police tape. The air smelled of soil and cut grass. There were three police cars in all, one ambulance and a bunch of what I assumed were police—but would later decide were forensics people—dressed in grey coveralls moving in and out of the building. I could see them through our front window: they were in our flat. Lots of them. Something had happened in our flat.

I thought back to Natasha's message: *You need to come home right now. It's about Oliver. The police really need to talk to you.*

Shit.

Because everybody knows that when the police are looking for you, there's only one thing you should do: comply. They're supposed to be on your side. If you tell the truth, everything is supposed to be okay. But as I stood there, dressed in a dark green satin jacket, white t-shirt and black jeans (all belonging to Tess), my hair in a ponytail at the nape of my neck, my bag (with a few things and my laptop inside) slung over my shoulder, doing my best to go unnoticed, I just couldn't bring myself to move towards them.

No, I was paralysed, stuck to the spot.

Because what if Natasha had told them we were fighting? What if they'd seen the scratch? What if they thought I had done something?

What was I going to do, just tell them that I hadn't and hope they believed me?

Fuck that. They didn't believe me last time, why would this be any different?

I needed to know what was going on first.

I'd call Oliver.

I was his wife, it was perfectly acceptable that I might call him, check on him. And then maybe he could tell me what had happened. Maybe he was fine. Maybe it was another break-in. Maybe it was nothing serious.

But it didn't look like nothing serious.

I pulled out my phone, went to my favourites and dialled his number.

Calling Oliver flashed up on my screen and I held the phone up to my ear. It rang. And rang. And rang. On around the fifth ring someone picked up.

"Hello?" But it was a woman's voice.

"Hello? Ummm, I'm looking for my husband Oliver. This is his number, isn't it?"

A breath was taken. It was audible.

"Is this Charlene Buchanan?" said the voice. She was northern.

I imagined her having dark hair, pointy features and light eyes that could see straight through me.

"Yes," I replied.

"Charlene, this is DCI Holland. Where are you?"

"Why?" I asked, my breath quickening.

"We need to speak to you immediately. It's extremely important." Her tone was short. Clipped.

"Of course," I said, trying to control the timbre of my own voice. Why wasn't Oliver answering his own phone? I swallowed hard. "What is this about?"

I was watching the scene in our flat, wondering where she was— was she sitting in a police car? Standing in our apartment? Sitting on Natasha's sofa? But she didn't need to answer my question.

Because a moment later I saw the answer for myself.

First came voices. Shouting to get out of the way.

Then came a stretcher being rolled out through the front door towards the ambulance. There was a red blanket covering a big lump. A body. No space for the face to breathe. And a navy-blue-covered arm hanging off the side. A hand. A gold wedding ring winking in the morning light.

It was Oliver's arm. His hand. His ring.

And I'd seen enough cop shows to know what that meant.

"It would be better if we spoke in person," DCI Holland said. "It's something of utmost importance. I can come to you if you tell me where you are."

My breath caught in my throat and I swallowed. "I'm just with my agent," I lied, my heart beating rapidly as I watched them move the stretcher into the ambulance. Bile filled my mouth, but I forced myself to speak. "I can come in afterwards. Where are you?"

"Charing Cross Police Station." And I could hear her voice in the distance, an echo, as she gave me the exact address and I pretended to note it down.

"Okay," I said.

And then we hung up.

All I could feel was the breeze on my face. My vision grew white.

How is he dead?

A ripple of what he would have felt in his last moments moved through me—it winded me. That awful realisation. The terror. The acceptance. Nobody deserves that. Did he know the face who did this? My hand instinctively moved to cover my mouth as though I knew a sob was coming. The enormity of what was happening was crushing. My eyes burned, I let out a small whimper and hot tears streamed down my face. I choked them back. I couldn't break down now. I wasn't safe.

What was I going to do?

Then came another sob. I couldn't control them. I needed to get away from the police. And so I moved as quickly and quietly as I could further into the park, away from their field of vision. As I did the sobs got deeper, louder, and I bit down on my lip to stop them, clenching my eyes shut. There was a bench up ahead of me and I couldn't see anyone around so I jogged towards it. It was still damp from rain the night before, droplets sparkling in the sunshine. As I lay down on it I could feel the cool water seeping into the fabric of my clothes. I huddled in a fetal position, my arms wrapped tight around me, and cried.

The world had gone cold. My sun had been eclipsed. My head was filled with cotton wool and I could feel my nose running cold as my tears ran hot.

I kept my eyes clenched for a good ten minutes as I cried it out. The breeze dried my tears just to have new ones fall and a siren blared in the distance. As I lay there I imagined the red light flashing as the ambulance pulled out onto the road and took Oliver to the hospital or the morgue or wherever they take dead bodies. I let out a whimper and opened my eyes, and when I did I realised there was a man nearby—a jogger—watching me. My stomach clenched. I couldn't draw attention to myself.

I sat up. Stiff. My face hot as I wiped tears away with my sleeve. He looked concerned. I smiled at him as if to say, *Breakup, you know how it is.* He nodded back and kept moving. My breath was quick and shallow as I looked around me through a blur of tears.

I could see the police were still there in the distance.

Nothing made any sense.

Oliver had been alive, probably still drinking a Peroni in his office, when I stormed out. What had happened after I left?

What was I going to do?

Because everybody knows the spouse is always a suspect. Even if they're cleared in the end, they're always a suspect in the beginning.

Always.

Especially if there was cheating. Especially if there was life insurance. Especially if the neighbours heard fighting.

But then, I had an alibi, a really strong one: I wasn't even there when it happened. Tess could vouch for me. Although, time of death is iffy at best (they use the contents of the stomach as a gauge—don't tell me movies aren't educational) and it could always be argued that I'd hired someone to do it for me. Someone bigger. Stronger. And by that hypothesis, my not being there ultimately appeared to be an attempt to *create* an alibi, thereby supporting my guilt not my innocence. I imagined DCI Holland going through Oliver's phone, reading my text messages: *I hate you . . . I know everything.* Had she gone through his emails yet? Found that screenshot of his dating profile Justin had sent him? Absolute proof he was cheating.

Shit.

The app.

I reached for my phone, navigated to the app, deleted Annabella's profile and then removed the app from my phone. The last thing I needed was DCI Holland getting hold of my phone and reading the messages between Oliver and "Annabella": *I want someone to tell her. I want her to know, I want it over.*

If that wasn't motive, what was?

And it would be bad enough when they spoke to Natasha and

heard about how she'd helped me move a load of his stuff into his car on Saturday, about how boozy my breath was and what I'd said to her.

Had they seen the scratch? Of course they would have . . .

My DNA.

I swallowed hard.

I needed to go and talk to the police, to find out what happened, tell them it had nothing to do with me and help them with their investigation.

I needed to trust that the truth would work out for me this time.

But even though the police were right there, I just couldn't bring myself to do it. I remained stuck in position. Scarred by experience.

Because I knew what it was to tell the truth and not be believed. And for all I knew that night when I was sixteen was on some file somewhere. It might be construed as a pattern of behaviour. Used against me.

I couldn't risk it.

And so, as I sat there statue-still and staring at the police, my synapses fired: white hot, faster than sound. Multiple narratives presented themselves simultaneously as I tried to figure out what to do, tried to predict the end result of each choice. If I went to the police and they didn't believe me, they could arrest me. And I didn't want to go to prison. But if I *didn't* turn up to Charing Cross Police Station? What then? Was I on the run from the police?

What do I do?

My mind was a swirl of pros and cons, fears and . . . well, then I was thinking of that random Google search on my work computer: *Where to buy a taser in London.*

What if whoever killed Oliver was setting me up to take the fall? What if they'd planted other evidence too, evidence I didn't know about yet, evidence DCI Holland was busy cataloguing?

Don't be paranoid, Charlie.

But the thought had been seeded. As I stared at the crime scene I could see two policemen coming into the park towards me. They were chatting. They weren't looking for me. But as the distance between us grew shorter my heart pounded louder and faster, so loud, so fast, I thought it might thrash its way out through its cage. I'm not sure exactly when I made the final decision, but a moment later I stood up from that park bench and began walking briskly in the opposite direction. I needed time to think. To figure things out. And so I was going to the only place I could think of where they wouldn't look for me.

Because a certain someone never did ask for his key back.

Episode 6

I was trembling, the keys gripped tightly between my fingers as I made my way up the five cement stairs that led to his front door. Josh's front door. Yes, my ex: #nevergoinghome #holidayspam #Biarritz. So that's where I was: Fulham. It was the only place I could think of to go. *Please don't let him have changed the locks.*

Up close, the white paint was still peeling off, just like it always had been, and a dusty breeze swirled around me as I pushed the key into the lock. Took a deep breath. And turned the key.

Click.

The door creaked as it swung open: the hallway smelled of wet cardboard or newspaper and it was empty except for a bicycle and a couple of taped-up boxes that had been left in the nook beneath the staircase.

I shut the door quietly behind me before anyone could see me. But it was mid-morning by then, so I figured that most people would be at work and wouldn't be back for hours. And Josh was away in #Biarritz according to Instagram, so I had a safe house.

I took the stairs two at a time. Old blue carpet turned grey in the middle from feet and dust and wear. As they creaked with my weight, I thought back to those moments in the week before, the ones when I'd felt eyes on my back, the little hairs on my neck standing on end, when I'd been certain I was being watched. Maybe I was. How else would whoever killed Oliver have known he was home alone?

And then I was thinking of that internet search on my computer in the shop again: *Where to buy a taser in London.*

My stomach turned to oil. *Could I be right?*

Could I really be someone's fall guy?

But who would do that?

By the time I got to the fourth floor I was out of breath and my eyes were burning with tears again.

I fumbled with the key at Josh's door. I was desperate to be inside. Safe. But the moment before I slid it into the lock, I stopped. What if he was in there? Sometimes people post holiday photos to social media after the fact, and the last thing I needed was to let myself in and find him sitting on the sofa, looking at me. I held my breath, listening for movement inside: creaking floorboards, the hum of a TV, muffled conversation, the shutting of a fridge. But no, there was nothing.

I pushed the key into the lock, turned it and went inside.

That was the first time I'd been back there since we'd broken up nearly two years before. The room was hermetically sealed, the blinds all drawn, his dirty scrubs lay in a pile beside the washing machine in the kitchen, and his bed was unmade. The Brita filter was still sitting in the same spot it always had—just beside the sink—and the air smelled of damp, dust and the stale citrus of Josh's cologne. There was something familiar, something comforting, about being there. It was as though I'd stepped into a time capsule to revisit an era when my life was simpler.

I closed the door behind me, dropped my bag on the counter,

then pulled out my phone. There was a missed call from *No Caller ID*. It was the police, I knew it. DCI Holland was calling to find out where the hell I was. Dizziness overcame me, and I held on to the kitchen counter to stop myself from falling. And then I couldn't hold it in anymore: the sobbing started up again. I crumpled to the floor, holding my hands over my mouth so if a neighbour was home they wouldn't hear me, clenched my eyes shut and hot tears streamed down my face.

Everything inside me wanted to call Tess—she'd know what to do—but I didn't want to put her in that position. To make her lie to the police for me. She was a lawyer—the stakes were higher for her. But she was also still my "in case of emergency" contact with Grace and so I knew eventually they'd call her. Eventually they'd start watching her flat. Which was precisely why I hadn't gone back there.

And also, if I'm going to be really honest here, there was another reason I didn't want to call her: I knew she'd try to talk me into doing something I didn't want to do. Something that sounded like a good idea but I knew in my marrow wasn't. Not yet.

I'm not sure how long I sat on that cold floor, muffling my sobs with my hands, but eventually the tears stopped and a strange calm came over me. Slowly, I pulled myself up and went to the kitchen sink. I turned on the tap, splashed cold water over my face, then dried it off with my t-shirt.

My bag was sitting right there on the counter, and my laptop was inside. So was that little silver USB stick with all of Oliver's files on it. I picked it up, moved over to the sofa, pulled out my computer and fired it up. The white Apple sign glowed bright in the darkened room as I chewed on my inner cheek.

So you see, the plan was not to run from the police—I wasn't trying to buy a fake passport and move to Mexico or Bora Bora, was I? The plan was simply to wait until I had something more to give them than just me on a platter.

Because the papers are always filled with articles about how the police are overstretched and understaffed, how things "slipped through the cracks." I'd already been one of those things once in my life. And if I was right and someone had framed me, then I knew the case against me would be strong. And even if they hadn't framed me, I was still the spouse, he'd still cheated, there was still a witness to say we'd fought, a scratch on his face, my DNA in it and a life insurance policy I'd organised all by myself.

So when I walked into that police station to see DCI Holland, I needed to have a strong alternate suspect.

Think, Charlie, think.

Who would want Oliver dead?

And why?

It couldn't just be a "why" I believed. It had to be one DCI Holland would buy into too.

And so I opened up a Word document and started to type: *s-u-s-p-e-c-t-s.*

Then I sat there, tears burning in my eyes, watching the cursor flash back at me from the screen. *Shit.* Why hadn't I watched more *CSI?* Because I had no idea what to write down.

My first reflex action (don't judge me, I'm simply giving you a true account of events) was to do what I always do when I'm confused: ask Google.

I pulled up a browser and typed in: *UK, homicide, men killed by.*

The first search result was an information page on homicide in the UK from the Office of National Statistics (mildly concerning that this happens so much that it needs a special web page). I clicked on it, my eyes scanning through the information for something that might guide me.

Seventy-six per cent of suspects convicted of homicide tended to be male.

So a man probably did this.

I scanned through the other stats hoping something would make sense to me.

While 50% of women are killed by a partner or ex-partner, men are far more likely to be killed by a friend or acquaintance (30%).

Well that's nice. But everyone loved Oliver. Everyone. Even me. Even after everything.

So it had to be about something else.

And to my mind, there were only two reasons people murder other people: love or money.

Was it some crazy woman he'd met on an app? Or someone's husband?

But that would be a crime of passion.

And a crime of passion is a gunshot, or a stabbing, or something you can't do silently. It's loud and messy. It's amateur. It's not a well-planned, slip in while he's all alone, kill him and then slip out again affair.

No, that's money.

It *had* to have something to do with Oliver's business dealings, with one of those AK-47 types he said he worked with sometimes.

I'd never truly understood what Oliver did for work, but does anyone ever really understand the inner workings of another person's job unless they do it themselves? He didn't understand why acting meant so much to me—the freedom to be my rawest self and have it applauded instead of shunned, to be absolutely in the moment, to forget my own pain for just an instant—and he didn't care about vintage dresses or how clever Chanel had been to sew little chains into the hems of her suits to make them hang so well. But what I did understand of it went like this: he was in private equity and he specialised in Latin America and West Africa. That meant he spent a lot of time in places like Brazil and Nigeria. There were others too, but those two were the main ones. As many of the companies he invested in were unlisted, he couldn't just do it via a screen. He had to go over there and negotiate directly with the boards. Most of it was straight up, but every so often he'd come back from a trip with this white pallor and an expression that scared me. I'd always suspected the break-in at our old flat had something to do with one of those people because he'd insisted on life insurance soon after that happened. And when I asked him why, he'd said it was nothing to worry about, but that there were people out there who weren't as scrupulous as he was. He was just trying to protect me if "the worst thing happened."

It makes my stomach shrink to admit it now but there was something sexy in the danger, in the mystery of it all.

A wave of love washed over me as I realised what he might have been up against: that he'd tried to protect me. Though, that didn't really tally with the dating apps and the sex parties and the lies he'd told me . . . It was as though there were two sides to him and I'd only ever been introduced to one of them.

My computer screen flashed back blue-white in the gloomy room as Tess's words from the night before banged around inside my skull: *Did you know Oliver had a company in the Cayman Islands?*

Because no, I did not.

And weren't offshore bank accounts always used for something shady? What did she call it? *Lucamore.* That was it. Lucamore Enterprises. And so I typed that into the search field of the thumb drive: *L-u*—But I didn't know how to spell Lucamore back then, I spelled it lukeamoore (that was how Tess pronounced it, with a "k") so nothing came up.

Back to staring blankly at a computer screen. And now I was wondering what good it would do me to find whatever Tess had been looking at anyway. If she didn't know what it was, I surely wouldn't either. No, I needed to sift through something I *would* understand.

His emails.

That seemed like the sort of place the police might start: what was he doing just before he died? And so I pulled up a browser window and went to Gmail. I still had all of Oliver's passwords as a photograph on my phone, but I didn't need to check them: I remembered. *We have one life to live . . .*

I entered his email address and then: *o-n-e-l-i-f-e-1-1*.

A white screen.

And then I was in. I glanced down his inbox but there was nothing of use there, so I clicked through to his sent box. What emails had he written in the days just before his death?

All three were to Justin. The first was about a meeting. The second was a question about a client. And then came the third.

The subject read: *RE: !!!*.

I remembered that email he was replying to with serrated clarity. It was from Justin. The one I found when I was copying his files:

Man, what the fuck are you doing? My sister just sent this through. Nobody cares what you do in your own time, but have a look at your LinkedIn profile! People are starting to figure out where you work and leave cute messages. We can't afford this kind of attention. Not after those emails. Fix it.

My heart was hammering in my chest as I clicked on Oliver's reply, imagining what he might have said. Had he apologised, told him he'd fix it? Had he given some context as to why he would have done that in the first place? Would I finally get an answer? I swallowed hard, focused on the screen, and forced myself to confront my dead husband's words:

Justin, it wasn't me. I didn't make that profile. But I think we have a problem.

My vision grew white at the edges as I stared at the screen.

What did he mean it wasn't him?

It was him! I'd spent all night chatting to him on the app, so he was clearly lying.

But why lie?

I could understand him lying to me, pretending to *me* that it was all some big mistake, but Justin had been his close friend for almost eight years and wasn't exactly Mr Morality himself. I knew he'd cheated on his ex multiple times, for instance. Oliver had told me. And the one time I met her before it ended, she'd confided in me that he had a bona fide porn addiction. That they were going to couples counselling. So I would have thought he'd have applauded Oliver's experimentation, Charlie-be-damned. Besides, he and Oliver had each other's backs.

Was Oliver just lying to *everyone* now?

I reached for the little silver USB stick and plugged it into a USB port. Up came the little orange icon. I clicked on it. *Open.*

But my stomach was rumbling and I needed food in order to think, so I went over to Josh's pantry and pulled out a box of yogurt-covered cereal bars. I took one out, ripping open the wrapper as I headed back to my laptop and Pandora's box.

I chewed on the cereal bar as I stared at the screen—all the files I'd taken from Oliver's computer back when I thought infidelity was the crux of my problems. The answer *had* to be in there somewhere, but I didn't know where to start my search.

I looked around the room as though the answers were in the yellowing plaster. My face was getting hot from too much concentration and the air in the room was stale. I needed fresh air, so I reached behind me and unlatched the window. The sky was covered in a layer of white-grey cloud now, the sun just a glary cotton ball behind it.

It was around then my phone started ringing again: Tess. I clenched my jaw as I watched it ring and ring and ring, clicking it onto silent.

A wave of guilt washed over me: we always answered each other's calls. That was the deal. But I was doing this for her own good, to keep her out of it. The call went to voicemail and I sat there, staring at the phone screen, until *one new voicemail* flashed back at me.

Focus, Charlie, focus.

I stared back at the screen and started clicking through files—it was a mishmash of client files, spreadsheets, statements, correspondence and other miscellaneous things I didn't understand. I scanned my memory banks, seeking out danger I hadn't seen the first time round. And all I could think of was one name.

Machado.

He was the client Oliver met with in the hotel on that night I thought he was cheating. I flashed back to the night I saw them together, trying to remember Oliver's energy, his facial expressions. Oliver hadn't seemed scared of Machado. But his face *had* drained of colour whenever he said that name to Justin over the phone. And he *had* put that meeting into his calendar as "private." His calendar was synced with his work computer so he would have done that so that nobody he worked with knew he was meeting with Machado.

Why?

Who was this man? Was he dangerous? He was clearly wealthy and influential. He obviously had enemies—otherwise why have bodyguards? He'd have "people."

People who could do this kind of thing.

People who don't make mistakes. People who wouldn't leave DNA. The sorts of people who'd already be out of the country. My mind flashed back to that guy in the shop, the one I told you to take note of. That was around the time the taser search appeared in my browser history. And he'd seemed uncomfortable. But surely Machado, or someone like him, would be more careful than sending someone into the shop I could later identify. No. The sort of person Machado would hire would leave no trace. And if there was no trace, I'd definitely get the blame.

A fresh wave of nausea washed over me.

I put down my cereal bar and went into the top right-hand search bar, typing in "Machado." *Enter.* I held my breath as I waited for something to come up.

Nothing.

That was strange. I knew he existed. I'd seen him.

But hang on. If it was Machado, or someone like him, why bother framing me?

Why not just make it look like an accident?

Still, maybe he *had* made it look like an accident.

I hadn't spoken to DCI Holland at length yet, there was no way I could know what conclusions the police had drawn. Perhaps I was totally off base and he'd slipped in the shower, perhaps it wasn't even murder.

Shit. *I should have gone to see DCI Holland.*

I bit down on my lower lip as I imagined her at Charing Cross Police Station, waiting for me, jumping to all sorts of incriminating conclusions. Was I making things worse?

And so I reached for my phone and pressed play on Tess's voicemail message.

"Hon, it's me, what's going on? Are you okay? The police are trying to find you." She exhaled loudly. *"Look,"* she said slowly, *"they didn't tell me exactly what happened, but I know how they operate. And whatever this is, it's really serious."*

Ba-boom. Ba-boom. Ba-boom.

My throat grew tight as I hung up the phone. It was only two hours or so after they'd found Oliver's body. For them to be tracking me down via Natasha-the-neighbour and Tess-the-best-friend with such fervour meant that no, they did *not* believe it to be an accident. And also: they'd sectioned off our building with do-not-cross police tape and there were far too many forensics people in grey jumpsuits wandering in and out for an accidental slip in the shower. No. They believed it was murder and that I was involved. And they wouldn't believe that without proper proof.

That was my hunch, at least.

And so I just sat there, on Josh's sofa, my mouth dry and my stomach now a strange mix of cereal bar and nausea, as I tried to figure out what the hell had happened and how I was going to get out of this.

There was only one other person I could think of who might know something about Machado, or Oliver's other dealings, someone who might be able to point me in the right direction. But it was the one person I didn't want to call. Still, I had no choice. I picked up my phone, scrolled through my contacts and called Justin.

12.36 PM

"Hornsby Private Equity, this is Meredith," came a singsong voice from the other end of the line as my pulse beat madly. If he didn't answer the work number I'd try his cell phone next. But it felt like he was more likely to answer my call if he knew Meredith was aware I was on the other end of the line. He'd have to explain why if he refused.

I'd met Meredith a few times—once at the office summer party and then a handful of other times when I'd gone into Oliver's office. It was comforting to hear her voice.

"Hi, Meredith, it's Charlie," I said, trying to keep my tone stable. "Is Justin available?"

A silence rang over the line. *Shit.* The police had already called them. I could tell.

"Charlie," Meredith's voice was crackly now, like she wanted to ask if I was okay but wasn't sure of the right thing to do in this situation. "Sure, I'll check."

The line went dead and I waited for Justin to pick up.

Tick-tock. Tick-tock. Tick-tock.

"Charlie?" Justin's voice. Finally. "Where are you?"

My ears rang with danger. Were the police there with him?

"Oliver's dead," I said, my voice trembling.

Beat.

"I know," Justin said, his voice dripping sympathy and warmth. "The police have already been here. What happened?"

"I don't know!" I said, my voice coming out five semitones higher than intended. "I wasn't even there. I was at Tess's place."

"Well thank god you're okay. We were all so worried about you. Have you spoken to the police yet?"

Beat.

Wait. Why was he being so nice to me?

"Not yet," I said, cautious.

"You really need to," Justin replied, his voice gentle. Paternal.

"Justin, I had nothing to do with this. And I really think this had something to do with your business stuff," I said, and I knew I sounded like the silly, inarticulate woman he'd always thought I was, but I didn't care. I was struggling. "I think . . . I think it might have something to do with that man. Machado. The one you guys spoke about all the time."

I could hear Justin breathing on the other side of the phone.

"Who?" he said.

"Machado," I repeated.

"Charlie, I don't recognise that name. Are you okay? Where are you? I can come and get you."

The room swirled around me. What did he mean he didn't recognise that name? I'd heard Oliver use it on the phone with him many times. For a brief moment I questioned my sanity. But no. I was not crazy. I knew what I'd heard. And I'd seen Machado with my own eyes.

"Yes, you do!" I said, and there was a level of hostility in my voice I hadn't expected.

"Charlie," he said slowly, "you've suffered a big shock." His voice was oozing a gentleness that threw me off kilter. "You need to go to the police and tell them what you know. That's the only way they'll find out what happened."

And I knew he was probably right. I *should* go to the police. But I was too scared.

"Look, this is horrible for all of us," Justin continued. "Oliver was my best friend. If I knew anything I would tell you. The whole thing is baffling. Everyone loved Oliver," he said, his voice trailing off. "Actually, wait, there is one thing." Pause. "It's a bit odd. But I've been looking through our things here this morning, through the safe, and I can't seem to locate some papers. Did Oliver have anything around the house you noticed? Contracts, printouts, that sort of thing?"

"What? Not that I know of."

"Okay, well please let me know if any papers turn up. They're really important."

"Sure."

"Shit, Meredith is buzzing me. I have to go, Charlie. But please speak to the police."

"Okay."

And then he hung up and I sat there staring at the wall.

He was being so lovely. So concerned. But he was also lying. I'd heard him talk about Machado too many times to believe he didn't recognise that name. So the question was *why* was he lying?

I was in the middle of one of those situations that no movie can ever prepare you for, that no textbook in school ever covers.

And I needed to pee.

So I took my phone and went through to the bathroom, flicking through Instagram as I sat there. It was jarring how the rest of the world was just going on like nothing had happened. Mine was the only universe in disarray. I scrolled down through my feed, shaking my head at how unfair it seemed, when I caught sight of something even more concerning.

Josh's most recent post.

Gatwick Airport.

Him and the blonde girl.

Waiting for the shuttle.

I stared down at the picture: it'd been posted over an hour ago. So, not only was he back in London but he was probably almost back at his flat by now. I grabbed for the loo roll, flushed, and ran through to the sitting room. I scooped up my computer without even turning it off, grabbed the cereal bar wrapper and threw any evidence of my being there in my handbag. There was a black baseball cap on the counter by the door. I reached for it and put it on. And then, with my heart a muted thud in my chest, I rushed to his front door, slammed it behind me and ran down the stairs to the building foyer.

When I got to the bottom, I looked through the peephole. I needed to make sure the police weren't parked out the front. They weren't. But something equally bad was about to take place: Josh and the bronze-limbed blonde were making their way up the front path towards the front door.

My breath caught in my throat: how could I explain being there?

Behind me was the nook beneath the stairs, so I crouched down against the inside wall, hiding myself behind the neighbour's bicycle. A moment later, the door opened and I saw legs: one set was wearing pale blue jeans, the other set were newly shaved and brown.

"Here, let me take that," came Josh's voice. "Why don't you just go open the door." I held my breath and all I could hear was the jangle of keys being passed to her, footsteps making their way up the creaking stairs. *Ba-boom, ba-boom, ba-boom.* Then came Josh's footsteps. And soon, they were gone.

I stared at the front door. I needed to get out of there before someone saw me. But I realised that I had no idea where to go next. The police would be watching Tess's place and there would be too many people milling around the shop in broad daylight, so what did that really leave me with?

Now, if you're thinking I should have just gone to the police, that I should have let DCI Holland do her job and sort it out for me, well, I can tell you right now that (a) you're wrong. It's really damned lucky I *didn't* go to the police like a good girl. And (b) that's nice. But let's see *you* hand yourself over to the authorities when *you're* the one who could end up in an orange jumpsuit or a blue jumpsuit or whatever the fuck they wear in British prisons. It's not as easy as you'd think.

—

2.04 PM

The atmosphere outside was thick and stifling, like I was stuck in a jar and someone had screwed the lid on too tight. I pulled open the heavy glass doors and went inside. I was hit by the combined smells of coffee beans, cinnamon and sweet vanilla syrup, by the layered sounds of pop songs and clinking ceramic mugs, milk being frothed and teaspoons being dropped onto tables and into sinks.

So where was I? Think: Where would you go if you were

wearing a black baseball cap and carrying a laptop? If you needed anonymity and free wifi?

Yes, I was in Starbucks.

The first thing I did was head up to the counter and order a coffee: black. But when the barista asked my name I didn't say "Charlie" I said "Annabella," just to be safe. God knows who I thought would be there looking for me, but that gives you an insight into where my head was at. Everyone was a potential threat.

A few minutes later I was collecting it and finding a seat far, far away from the smudgy window and the darkening clouds outside. It had been sunny that morning and already it looked like rain.

I put down my coffee, reached into my bag just beyond the headshot and script from my audition a few days before, pulled out my laptop, connected to the wifi and opened a search browser: *Machado, South America.*

If Justin wasn't going to help me, I'd figure it out for myself. If I knew exactly who Machado was and who he worked for, maybe I could find something to show DCI Holland in Oliver's files.

I pressed "Enter" and 4,120,000 results appeared.

A couple of hours and a lot of clicked links later, I was on the verge of tears again. Because as quickly as hope had filled my veins with every click of a new lead, it had been replaced by icy disappointment—none of them were him. They were either too young or the photo looked nothing like him. There was nothing on social media. Nothing on LinkedIn. No mention of him in journal articles or the news.

It was as though he was a ghost.

A ghost I'd seen.

But all this made me even more certain he was somehow involved.

My phone started ringing from my bag—people on tables nearby were looking at me now, giving me that put-it-on-silent look—and I pulled it out into view: *No Caller ID*. It would be DCI Holland again. My face flushed hot as I flicked it to vibrate and let the call go to voicemail. It felt like I was close. She'd have to wait.

So I was holding my phone when it buzzed with a reminder:

CALENDAR

Pilates!

I thought of Brooke, lying on her Pilates reformer bed on Wednesday morning, water bottle beside her, waiting for me yet again. And my throat tightened as I thought of the story I'd told her of how perfect my marriage was. I thought of her in our flat: me crying, black bags, gin. My flimsy story about moving to a new place that was so fucking fab. What would she think if she saw me now? If she knew how things had gone in the last forty-eight hours? If she knew the truth of my marriage in comparison with the us-against-the-world version I'd peddled?

I bit my lip and stared at the screen.

There had to be someone out there who could point me in the right direction. Someone who knew what had happened, about

Justin and Oliver's business dealings. Someone else who knew Machado existed. The first person I thought of was Meredith, the woman who answered the phone. She was the team assistant after all. She'd have been instrumental in creating the paperwork for most of their deals. Would have read most everything that came in and out of their office. All the financials of every business they invested in. And so it stood to reason that she might know something. But there was no reason for her to part with that information and she might lose her job if she did.

Which left only one other person who might possibly know something.

She wouldn't be thrilled to hear from me, that much was certain, and there was no way of knowing whether she'd be able to help. Maybe Oliver had shared no more with her than he had with me. But she'd lived side by side with him for over a year so perhaps he'd mentioned Machado before he became a threat. And the police wouldn't have called her yet so there was no real danger in trying . . .

I pulled up a new browser window and typed in *Alyssa Shaw*.

It was a name I hadn't googled in a very long time, not since I followed Oliver to that hotel, realised I was wrong and promised myself I'd stop.

Which is how I didn't know the truth before now.

Because the first few results weren't her at all. It was easy to discard them one by one because I knew all too well what she looked like. I could still see her there in Sainsbury's with her long, lank hair.

Her jaw gripped to stop the tears. And I was hoping I'd find out that life had worked out well for her in the year and a bit that had passed since then, that she'd landed her dream job or started posting pictures with #couplegoals on social media. I needed her happy, and not just for altruism's sake. Happy people are more willing to help.

But I couldn't find an email address, nor a phone number. I already knew she wasn't particularly visible on social media, but she *did* have a Facebook page. And so, for the first time in over a year, I went to the search field and entered her name.

Up came a page of profiles.

The first three weren't her.

Hers was the fourth one down. I recognised her immediately.

But as I stared at it, the world seemed to warp around me. A real-time Snapchat filter.

Because it had changed.

Now it read: *Alyssa Shaw Memorial Page*.

You know what that means, right?

Alyssa Shaw was dead.

The air remained filled with the smell of coffee and the sounds of clinking cups and spoons, but all that was muffled by *ba-boom, ba-boom, ba-boom*. I clicked and up came her page. There she was, smiling back at me. She was sitting on a navy-and-white-checked picnic blanket and the light on her face had that red glow it always does in summer when the sun is going down. My pulse sped up and my throat grew tight.

Did Oliver not know she was dead, or had he actively hidden

that from me along with everything else? What about Justin? Had he known when he called her batshit crazy? Or was that before she died?

And how did she die?

The earth began spinning double time. I sat perfectly still as I tried to get my head straight. There were so many moving parts to my life I hadn't been aware of before now.

I needed one of those corkboards they use in TV shows to catch serial killers to make sense of it all.

Alyssa. The dating app. @*lover7*. Lucamore. Machado. DCI Holland. Whatever documents Justin was looking for.

Who the hell had I married?

Tears pricked behind my eyes as I stared at my screen, trying to control any sobs so that I didn't draw attention to myself. I thought back to my phone call with Justin. He was lying. I *knew* he was lying, but why? Was he scared of whoever did this? That if he said any-thing, something might happen to him too? Maybe if I was sitting there in front of him, not worried about who might be listening in on his call, maybe then it might be different. I needed to try. But thinking back to our conversation, he kept mentioning the police. I needed to talk to him *without* the police. And so I picked up my phone and dialled his number for the second time that day.

Ring. Ring. Ring.

"Hornsby Private Equity, this is Meredith," came her singsong voice once again.

"Hi, Meredith, it's Charlie again," I said, my voice stronger this time. "Tell Justin I think I've found what he's looking for. I'll come meet him outside the office in an hour."

"Ummm, okay," Meredith said. "I think he has a meeting in an hour."

"It's important, Meredith, he'll want this."

—

5.57 PM

I stood across the road for about five minutes watching Justin pacing back and forth in his overpriced suit, lingering outside his building. I was checking for signs of the police. Had he called them? Were they waiting for me? But by now, I was pretty sure it was safe. Whatever documents Oliver had taken mattered to Justin far more than his civic duty. I waited for the light to turn green and crossed the road. He looked up just as I got to him.

"Hi," I said, my voice flat.

"Charlie," he said, looking at his watch, "I don't have much time." His eyes were on my bag now. He was wondering whether what he wanted was in there. I needed to bluff so I held on to my bag like it was full of valuables, not just old cosmetics and a big manila envelope I'd bought at a post office on the way over here, now filled with the script from my failed audition and my headshot.

It's always good to have a prop, something to do with your hands.

"I think we need to go somewhere to talk. It's important."

Justin had never seen me in command like that and I think it took him by surprise because he did what I said.

"Why don't we go to the place we usually go," he suggested.

The black walls, black ceilings, chalkboard menus place I'd gone to just the week before with him and Oliver. The place beneath his building.

"Sure," I said, and we headed there quickly, both of us hurrying, neither of us speaking. Then it was down the stairs, through the heavy door and over to a free table in the corner. There was a candle that had been lit and it felt like a betrayal to be sitting there with him instead of Oliver, even after everything. I took off my jacket, hung it over the back of my chair and sat down. Justin did the same.

"What can I get you, Charlie?" Justin asked, calling over the waiter.

"Just some water."

"Sparkling water for the lady and a Glenfiddich for me," he said, fiddling with his signet ring.

The waiter left and it was just me and him.

"Now, Charlie, Meredith said you found the missing documents. What a relief," he said with his smarmy smile.

I looked at him. Took a mental snapshot of his expression. Then I pulled the manila envelope out of my bag, laying it on my lap. "Yes, it was only after we hung up that I thought of it." So far: true.

"Well, thank you *so* much, Charlie," he said, reaching out for the envelope.

"Not yet," I said, patting it. "I have some questions first, Justin."

"Of course, shoot," he said with a smile as the waitress delivered our drinks.

I took a sip of sparkling water, the wedge of lime touching my upper lip, and his eyes followed my movements.

"Who's Machado?" I asked, my gaze on his features. I watched his face change. It was incremental. The flicker behind his eyes flamed up. The muscles in his jaw tensed, his pale blue eyes opened just a fraction, and the pupils got small—very, very small. He knew exactly what I was talking about. No matter what came out of his mouth next, he *knew*.

"Why are we going through this again?" he asked gently. Like I was torturing myself with unnecessary trains of thought.

My eyes remained on his. "You can't say you don't know who he is, Justin. I heard you on the phone to Oliver loads of times when his name came up. So why are you lying to me? Do you think he had something to do with this?"

"No," he said, taking a sip of his Scotch, his eyes darting to the envelope, then back to me. "Look . . . If you must know, he's someone we do business with. However," he said, lowering his voice to a whisper as if to impart how big a deal it was, "it's pretty bad form for me to even tell you that."

My mind swirled. Was he telling me the truth? I mean, I'd heard of doctor-patient privilege and lawyer-client, but I wasn't entirely sure private equity guys had to swear a similar oath.

"Now," he said. Smile. "Can I have those documents, please?

Oliver shouldn't have even taken them home. We could get into big trouble if anyone found out." He was looking at the envelope on my knees. "It was a total breach of privacy."

"What's in here?" I asked.

"Haven't you looked?" he asked. What was that in his eyes? Relief?

"I did, but I couldn't really make head or tail of it." I could all but see the tension flow out of him. What was he looking for that would make him so worried? "Don't *you* want to know who killed Oliver?" I continued.

Justin let out a big sigh.

"Of *course* I do. I'm still in shock. But like I said before, I really think the best thing you could do would be to go to the police. You're not helping things by running around like this. You need to go talk to them and try to help them figure out what happened."

I nodded. Small.

"But I'm scared."

"Oh, Charlie," he said, reaching across and touching my hand; he'd never done something like that before. "Of course you are. But you can always call me if things get sticky." Something panged in my chest.

Maybe he was right. I mean, what had I discovered so far? Nothing. Maybe Machado really *was* just a client. Maybe I was making a big fuss over nothing. Seeing red flags where there were none. But I knew I hadn't killed Oliver. There had to be another answer out there, so now I was wondering whether I should ask Justin about the dating apps, about what Oliver meant when he said, "We have a problem." But for all I knew the police were on their way and I had other questions that were far more pressing.

"What was Lucamore?" I asked. I did it just like that, with no warning shot.

"What?" Justin asked, his face contorted now.

"Lucamore," I repeated. The air around us grew thick with tension. "Oliver mentioned it a couple of times."

Beat.

"What did he say?" Justin asked, his eyes narrowing just a tad. I was onto something.

"Not much, I just wasn't sure what it was," I said, trying to play it down.

"Right, well, that too is a confidential business thing and he shouldn't have been talking to you about it," he said slowly, enunciating his words. "That's all I can say."

"Oh, so it's not something that will be in Oliver's will then? Not something I might inherit from." You see what I was doing, right? I was asking him outright if Oliver had a stake in it. I was just doing it in a sneaky way, giving him the chance to lie. Disguising it as my wanting to know what cash was coming my way.

"Lord no, it's a Hornsby project," he said, tangible relief in his expression.

So there it was: he'd tried to lie about Machado existing, and now he'd lied about Lucamore too. Something very strange was going on. The only reason Justin would lie would be to cover some-thing up. So what was that "something"?

Shit, did he have something to do with Oliver's death? But why would he do that? I looked around the restaurant, reminding myself of the nearest exit.

"Can I have that envelope now?" Justin asked and my gaze snapped back to his.

What were the documents he was so keen to get his hands on?

"I have one more question." I didn't want to ask it, but I knew if I didn't I might never know. "Did you know Alyssa Shaw was dead?"

He was quiet. Stationary.

"Oliver's ex," I continued, as though to jog his memory.

His eyes moved down to the table, then flashed back up at me.

"Yes, Charlie, I did. It was very sad," he said, shaking his head with supposed remorse. "I told Oliver he should tell you about it, but he seemed to think it might upset you. That you might feel responsible."

"What do you mean? How could I be fucking responsible?"

"She took her own life, Charlie," he said. "She was always quite vulnerable, but after Oliver left she really went off the rails. It was very, very sad."

My throat tightened and the walls swayed in towards me. This news had caught me entirely off guard. Was this somehow my fault?

All I could manage was "When?"

He shook his head as though in mourning, even though he'd never had a good word to say about her. "It was last summer, I think."

That was just after she saw us in Sainsbury's. And that made sense. There was a sadness that clung to Oliver around that time. I'd thought it was because of me, because I hadn't trusted him, but this made more sense. He'd felt guilty. Responsible.

Was that why he'd asked me to marry him so quickly? A way to atone?

"Now, I really do need those documents," Justin said, his blue eyes boring into me.

"Oh," I said, my eye on the exit. Standing up, I took the envelope and left it on the table. "Here you go."

And then I all but ran to the stairs as fast as I could. When I got to the top I looked around. There were red London buses and beeping motorbikes and a cab right there in front of me dropping someone off. I needed to get out of there before Justin had time to call the police (or come and yell at me), so I lunged towards it, plastered on a fake smile and said to the driver, "I'm heading to Notting Hill Gate."

—

7.22 PM

I walked down the alley to the back entrance of the shop, keeping my face angled down and my pace unremarkable, unmemorable.

An irate text message had come in from Justin in the cab. *What the hell are you playing at?* Attached was a snap of the headshot and script I'd left in the manila envelope. But I didn't care if Justin was angry with me. I could see through his façade now: he was hiding something, something that could keep me out of prison. And his words haunted me: *She took her own life, Charlie.*

How had all this happened?

Oliver was dead. Alyssa was dead. Justin was lying. I was going to have to chat to DCI Holland soon, but I still had very little to tell her.

The sun was going down and I was getting cold, but the shadows left me feeling a little less exposed. Almost everything had closed an hour and a half ago so there weren't many people around. It was risky coming to the shop—the police might be watching it, but surely they couldn't watch everywhere all the time. Besides, only an idiot would go somewhere they worked when they were on the run from the police, right?

The other option was to use my credit card and book into a hotel, but that seemed even riskier. They'd be watching my cards if they had any sense. They might be tracking my phone soon too. But as it was still within twenty-four hours of the murder I figured I probably had a little longer before that happened. There would be paperwork to sort through, red tape to navigate. And I hadn't formally been arrested or charged so there might be privacy issues that could stand in their way at this point.

I lifted my keys from my bag, slid the big one into the lock and pushed it open. The air smelled comfortingly familiar—like dust and dry cleaning and the Pomegranate Noir room spray from Jo Malone that Grace loved. I closed the door behind me as quietly as I could and crept through to the front room. Reaching into the front display I'd put together with so much love, I pulled out the grey blanket that lay on the floor and then reached for the light blue velvet cushion that sat on the chair before heading out the back to the storage room.

I was exhausted. I needed to sleep. I needed to be left alone.

I pushed open the door and flicked on the light. It was too bright and startling after my eyes had become so accustomed to the shadows. There was a green velvet sofa with stained cushions against the far wall. I was planning on sleeping on it, but as I drew near I realised there was something there, sparkling under the globes. I moved towards it: a chocolate bar, a salad from M&S with a little plastic fork and a folded piece of paper.

I opened it, my pulse quickening.

Just in case you come here. Grace x

You see, that's the thing with people: they always surprise you eventually. Every single person in your life right now is a stranger you know. But every once in a while, the surprises are good.

So, nestled under that grey blanket, I peeled back the plastic from the top of the salad—baby spinach, salmon, potatoes, cherry tomatoes—and took a bite. I needed my blood sugar to be stable before I could do what needed to be done next.

I needed to know if anything had been reported yet. I needed to know how bad things were. So I pulled out my phone, and with a mouth full of potato and mayonnaise, I conducted a garden-variety Google search: *Charlene Buchanan; Oliver Buchanan.*

All that came up were my IMDb page, some outdated minor press, Oliver's LinkedIn page, Hornsby Private Equity and, two pages in, our wedding notice. So far, so good. So I took another bite of salad and navigated to the *Guardian* website. A quick scan of the UK News page revealed nothing about me, nor Oliver.

Next, I went to the *Evening Standard*. Clicked on News, then Crime.

Nothing.

Finally, I checked *The Independent*. Again, nothing.

For all DCI Holland's missed calls, for all her tracking me down via Tess and Natasha, it appeared I wasn't important enough to make it to the news. This was a good, good thing. And so I went to sleep that night in a state of almost calm. But that didn't stop adrenaline waking me at 4 am. We always know when something big is about to happen, even if we don't know what it is.

Episode 7

TUESDAY, 12 JUNE 2018 (7.14 AM)

The café across the road opened at 8 am and I couldn't afford to be seen by Meg when she arrived. So I put the blanket and cushion back in the window display, stuffed a black polo neck in my bag in case I needed it, and headed quietly out the back door by around 7.15 am. I may not have been the subject of press conferences and manhunts yet, but I wasn't taking any chances. The only sign I'd been there was the note I'd left for Grace on the sofa: *Thank you xxx.*

Then I headed to Ladbroke Grove and called an Uber. I got inside and slammed the door with relief.

Next, I posted a picture to Instagram. That might seem like an odd thing to do, given the circumstances, and you're right, it is. But I wasn't sure if the police were watching my Instagram page or not, and it seemed like I should at least *try* to throw them off the scent, send them to a different part of London. So I'd been trawling through my photo reel, looking for something relevant, and I found a picture of a graveyard that Oliver and I used to walk through. It was near our old flat in Kensal Green, the one we moved out of after the break-in debacle.

It was: One. Two. Three. Big breath. Post.

And it was done long before I got to where I was headed, the other side of town—far from where anyone would be looking for me. Somewhere I could get lost in *I Heart London* tourist t-shirts and people staring down at maps on phones. I was heading to Carnaby Street.

Soon I was sitting in the same diner Tess and I used to go to all the time when we were regulars at Tramp. The air smelled of frying bacon and maple syrup, and I was drinking the familiar filter coffee that had been sitting in the pot getting stale for far too long, staring at my computer screen. Oliver's files were all there in front of me and I was pretty sure that Justin had something to do with it all by now, but I was losing faith in my ability to join the dots. Maybe if I were to hand everything over to DCI Holland together with my suspicions, she'd be able to make head or tail of it.

Perhaps I should just do that. Go to the police station right now. Trust.

I closed my eyes, imagining how it might play out in Utopia: DCI Holland might meet me at the door, tell me she was so sorry for my loss, be kind. She might tell me they had a couple of leads and then pass me a card for a grief counsellor. My heart slowed to a slur of a beat as I realised it could all be okay.

But then, it could also go very wrong, just like last time. She could take a few DNA swabs, present me with the evidence and caution me on my rights.

Still, I wasn't delusional—I knew I couldn't run from the police forever. That had never been my intention. I just wanted to give myself the best chance I could at getting out of this mess.

I took a sip of stale coffee and picked up my phone. A few more texts had come in from Tess and one from Grace. I ignored them all and clicked through to my emails. Tess had emailed me as well and guilt washed over me. I was about to deviate from the plan and reply when a new email popped into my inbox.

It was a Google alert.

I'd set them up a couple of years before in an attempt to not miss any of the glowing acting press I never ultimately received. But this one had nothing to do with acting.

The headline read: WOMAN SOUGHT BY POLICE FOR QUESTIONING OVER HUSBAND'S DEATH.

Ba-boom, ba-boom, ba-boom.

It linked to an article that had been posted two hours before on the *Evening Standard* website. My vision blurred as I clicked the link. Another window opened. And there I was. Blonde hair to my shoulders. White shirt. Light pink lipstick. Smiling amber eyes. A picture which could be described as "pretty and angelic" was now rendered sinister and deceptive beside that headline.

I looked around me at all the other people sitting in that diner. *Shit.*

I minimised the browser window so anyone looking over my shoulder wouldn't realise that the face on the screen matched the face that was looking at it.

London actress Charlene Carter is being sought by police over the death of her husband, Oliver Buchanan, on Sunday night . . . My heart was racing as my eyes scanned down through the words: *Neighbours report hearing a domestic row and a woman's scream at around 7 pm.* Fucking Natasha. *Mr Buchanan's body was found early Monday morning when a neighbour noticed the door had been left ajar.*

I closed the browser and immediately cleared my search history. There was no reason for this—I was just in that sort of mindset. My synapses were zinging, my forehead covered in a thin layer of sweat.

The article said the door had been left ajar. That sounded a lot like someone wanted him to be found. Quickly.

Someone who wanted me framed before too many questions could be asked.

I realised that everything I feared most was true: I *was* the prime suspect. And all signs pointed to the fact that someone had set me up.

And if I'd gone to see DCI Holland when she'd asked me to, I'd have been blamed. And so, no, I wouldn't be going in to see her just yet. I needed a little more time to get my head around what this meant for my life.

Was I really going to go to prison for my husband's murder?

Was there really nothing on that USB full of Oliver's files that could help me? And if I didn't go to the police, where was I going to sleep that night? If I was in the paper they would definitely be tracking my cards. And I couldn't risk going back to Boulevard again. I'd been lucky to get away with going there once. Shit, were they tracking my phone by now? I should turn it to airplane mode. Or take out the battery.

But as I went to reach for it, Brooke's call came in.

I almost didn't answer, you know. But then I realised this was it: my out. I could go and stay with Brooke.

"Hello?" I said, keeping my voice down.

"Hey sexy, just checking you are coming to Pilates tomorrow," she said.

"I don't think so," I said, my voice quivering. "Fuck, Brooke. My whole life is falling apart."

"Huh? What's going on?"

I took a deep breath. "Oliver's cheating on me." As I said it I clenched my eyes shut, knowing that the illusion I'd woven was shattering in her mind, and praying that she hadn't seen the *Evening Standard* story.

"Wow," she said. "I'm so sorry. Wow."

"I know."

"Well, do you need somewhere to come stay?"

Relief pulsed through me. That was perfect. Nobody would look for me there. "Yes, that would be so helpful," I said, a wave of guilt rushing through me because I hadn't told her Oliver was dead and I was being chased by the police. But how could I? Nobody would be comfortable harbouring a fugitive.

"It's all the way in Bow though." She laughed.

My phone pinged. A message had come in. I assumed it would be Tess, checking on me again, and my stomach clenched. I wanted to tell her I was okay but I also didn't want her to need to lie if they asked if she'd heard from me.

"I know. Totally worth the journey." I'd always refused to make the long journey before now, but when I needed her I was willing to. That made me selfish, right?

"Okay, I'll be home at around five-thirty. I'll send you my address," she said.

"Thanks." And then we hung up and I glanced at my messages. But it wasn't from Tess at all. It was from Justin: *Hi Charlie, just checking if those documents had turned up yet. This is important!!!*

I stared down at my phone: what was wrong with him? His best friend had died thirty-six hours before, and *documents* were his highest priority? But it was good that I had that message now. I'd show it to DCI Holland, along with whatever else I discovered about him when I finally went to the police. The time clicked over to 8.23 am. I wasn't meeting Brooke until 5.30 pm. What was I going to do all day?

I had no idea. But I did know one thing: the moment Brooke's address arrived in my inbox I'd memorise her postcode, remove the battery from my phone so nobody could track me, pay my bill and go somewhere far, far away from here.

It was a strong plan.

—

5.32 PM

Here's something you probably don't know: in real life you can't just whip a battery out of an iPhone. You need multiple tools, the hands of a surgeon and complicated instructional videos off YouTube. I had only one of those three things, so I'd settled instead on turning it onto airplane mode, turning it off and then hoping for the best. The driver took a sharp turn to beat the lights and my stomach got left behind. I looked up: the windscreen wipers were going and red tail lights reflected off the mirrored tar.

temp's flat. The sitting room was all cream curtains, with a brown, comfortable-looking sofa and chair set, a big rectangular TV and a glass coffee table. The carpet was that sort rental properties always have, the black-white-brown-beige-swirl type that doesn't show stains, and the wallpaper was yellowing around the edges.

"Tea?" Brooke asked as she walked into a small kitchen at the other end of the room: turquoise and white tiles on the walls, ageing white wooden cabinets and a white tiled floor. She flicked on the kettle and its hum filled the room.

"Sure, that'd be great," I replied, sitting on a chair and glancing down the hallway. It led to what I assumed was her bedroom because I could see the end of a double bed, white sheets and a flash of turquoise inside. The bathroom, I decided, must be down that way too.

"How do you take it?" Brooke asked as she opened the fridge.

"White, no sugar," I said. The room filled with the sounds of fridge doors being closed and cupboards being opened and cups being laid down on the counter.

I was thinking of the phone in my bag. Tess had probably called again. She'd be so worried by now.

"Here you go," Brooke said, handing me my cup and sitting on the sofa.

I took it from her, my fingers burning from the heat.

Brooke was looking at my bag sitting on the floor by my feet. "You pack light," she said, and I thought of how I went to Tess's place just forty-eight hours ago thinking it would only be for the night.

"I know—I sort of left in a rush," I said, taking a sip.

Brooke was frowning. "So how did you find out he was cheating?"

I shook my head and blinked back tears. But they welled in my eyes despite my best efforts. I was thinking of his body being wheeled out of the building and my helplessness, knowing I'd never see him again. But I couldn't tell Brooke that and I needed to explain away my tears. And so I told her a half-truth.

"I found him on a dating app."

Her eyes got big for a moment. She took in a deep breath. "Shit. That's awful. When?"

I shook my head as if trying to pry loose the memory. "A week or so ago."

"I'm so sorry, you didn't say anything . . ." Brooke said, taking a sip, her gaze shifting to my hand and then my wrist.

"So that's why no rings? Oh, and your wish bracelet's gone . . ."

I looked down at my bare wrist, remembering the night he put it on. The wishes.

"I cut it off," I said. A hot tear rolled down my cheek and I wiped it away with the back of my hand. "You should have seen all the messages, Brooke, in his Facebook account." I was playing the cheated-on wife well.

"You poor thing. You must be so angry. Wait—so you have his passwords? Amazing! Let's use them and get our own back."

"Thanks," I replied with a faint smile. "But honestly I just want to think about anything else but all this for a bit."

Beat.

"Of course, hon. Well, make yourself at home. I'm afraid all I have is this sofa, but it's quite comfy." She tapped the sofa she was sitting on. Then she stood up and went over to a big cupboard by the bathroom and pulled out a dark blue towel. She came back and laid it over the edge of my sofa.

"Why don't you finish that up and go take a long hot bath. I can lend you some pyjamas. They might be a bit long"—she was a good three inches taller than me—"but they'll do."

"Thanks, Brooke, that'd be great," I replied. And then I took my tea and headed to the bathroom.

I closed the door behind me and turned the taps on and, as steam began to fill the room, I stared at my reflection in the mirror. My hair was hanging loose around my shoulders and needed a brush. My eyes were bloodshot. And my expression was tense. This was the first time since I'd seen Oliver on that stretcher that I'd had a chance to relax. To feel safe. The sound of water crashing into the bathtub echoed off the white tiles. As I sat on the cool porcelain and reached my hand into the water to test the temperature, my shoulders slumped forward and I started to sob.

I wasn't sure if Brooke could hear me on the other side of the door or not, but it was okay if she could: I had an excuse. I'd found my husband had been cheating on me. I'd found him on a dating app.

I peeled off Tess's olive-green jacket, my white t-shirt and jeans, leaving them in a pile on the floor. Then I unhooked my bra and took off my underwear.

And that's when I saw it.

My period.

Of course I had my period: because I didn't have enough prob-lems right now. And my bag was in the other room, wasn't it? I stared at Brooke's bathroom cabinet. Was it very off-form to go through it looking for a tampon? I decided it was so I let out a deep breath, wiped the tears from my eyes, wrapped myself in that dark blue towel and pulled open the bathroom door. Brooke was sitting there on the sofa again, looking up at me quizzically. "Everything okay?"

"Just need my bag." I smiled, taking my laptop out—water dam-age was not what I needed—and rushed back into the bathroom.

I got there just in time to turn off the taps and avoid flooding Brooke's bathroom. I hung my towel over the rack and, sitting on the loo, rifled through my bag. I felt my wedding rings, the USB, the red pen I'd taken to the audition, a little can of hairspray, some bits of paper—receipts?—and pulled out a hair band to tie back my hair. There had to be a tampon in here somewhere. Please, dear god, don't let the plastic be broken.

And then there it was, a small box.

It wasn't the brand I usually bought, but I assumed it was one of Oliver's panicky buys and that made me ache just to look at it. I opened the little black-and-blue box. It was full. Eight white tam-pons all neatly packed together. So when I pulled one out the other seven loosened, fell about the box a bit.

Which meant I saw it.

A little white circular disk.

Ba-boom, ba-boom, ba-boom.

I blinked hard as I stared down at the inside of the box.

What the fuck is this?

I reached in and pulled it out, squinting down at it, my breath fast, my heart thumping. I turned it over, looking for some sort of logo or text. There was a rough bit on one edge, sort of like braille, which read "Zoomzo." I reached for my phone and watched the screen flash white as it slowly powered up. Then I turned it off airplane mode and pulled up Google.

With shaking thumbs I typed in *Z-o-o-m-z-o.*

And there it was: *Zoomzo—the safest way to track your child or elderly parent via your smartphone.*

It was a tracking device.

I immediately turned my phone back onto airplane mode, then shut it off.

I'd been right. Someone had been watching my every move.

The room was thick with steam and I was glad that I was already sitting because I felt dizzy. I searched through my memory banks, through every film I'd watched, but there was nothing to guide me. No heroine's journey for me to mimic, no scene to help me work out what to do next.

It was just me, alone.

I was in uncharted territory.

I stared down at the disk. What should I do with it? If I left it here, wouldn't that make it easy for Machado or Justin or whoever put it there to find me? But what excuse could I give Brooke for going out and dropping it somewhere?

And I was very fucking scared to go outside in the dark alone. Inside this house, with the door locked and a witness, was the safest place for me.

Shit, shit, shit.

All I knew for sure was that I couldn't tell Brooke.

If she realised what sort of danger I'd brought with me, she'd never help me. She'd make me leave. And so I slid it back into the tampon box where I'd found it and got into the bath.

On the day I finally realised what was going on, I woke up early.

Brooke's bedroom light was still off so I guessed that meant she was still asleep. I was propped up on the sofa I'd slept on, my laptop balanced on my knees, screen glowing blue-white in the dark as I stared down at yet another bloody Excel spreadsheet. It was plugged into the wall—the battery had died, but thankfully Brooke had a Mac charger. I'd been up for a couple of hours by then and could still smell the pizza we'd ordered when I got out of the bath. Mushroom. Capsicum. Cheese. First it made me hungry. Then it reminded me of Oliver. Of the pizza place on our corner we'd always loved—and the memory made something in my chest twist just a little more. Like my heart was being wrung out.

Ouch. I shuffled my weight. My back ached and my bones felt out of whack. I must have slept in a weird position. But I was almost there, almost through all his files. I hadn't found anything yet, but that didn't change what I was going to do that day. Finding that tracking device in my bag—finding it hidden in a fucking box of tampons—had filled my veins with ice and left me with no doubt as to what I needed to do: go to the police.

That USB stick was my last chance, but so far nothing on it looked suspect to me.

I closed the spreadsheet and stared down at the list of folders as the time winked back at me from the upper right-hand corner of my screen: 6.07 am. *Shit.* Brooke would be up soon.

I told myself not to be mean, that she was well-meaning and everything—she was even missing Pilates this morning to be with me—but, even so, I knew she'd slow me down again. Instead of being able to go through the rest of Oliver's stuff strategically the night before, I'd spent it trying to fabricate reasons why I didn't want to go through Oliver's emails with her to "see what he'd been up to and how we could get back at him." You see, it had occurred to me that I'd been really daft to log into his emails two days before in Starbucks—what if the police checked and saw they'd been accessed after his death? It wouldn't look good. They might find out it was me. So I didn't want to do it again. Which was why I'd been awake for two hours doing this alone in the silence and peace of dawn.

But yes: 6.07 am. I was running out of time. I'd need to hand myself in soon or the police would issue an arrest warrant, if they hadn't already . . .

And so I scrolled down and clicked on the only folder I knew I'd be able to decipher quickly: "Photographs."

It was organised by events like "Christmas 2018," "Honeymoon" and "Wedding," the other folders simply named by year.

They dated back to 2012, but I didn't have that sort of time so I started at 2014. I was looking for a picture of Machado. The plan was simple now: I'd give DCI Holland the USB stick full of Oliver's files, tell her of my suspicions about Justin, and hopefully show her a picture of Machado. Because, no matter what Justin said, I'd seen Oliver's expression whenever Machado's name came up: hollow, twisted, pale. He wasn't just an ordinary business associate. And Justin wouldn't have tried to pretend he didn't exist if there weren't a suspicious reason.

But all I was scrolling through were coffee cups and wine glasses, sunsets, shots in the dark where only partial faces were visible, shots with people I'd never seen before. It was frustrating—at this point I would have settled on a shot of that man who'd come into the shop that day. Something. Anything. But I kept going. Watching. Waiting. Soon I came to 2015. A holiday. Summer. His brother and mother. They were in Greece somewhere: lots of white paint, blue seas and red and pink flowers in terracotta pots. I never got to know Oliver's brother properly—we'd met once, briefly, just after I met Oliver— but I knew he was always in some sort of trouble and so Oliver had always felt the full burden of trying to take care of his mother. I was pretty sure that was what drove him in large part to be so successful despite the odds—there were people relying on him.

I stared down at his mother's face: dyed auburn hair with grey roots, green eyes like Oliver's, deep furrows above her brow. She was a kind woman. The last time I saw her was at her home in Norfolk. Sunday lunch in early January. Beef Wellington. Then we'd smoked a cigarette in the garden, she said how sad she was that she hadn't been at the wedding. I'd told her I was sorry, then tried to make up for it by gushing about how much I loved her son. My chest contracted at the thought of her hearing the news. It would kill her. God, she wouldn't think I'd done it, would she? Wouldn't believe that of me? Surely she'd stand up for me, her daughter-in-law.

I kept scrolling. There were some of Oliver and Justin in Brazil on a business trip. They looked happy. Victorious. Like they'd just done something clever. Oliver was tanned, just like when he got back last time: his eyes sparkling green against the bronze of his skin. And in that moment I could smell him again: ylang-ylang, spice. We were back in our bed again. Everything ached. I kept scrolling.

Brooke's bedroom door creaked open. She was up.

"Hey," I said, my voice crackly from lack of sleep.

"Hey," she replied, wandering through to the bathroom as I looked back to my screen.

I was at 2016 now. The loo flushed from the bathroom and the shower was turned on. I reached beside me and took a sip of water.

I scrolled back to pictures of Christmas 2015, one of Oliver sitting on a roller coaster with his arm around a girl, and I recognised her: dark hair, long sun-kissed limbs, happy smile.

It was Alyssa.

My throat tightened as I thought of her Facebook memorial page. I thought of how Justin described her: unbalanced, batshit crazy. How he said she'd committed suicide. Was I really somehow responsible for that?

I scrolled slowly, drinking in her form, her lines, the woman Oliver had loved before me, and I winced. He looked so happy with her. And Alyssa, she was so vibrant in those pictures, so different to the woman I'd seen in Sainsbury's. How does a transformation like that happen?

A few minutes later the bathroom door opened and Brooke emerged in a white towelling robe, her hair wrapped in a blue towel. I was still staring at the screen but was aware of her moving into the kitchen.

"Tea?" she asked, flicking on the kettle.

"That'd be great," I replied, still scrolling through the years, staring back at the screen.

It was March 2016. Alyssa was with the daffodils now. Alyssa in Paris—I didn't know they'd gone to Paris. Oliver had never mentioned it. But he'd left her for me, so he must have loved me more. Then there was the two of them in a vast green field, hills behind them, a crisp blue sky with just a wisp of cloud. Where were they? Then came another, this time indoors, and it must have been taken at Easter because Alyssa was holding an egg, sunshine flaring off the tinfoil.

The hum of the kettle filled the room. Then the sound of the fridge being opened, a drawer. I scrolled down through the pictures. And it was in a strange sort of slow motion that I saw the next shot. Because this one was not of Alyssa and Oliver at all.

This time Oliver was standing with another girl.

A girl in a red jumper and a short black skirt.

Her face, her features had been reshuffled slightly, hardened by time, but I recognised her face immediately.

Ba-boom, ba-boom, ba-boom.

It was Brooke.

Yes.

The same Brooke who was making me a cup of tea.

My breath caught in my throat as I squinted at the screen.

I had to be wrong.

I looked up at Brooke and back down at the screen.

My throat grew tight as I tried to set my expression so she wouldn't know what I was looking at.

Because it was definitely her. She was a bit younger, her hair was a bit longer and messed up by the wind, but there was no doubt about it. My stomach clenched as I looked up at Brooke.

Everything was in high definition now, like I was stuck in one of those clever TVs where you can see the actors' pores.

The sound of water being poured onto a teabag was crystal clear. As she came over to me and handed me my cup, it was as though she were moving in slow motion. I focused on my breathing and did what I could to control my thoughts. I needed to think good things or she'd know something was wrong: *Brooke is my really good friend, Brooke has helped me, Brooke is lovely* . . .

But even so, I could feel my jaw shake.

"Are you okay?" she asked.

Fuck.

"Yeah," I said, forcing myself to meet her eye. *Brooke is my really good friend, Brooke has helped me, Brooke is lovely* . . . "I'm just really upset about Oliver. And I didn't really sleep."

I took a sip of tea and my ears rang. *Shit, should I be drinking this? What if she had put something in it?* But she was watching me so I had no choice but to swallow as I wondered why in the hell was

230

there a picture of Brooke with Oliver in his files. How did she know him? How did she know him *all the way back in 2016*?

I scanned my mind for a logical explanation. Perhaps this was some sort of six degrees of separation phenomenon at play?

But no, that didn't make sense. I'd shown her pictures of Oliver before so she knew what he looked like. If she'd met him, she would have recognised him. So why hadn't she mentioned it?

Now, there's an instinct in all of us that wants us to survive. It's the same instinct that kicked in when I was sixteen—once his hand grew so tight around my mouth that I couldn't breathe, it told me to submit. And right now it was screaming, *No, Charlie, do not say anything.*

But Brooke was looking at me funny. So I closed down the photographs, shut the lid of my computer, picked up my towel and said as calmly as I could, "I better shower." Then I picked up my bag, the small pile of folded clothing I'd left on the floor from the day before and headed through to the bathroom.

I just needed to get away from her. I needed to think.

I closed the door behind me and looked around. I turned on the shower and quickly pulled off Brooke's pink pyjama set, dropping it on the floor.

Ba-boom, ba-boom, ba-boom.

I ran through everything in my mind. Brooke had met me at Pilates. Had that been on purpose? Had she intentionally befriended me? I thought back to all our conversations, to how she'd probed about Oliver's business. To how she'd seemed such a willing audience when I told her about what we did together, what our couple-y routines were. *Shit.* Was that why Oliver had wanted me to be so careful on Instagram, so she couldn't find us? Was she some insane stalker who was in love with him?

But I'd been careful. How could she possibly have known which Pilates studio I went to?

I racked my brain. I'd posted a photograph or two on Instagram but they had always been bland, lacking in identifying features, just feet in straps, so how had she known?

I tested the temperature, then stepped into the shower, letting the water flow over my face. If she was listening at the door I needed her to think I was showering, like nothing was wrong.

As I closed my eyes and let the water cascade over my face, I could see in my mind's eye the pictures I'd posted on Instagram. One was a selfie, lying on the bed. Just the black leather of the reformer bed behind me. The other was of my feet in the straps. Behind them was just a ceiling and a fan . . . nothing. Hang on. The straps. *Shit.* My memory was recalling something white on them. The studio's name was printed in white on the straps.

Holy fuck.

She was properly crazy.

I looked up at the door, the same door that she was on the other side of, as I thought through the rest. What did all this mean?

So Brooke had befriended me to get to Oliver. A man she was in love with. That's why she'd been so interested in what we did and where we went. But wait—Oliver was dead.

Surely Brooke couldn't have killed him.

It seemed too big. Too wild. Too insane to be true. And how would she have even pulled it off? How did she get into our apartment? Had she broken a window? Had she pressed the buzzer? No, surely not. What if I'd been there?

But hang on, that wasn't a risk for her: She *knew* I wasn't there. Because Justin wasn't the one who'd been watching me, nor was Machado. It was Brooke. She already knew Oliver was back in the UK—I'd told her just the day before—and thanks to that tracker, she knew he was alone.

But when had she put it in my bag? At Pilates? At the shop when I was out back? And how long had she been watching me?

Shit. I thought of how I'd told her we were moving. If she'd been stalking him, that would have worried her: the thought that she might lose track of us. Of him. Was that why she went there that night? Because she loved him? Or was it a if-I-can't-have-you-nobody-can scenario? If she was planning on killing him, the thought we were moving would definitely have expedited her plan. She already knew the layout of our house. She'd already had a plan. She wouldn't have wanted to do all that legwork again.

Had *my* lies been the thing that killed Oliver in the end?

But if she killed Oliver, she knows he's dead. That I'm lying to her about why I'm here. And she's playing along, toying with me . . . Why?

And then I thought of her interest in Oliver's emails, his files. Why? What did she think was in there? And if all this was true, why had she reached out to me and pretended to help? And then, just like that, I knew: it was to cover her tracks.

If my new friend disappeared directly after Oliver died, wouldn't she immediately seem suspicious?

No. She needed to continue as though she had nothing to hide. She needed to hide in plain sight.

Which she would have managed to do if I had never seen that picture. Because in my mind she had never even met Oliver, so why on earth would she kill him?

It was the perfect crime.

I struggled to control my breathing, holding on to the wall for support and looking over to the white door even though I knew I'd locked it.

The room was spinning like I'd downed half a bottle of Scotch as all the pieces fell so perfectly into place. I could hear her voice echoing in my head: *Oh, and your wish bracelet's gone.*

I'd never mentioned my Bahia bracelet to her.

Had she seen it on my Instagram story?

Was she *@lover7*?

The one who'd been watching me on Instagram?

But what had I ever done to her? And how could she really have believed she could get away with it? That she could go into our house, kill Oliver and blame me?

Because, you know: DNA. Her DNA would be in our house, they'd know she'd been there. It would all be okay.

But then: *Oh fuck, she'd covered her bases.* She had a really good excuse for her DNA being in our house if it ever did come to that. She'd been there just the day before he died. She could explain it away that way.

Why is she doing this to us?

Then I thought of Alyssa. Had Brooke targeted her too? Was that why she'd killed herself?

My stomach turned to oil as I looked around the room. What the hell was I going to do? *What would Amy in* Gone Girl *do?* Or that blonde woman in *Killing Eve?* That's who I needed to be right now, a little less me, a little more sociopath.

There was a window, a small rectangular window that looked out onto the back garden. I could fit through that. I knew I could. I left the shower running, then got out and quietly unlatched it. But what the fuck—my computer and any proof I had that Brooke had ever met Oliver was in the other room. And what was I going to do: jump out the window, hope she didn't notice and just run? Of course she'd notice.

No. The only way I could get out of this was to play her at her own game. I'd need to just pretend I had no idea it was her.

And so I turned off the taps, dried myself off, dressed in my clothes from the day before, adding the polo neck this time as it looked cold outside. There was nothing for it other than to play along. My bag was lying there on the floor, dangerously close to a puddle, so I picked it up, rifling through it until I found my phone and frantically turned it on, desperate to see the screen flash white, that little Apple sign appear, and to turn it off airplane mode for good. How quickly things had changed.

Now I *wanted* the likes of DCI Holland to be able to find me if things went wrong.

Staring at the bathroom door, I took a deep breath to calm myself, opened the door and went back to the living room.

I could hear the hairdryer going—so Brooke was back in her bedroom now. My eyes immediately moved to my laptop to check for the USB stick I'd had in it with the photograph—the only thing I had linking Brooke to Oliver, to Alyssa.

It was gone.

I had a split second to decide what to do: say something or pretend I hadn't noticed.

I needed that USB—without it, I had nothing. But she wasn't going to give it back to me, was she? And she'd killed Oliver. She had that in her. And I was in her flat. I didn't know about the locks. They could be double-bolted. And if she was smart enough to plan all this, I needed to be careful. Who knew what sort of contingency plan she had in place if things went wrong.

I needed to make her believe she'd got away with it. Otherwise, she probably would.

—

7.59 AM

It'd never made much difference to me whether I was three minutes from the station, four minutes from the station or eight. I'd read those sorts of descriptions in Flatshare ads: *Only three and a half minutes walk to the station* and thought, Wow, *because that extra thirty seconds really matters.* But that morning, it *did* matter.

The eight-minute walk to the station with Brooke felt like eighty. Eight hundred and eighty.

Stilted conversation. Hot cheeks. Blurred vision as I visualised the Tube map in my mind, trying to figure out whether we were going to be heading to the same platform, all the while trying to hold a polite conversation. Then came the realisation that I'd fucked up: I'd said I was going to the shop (Notting Hill Gate), but now, thinking of the Tubes and which ones we'd each be catching, I realised I needed to change tack. Brooke's temp assignment was in Moorgate and that would mean we'd both be taking the Hammersmith and City line for at least part of the way. I couldn't have that. But what could I say?

Clarence.

I'd need to pretend I was going to Clarence because he was in Monument. That meant a different Tube. And so about four minutes into our eight-minute walk I pulled out my phone, pretended to see a new voice message and, as Brooke watched, I listened to one of DCI Holland's messages from the day before.

"Charlene, it's DCI Holland calling again. We need to speak to you immediately. It's about your husband, Oliver. It is extremely important. Call me."

"Oh, shit," I said, hanging up.

"What?" Brooke asked.

"I have to go and see my agent. Can I get to Monument from your station?"

"I think so," she said. I don't know if she knew I was lying. But it didn't really matter as long as she didn't know why. So I spent the rest of the walk staring down at my phone, zooming in on a TfL Tube map, pretending to check my journey.

But I wasn't doing anything of the sort. I was deflecting.

The effort of keeping up that act, combined with the muffled grief and fear brewing just below my skin, made me feel like I'd run a marathon by the time we got there and headed through the turnstiles with the crowds.

A man in a charcoal suit bumped into me as I got through and I almost fell. I steadied myself. Then Brooke was through, her Oyster card still in her hand, saying, "Shit, are you okay?"

She seemed so nice. This woman in my husband's photographs. This woman who had lied to me. Who killed him.

"Yeah, fine," I said. "Thanks so much for last night, hon." I air kissed her cheek and every single one of my cells recoiled.

"No problem. I hope everything works out." She smiled, her brown eyes flecked with orange, steady on mine. I studied the thoughts behind them. There was nothing readable in her eyes or her mood. She seemed calm, like she didn't know I'd seen that photograph. She didn't know I'd noticed the USB was gone. She didn't know what I was planning.

But could I trust that? Because I'd only ever seen the version of her that she'd shown me: my friend, a girl new to London, a harmless stylist. And she'd only seen what the entire world saw when they looked at me: the token-blonde wife with the movie-worthy marriage.

"Thanks," I said, and then I turned and moved towards the platform for the District line. I didn't look back—it would be too obvious—so I just needed to trust that she was heading to her platform too.

There was a busker playing a violin at the bottom of the stairs, and the air around him was damp and mossy. I moved past him and onto the platform, my pulse racing. It was rush hour, so soon the platform was almost full. White shirts. Shiny shoes. And there we were, a platform full of strangers. All of us living out our own stories, each of us just the background extra for someone else.

Everyone was either texting, scrolling or standing at the edge of the platform, listening to music and trying to avoid eye contact. I was the only one looking around.

There was a dark-haired woman with a small burgundy handbag hanging from her shoulder to my right, but I couldn't tell if it was zipped shut. There were lots of men with briefcases and pockets. But that was risky. Then, to my left, I saw a blonde woman with a charcoal-grey Longchamp bag over her shoulder. There was a white rolled-up piece of paper sticking out one side, making it impossible for the zipper to shut properly. She'd do.

As I moved closer to her, I reached into my bag for my box of tampons, opened it and pulled out the little white tracking disk, clenching it in my fist.

It was then that a distorted voice came over the loudspeaker announcing that the next train was approaching. I followed the woman with the Longchamp bag to the edge of the platform, standing close behind her in the queue, and stared down the darkened train tunnel. A white light. A rush of air. Dust in my throat. The screech of brakes. I grimaced at the sheer volume and then the doors pinged and opened.

The carriage was already sardine-tin full—I could see that through the windows. Then came "Please mind the gap," a few people got off and then we all kept our eyes down as we slowly pushed to get on. But the moment I could, the moment I felt sure nobody would see what I was doing, I dropped the tracking device into that woman's bag. Then I turned and pushed my way off the train again, moving towards the back wall.

I stood there, listening to the doors beep and close, and watched as the train, the woman with the Longchamp bag and that little white disk disappeared.

Now, if Brooke checked the tracking app, I would be somewhere far, far away.

—

8.21 AM

The wall was hard and cool behind my back—I was pretty sure I was standing in (or near) a puddle of dried urine—and I needed coffee. My eyes were strained by lack of sleep and as I stared down at my phone, a new set of passengers filled the platform to wait for their train. This would be the third train since I arrived down here. It'd been around ten minutes since Brooke and I parted ways.

I re-read the instructions on my screenshot for the fifth time, committing them to memory. People gathered by the edge of the platform, a high-pitched screech filled the air and then: *beep, beep, beep, "Please mind the gap."* But as everyone else on that platform piled onto the train, I switched my phone to airplane mode, turned it off and headed back out through the exit.

Brooke should be gone by now.

Soon I was heading back past the spot we'd said our goodbyes, and out into the cool morning air. I turned left and moved quickly towards Campbell Road. When I was past the pub I could see the signage of the Texaco to my left. People bustled past me on their way to the station as I crossed the road and headed all the way back towards Brooke's black front door.

But I turned right just before I got there. I wasn't going in through the front.

My blood rushed through my veins as I unhooked the latch on the dark green gate. I reached for a wheelie bin and pulled it behind me, closing the gate before anyone could see. I knew the layout of her home now, the way she had known the layout of mine by the time she let herself in to kill Oliver, and so I pulled the bin beneath the bathroom window that I'd unlatched before I left.

I stared up at it, then around behind me: nothing but fences and neighbours who wouldn't see me unless they were peering over. I made a quick assessment—no movement, so hopefully they were probably all heading to work by now.

But shit, was I insane?

I ran the information through my mind one more time. I was

about to potentially add "breaking and entering" or "trespassing" to my current list of charges. Did I really want to do that?

The problem was, I didn't see any other way out of it. There was only one thing I had linking Brooke to Oliver, and it was on that USB stick. The one she'd taken. Yes, the police could probably piece it all together, find the connections for themselves, but that all depended on them believing me in the first place. On them doing the digging. And as there were no strong links between Brooke and Oliver, they weren't just going to bash down her door with a warrant. They'd call her first. Have a nice polite chat. And she'd have plenty of warning, plenty of time to come up with excuses and ditch the evidence.

I placed my hands on the cool plastic of the wheelie bin, took a deep breath and hoisted myself up onto it, scrabbling for balance and taking care not to break through the weak spot in the middle. I gently pried open the window, then held my breath, stood dead still and listened.

There was still a chance she was in there. That she'd clocked the change in me and had returned from the station too.

But there was no sound coming from inside.

And so I peered through the window: there in the far corner was the bath-slash-shower I'd stood in just that morning when all the pieces of the puzzle had first fallen into place. There was the loo to the right of the window. And beneath the windowsill was the basin. I'd stand on that. But first I needed to get my bag inside.

I lowered it gently into the sink, letting it fall into the middle.

I'd never actually broken into a house before, but I'd seen it done in movies. It didn't look that hard.

Well.

Let me tell you something about pulling yourself through a little window: it's very, very, very hard.

You need a lot of upper body strength.

Upper body strength I didn't have.

I placed my palms on the cool and dusty paint of the windowsill and tried to pull myself up. But I was too heavy. *Shit.* So now I was breathless. But I needed to do this. Not just because of all the reasons I had before, but because now my laptop was inside, wasn't it? And it was going to look pretty bloody suspicious if I just left it there.

I clenched my eyes shut and ran through every movie scene I'd ever watched: how did they do it?

Legs.

Legs first.

Thankfully, what I lack in upper body strength, I make up for in flexibility. So I reached one leg in first, using my arms to pull me up until I was straddling the windowsill, then, with a bit of contortion, in went the other. My feet hit the basin—*Shit, is that my computer?* I quickly moved them to the edges as my body followed through. I stepped off onto the bathroom floor quickly, before I could break anything. My heart went wild in my chest, like a butterfly caught in a jar.

But I was in.

Ba-boom, ba-boom, ba-boom.

Now what?

I stood dead still, adrenaline zinging through my veins as I listened again for sounds. Someone else breathing. The creak of a floorboard. But there was no movement in the flat. No noise. Not even the sounds of traffic. Just me. My beating heart. My breathing.

She definitely wasn't here.

I swallowed hard, grabbed my bag and moved out into the hallway. To the left was the living room and kitchen, the sofa I'd slept on. And to the right was Brooke's bedroom. I tiptoed in even though I was alone. I dropped my bag by the door so I wouldn't forget it and looked around. She'd made her bed that morning while I was having a panic attack in the shower. The turquoise bedspread lay perfectly centred over white sheets below a set of three gold throw pillows. Beside the bed was a big oak closet and a white IKEA set of drawers.

I was looking for a computer: if there were answers, they'd be on there.

And so I began in the place where I hid mine: the set of drawers.

I pulled open the first one: a tangle of underwear, balled socks, unclipped bras and loose stockings. I felt around. Nothing.

The second: long-sleeved polo necks and the like, all in perfect Marie Kondo rolls. I reached beneath them, but all I felt was wood and potential splinters.

Then the third: workout clothes, old t-shirts, pyjamas . . .

Then something hard.

Maybe plastic.

I pulled it out into the light.

It was black.

It fit in my hand.

A taser.

And now it had my prints on it.

Fuuuucckk.

I ran to the kitchen, looking for something to wipe it down with. But I needed to make sure there was not a single trace of me on it, and so I did the only thing I could think of: I filled a sink with water, squeezed in some soap, swished it around and then dropped the taser in there. I stared down at it, submerged beneath the bubbles. It was probably broken now, but that was better than creating more evidence against myself. There was a dishcloth and a small grey washing-up brush sitting behind the taps, so I covered my hands with the cloth and roughly cleaned off the outside with the brush.

Then I pulled the plug, let out the water, and once the water had all drained out, I squeezed the moisture out of the cloth and dried it off. Holding it over my sleeves so I didn't leave prints, I took the taser back to where I'd found it, and I thought of that Google search: *Where to buy a taser in London . . .*

That had been Brooke. But when? And how?

It was as I nestled it back under her pyjamas that I found the answer.

Cool and metal.

Keys.

I pulled them into view. There were three on the ring. *Ba-boom. Ba-boom. Ba-boom.* A big one and two smaller ones. And they looked terrifyingly familiar. Yes, they looked just like *my* keys: one to the shop, one to the security door of our building and one to our front door.

I ran over to my bag and pulled out my own set to compare and my throat grew tight. They were exactly the same. My memory flung back to the day I lost my keys and found them again beneath my computer. She'd been there on the day I lost them. She could have copied them and then let herself into the shop. After conducting her little taser Google search all she had to do was leave them there on my desk and let me assume it was my oversight.

Those keys were also how she got into our flat.

Shit.

Because that posed a new problem for me: I'd been right, there would be no forced entry. Which, I assumed, was intentional. Because that would make *me* look even more guilty. She most definitely had set me up. But why?

I clenched my jaw and pushed the keys back where I found them, then looked around the room. The closet. She might have hidden it in the closet.

My hands covered by my sleeves, I pulled open the doors. The rails were filled with an array of dresses, shirts and skirts all hanging on misshapen wire hangers. Beneath those lay rows of shoes—nothing there. And above those, a series of sweaters. Mustard yellow. Pink. Red. Just like the red one in that photograph on the USB stick I no longer had.

Holding my breath, I reached beneath them, feeling around.

Nothing.

I clenched my eyes shut. *Where would she keep it? Where would she keep it? Where would she keep it?*

Because I knew she had a computer. A Mac. I'd used the charging cord. And her handbag wasn't big enough for her to have taken it with her, so it had to be here somewhere. I closed the cupboard doors again and faced back to the bed.

The bed.

I knelt down and looked beneath it.

It was dark and dusty, the rough outlines of balls of hair and fluff just visible in the low light.

And then there, towards the wall at the head of the bed, lay something rectangular.

Something the size of a laptop.

I reached for it, pulling it to the light.

Yes. It was a laptop. In an old grey zip-up case.

I pulled it out, the noise of the zipper opening echoing off the walls. I pulled the grey metal laptop out. Balancing the laptop on my legs, I powered it on and, as the white Apple logo glowed in the dimly lit room, that's when I saw it.

The "W" key was missing.

The walls warped inwards.

This was Oliver's computer.

The one that had been stolen months before.

It was Brooke who had broken into our flat while we were away on honeymoon. Brooke who had stolen his computer. *Only* his computer.

Why?

What had she hoped to find on there? What was all this about?

As I closed my eyes I tried to recall the screenshot I'd been studying on that train platform: *How to reset a Mac's password.*

Because nothing in life is an isolated incident, is it? Everything seeps into everything else.

Everything is useful in the end.

I held down two keys.

Step one: *Hold down command and R at the same time.*

Step two: *Go to "Utilities."*

Step three: *Click on "Terminal."*

Step four: *Type in resetpassword.*

Step five: *Enter new password.*

I entered the only word I had on my mind right then: *Oliver.*

Step six: *Save.*

Step seven: *Restart.*

Step eight: *Re-enter password: Oliver.*

A moment while the computer loaded, and then, just like that, I was in.

Episode 8

WEDNESDAY, 13 JUNE 2018 (8.58 AM)

My throat tightened as I stared at Brooke's desktop. The face staring back at me in that darkened room was one I recognised. But it wasn't Oliver's. And it wasn't Brooke's either.

It was Alyssa's face.

The same picnic-blanket-red-glow picture that was used on her memorial page. The room rang with silence and adrenaline pumped through my veins. What was going on? Everything just kept getting weirder and weirder.

If Brooke was some stalker in love with Oliver, why would she have Alyssa's picture as her screensaver?

I stared at her desktop: it was much like mine—like Oliver's—a mess of documents and blue folders, and I didn't know where to start. What was I even looking for? How do you prove someone killed your husband?

What I needed was direct access to her twisted mind. Her every little secret. But I'd have to settle for the next best thing: her social media feeds and emails. Because, thanks to Oliver, I knew exactly where to find the passwords to those.

Chrome was the only browser on the ribbon at the bottom of the screen, so I clicked on it and went to "Preferences," then "Passwords."

I scanned the list, looking for her Facebook login and my breath caught in my throat. Because Brooke had told me her last name was Thompson—*Brooke Thompson: Personal Styling*—and I'd never had any reason to question it. And yet, there was her email address: *BrookeyShaw007@hotmail.com*.

Yes: Shaw.

The same last name as Alyssa.

And, in that moment, everything I'd been missing came tumbling into view all at once, like someone was adjusting the focus on my lens in real time. Now that I thought about it, there *were* some similarities between the two: same colouring, same build. And with the same last name, only one thing made sense.

They were sisters.

So, had Brooke met Oliver when he was dating Alyssa? Was that when her obsession began?

My heart thudded in my chest as I clicked on the eye beside her email address and, when prompted, entered *O-l-i-v-e-r*.

A moment later, there it was. Revealed. Her email password.

The floor spun beneath me as my mouth sounded it out: *AlyssaRIP*.

I clicked on the eye beside her Facebook login and the same password flashed up: *AlyssaRIP*.

My stomach clenched. I was no expert on the subject but it seemed to me that if you were stalking your dead sister's ex, you wouldn't want things around that might remind you about your sister at every turn. You wouldn't, say, have her picture as your screensaver and her name etched into your passwords.

Which meant I was missing something.

Keeping the passwords tab open, I opened another window

and logged into her Facebook account, the Facebook account she'd pretended not to have all those weeks ago when we'd first met and I'd wanted to add her on Facebook. *Oh please, Facebook is for my mum. But you can add me on Instagram.*

Slowly, I entered her password: *A-l-y-s-s-a-R-I-P.*

And then, after a moment of white, the screen filled with her secrets, the true Brooke I'd never seen. Brooke Shaw didn't post to Facebook that often. But a quick click through her photographs showed a number of images with her and Alyssa together. They were definitely sisters. And more than that, they were close.

I clicked through to her Facebook wall and scrolled down. She hadn't posted anything in a few months, not since April, around the time she wandered into my Pilates class. I guess she'd been busy with me. But my heart clenched when I saw what she'd posted back then. It wasn't the subject matter that scared me: a coffee cup (innocuous enough). It was *where* it had been posted from: Instagram.

From an account named *@lover7.*

I'd been right. It *was* Brooke who'd been watching me.

I was filled with a need to see what was on that account. Everything I'd not been able to see before.

Her Instagram password wasn't listed there with the others, but I was pretty certain I knew what it would be. People often think Instagram is only a mobile app, but you can use it from a computer too. I used it that way every day at my job at Boulevard. So I didn't need to turn on my phone and infect it in a way that might later be used against me.

I opened a third tab and went to Instagram.

I knew her username: *@lover7,* so I entered that. And then I took my chances with her password and entered *AlyssaRIP.*

Two seconds later, the screen filled with photographs of her and Alyssa together. Each had a caption beneath it, all variations on: *I'll never forget you*; *I will never stop looking for the truth*; *When you lose a sister you lose half your soul.*

Brooke wasn't a woman in love.

She was a woman in mourning.

But why take it out on us?

Did she blame us for her sister's death? Oliver for breaking her heart? Me for stealing him away? It wasn't like that, but Brooke didn't know that. I could hear the words rattling around in my head: *He left his ex for me. She was batshit crazy though. We bumped into her once at Sainsbury's—Wow, she was a mess.*

Shit. No wonder she hated me.

The room spun as I thought of that taser search in my browser history. What else had she planted for DCI Holland to find?

And how the hell was I going to get out of this?

Because it's one thing to *know* someone killed your husband, but it's quite another to be able to prove it. I didn't have the photograph of her and Oliver together anymore, so for all intents and purposes I couldn't even prove they'd met. I could tell DCI Holland that Alyssa was Brooke's sister, but being sisters with someone doesn't exactly make you a criminal. Not as much as, say, breaking into someone's flat and accessing all their social media and email accounts. And if Brooke had planned things well enough to copy my keys, drop that tracker in my bag, and put the taser search in my work computer search history, it was highly likely that she'd have an excellent excuse in case any connection was made. She'd have an alibi.

No, I needed more. A lot more. And so I went back to Hotmail and entered BrookeyShaw007@hotmail.com and then typed in *A-l-y-s-s-a-R-I-P.*

My ears roared as the screen flashed white and her inbox came into view. It was as though I already knew I was about to learn something I couldn't unlearn. My stomach grew tight, my breathing shallow. Whatever was in there, I suddenly didn't want to know. But that didn't matter. I *needed* to know. It was potentially the only thing that would keep me out of prison.

The first message I saw was a helpful one from Instagram alerting Brooke to the fact that her account had been logged into from a new location. I deleted it immediately, before she spotted it on her iPhone, and then removed it from the deleted file too. No point leaving an e-trail.

Back in her inbox, I scanned the unopened messages, their titles still bolded. As I read them, the entire world lapsed into slow motion. The top two read: *Oliver1982 you have a new message.*

The third read: *@Oliver1982 somebody likes you.*

The senders differed, but all three came from dating apps.

All thoughts in my head were now on mute and all I could hear was *ba-boom, ba-boom, ba-boom.* What was going on?

Why would Brooke have emails from Oliver's dating apps in her inbox?

My eyes burned with tears as I blinked quickly, staring at those messages on the screen, struggling to compute.

The walls swayed in towards me. Could this really be happening? No. Surely not. My hand moved to my mouth and I swallowed hard. Because there was only one reason I could think of: it wasn't him I'd seen on that app after all. He *wasn't* cheating. He *wasn't* going to sex parties. It was all a lie.

It was *her*.

I clenched my jaw and my eyes burned with tears as I remembered Oliver's reply to Justin: *I didn't make that profile. But I think we have a problem.*

I should have trusted him.

My eyes blurred with tears. What had I done? If I'd believed him I'd never have stormed out, he might still be alive.

Battery acid filled my mouth.

But why was she doing this to us? People get their hearts broken every day. We didn't mean to hurt anyone—we just fell in love.

Then came the next thought. If Brooke made those profiles, then it was Brooke, not Oliver, who was messaging me that night I went out with Tess to that gallery. It was *her* I was sexting with, not him.

The messages she sent me came flooding back: *I want someone to tell her. I want her to know, I want it over, but I don't have the heart to let her down.*

Was Brooke doing that with every woman she matched Oliver with? Encouraging them to tell me, Oliver's wife?

And then I realised—yes, if she was planning on killing him, that's exactly what she'd been doing. Because Brooke wanted someone to tell me, for me to think he was cheating. She wanted me to have a motive. She wanted us to fight.

No, she *needed* us to fight.

For me to tell people he was cheating, for the neighbours to hear us argue—she'd have known there was a good chance there would be a screaming match at some point. Who wouldn't get angry if they found a garter belt in their husband's pocket on top of everything else? A garter belt she knew Oliver would deny any knowledge of, which would make me doubt him even more.

A garter belt she'd planted because, as I now knew, she had keys to our flat.

But when?

I thought back to that night I went through Oliver's computer. Something had felt different about the flat. About the air. The faint smell I couldn't put my finger on. I knew what it was now: Moroccan hair oil. Vanilla.

I clenched my eyes shut, trying to stop the thoughts, but it didn't work. A hot, thick guilt was pulsing through me.

Because *I'd* done this. I'd made it possible for her.

She'd found the pictures for his profile on *my* Instagram page.

And he'd warned me.

He'd tried to tell me and I hadn't listened. A small cry escaped my lips and something deep within me punctured: he *had* loved me, he *hadn't* cheated on me, I'd never see him again and it was my fault.

The room was spinning now and my face was wet with tears, but the time in the top right-hand corner read 9.22 and I needed to leave before someone realised I was here. Roughly wiping my cheeks with the back of my hand, I focused on the screen and scanned down through the rest of her emails. There was nothing there. Nothing I could use. And that's when I noticed the highlighted messages at the top. Five of them. They'd been pinned; they *had* to be important.

The first one was from "Alyssa Shaw," so I clicked on that one. Of course I clicked on that one.

The subject read: *This is what I sent him.*

I clicked through to the body of the message and quickly scanned the words.

Dear Oliver,

I still can't believe you did this to me. To my parents. They're going to lose their house if we don't pay them back. Please, I'm begging you. I know this isn't who you are. Because I fell in love with the most wonderful man, a man who would never use me like this, who would never lie to me like this. Please, be that man. Please get us our money back. You promised me we couldn't lose it. You PROMISED me. And I promised them. And please, for the love of god, reply to me this time. I miss you. I'm not even sure if you're coming home again. Please.

I love you, Alyssa

Okay—what?

My eyes darted to the date: 11 November 2016. They were still together at that point. But why would Oliver have borrowed money from her, from her parents, for an investment?

It made no sense.

And not just because using personal money for a business venture was a risk Oliver would never take, because I *knew* my husband at least that well: he wouldn't have bet on a horse that would lose. He was too ambitious, too capable.

If he'd taken her money and not paid her back . . . he'd meant to.

But why would he do that?

I clicked on the next message. It was from Alyssa again and it was dated early June 2017. It read:

> *I saw them together, Brooke. I can't do this. She looks so happy, just like I did. He's never going to talk to me again or give me anything back. Mum and Dad are never going to forgive me. I'm never going to forgive myself. I can't sleep anymore. I just don't know what to do.*

My pulse tapped against the soft spot in the middle of my throat and my hand shook as I clicked on the next message. It was from a lawyer this time, dated January 2018, just a few months earlier.

Dear Ms Brooke Shaw,

As per our conversation today, I regret to inform you in writing that we cannot take your case any further as there simply is no proof to support your allegations against Mr Buchanan.

In addition, it is vital that you cease emailing Hornsby Private Equity immediately—they're threatening to take action against you for harassment. We offer our gravest sympathy for your situation and your loss, yours sincerely . . .

Were those the emails Justin had mentioned? *We can't afford any more attention after those emails . . .*

Oliver made it clear he never wanted to talk about her. About any exes. No wonder.

I sat there in the stale air trying to piece it together simply for myself—a colour by numbers attempt. So Brooke was Alyssa's sister. Oliver had dated Alyssa, he'd invested money for her and her parents and lost it. Or kept it. Or something. But whatever it was he hadn't paid her back. Then he'd left her for me. Alyssa had killed herself. And Brooke blamed us. When lawyers couldn't help her, she took matters into her own hands. She'd broken into our flat and taken his computer.

Did Oliver know it was her? And what had she hoped to find on his laptop when she stole it? Proof of what he'd done? Proof of that shady investment?

And when he remote wiped it and she didn't find what she was looking for—what, she'd formed a new plan?

A plan to kill him?

I minimised the browser window and went through to Brooke's recent files. And that was when the next thought hit.

All those times I told her how close Oliver and I were, how we told each other everything, how I was his "problem solver"—no wonder she wanted to frame me. She probably thought I knew what he'd done. That I'd stood by him and did nothing.

Yes. The very shell I'd created to protect myself—the image, the armour, the token-blonde wife, all the lies I'd told Brooke—was precisely what had landed me here.

But couldn't I just take this to DCI Holland? Couldn't I just tell her? I considered how that conversation might run.

Me: *Oh it wasn't me* (with all the motive in the world) *who killed my husband—it was a girl named Brooke I met in Pilates two months ago. She was the sister of a girl my husband used to date, Alyssa. Brooke blamed us for Alyssa's death and was after vengeance.*

Maybe. It didn't sound too bad . . .

DCI Holland: *Charlie, how did she get into your house? What evidence do you have that she ever even met Oliver? What about that taser search on your work computer—did she magically get in there too?*

Me: *She had keys. She copied them.*

DCI Holland: *Oh, well that's convenient, isn't it? Do you have any proof of that?*

Me: *Yes, I have them right here* [pulls Brooke's copy of the keys].

DCI Holland: *Ummm, how can you prove you didn't make those copies?*

Me: *Oliver's computer is in her house. She stole it from our flat. So is the taser! You should go and look.*

DCI Holland: *Okay, well (a) it's slightly concerning that you know that—how can we be sure you didn't plant those things there yourself to shift the blame? And (b) we'll need a search warrant for that. Let's give Brooke a call and see if she'll chat to us in the first instance.*

Brooke: Denies everything.

No, I needed to somehow *show* DCI Holland the truth, have her reach the conclusions herself, that was the only way. I swallowed hard, staring at the screen: the files were listed in order of "date last opened."

There was a spreadsheet at the top so I clicked on that and while it was opening I checked the titles of all the other files. A little further down, there were three image files named Oliver1.jpeg, Oliver2.jpeg and Oliver3.jpeg. I didn't need to open them to know they were the images she'd used on his dating app profile, but I clicked on them anyway. Up they came in quick succession: the first was the one I'd taken on our honeymoon. I'd posted it an hour after I took it. Then the next: him tanned, green eyes gleaming, grinning. And the third: him in a tux, my hand around his waist, just my red nails and bangles visible.

Brooke had used our happiest memories against us.

The spreadsheet had opened by then. Down the left-hand column were dates. Then beside that were two columns. One was titled "Charlie"; the other "Oliver."

Beside the most recent Monday in my column was written: *Nothing of interest.* In Oliver's column: *He is still away.*

Beside Tuesday in my column: *Didn't come home at usual time.* In Oliver's column: *He got home just before nine. Unpacked. Went out for pizza. Think in UK until mid-next week. Need to check.*

Wait . . .

How did she know he got pizza? Or that I didn't get home at my usual time? Was she there? Watching him? That made sense . . . Because on the night I saw Oliver on Tess's dating app, she'd changed the radius of her matches to within three miles. If Brooke had been in Bow, she wouldn't have fallen within that range. But if she'd been at our house in Battersea . . .

I quickly scanned the document—she'd been watching us for months. Tracking our patterns. Making notes when I told her things.

See? I told you we should have closed our curtains. She must have found a place nearby to watch us.

But I knew what I needed to do now: make sure I wasn't the only one who had seen this information.

However, I couldn't just send it to the police. I was too involved and, like I said, they might think I'd created it. Planted it. Whatever.

Even though I had access to Brooke's emails, I couldn't send it from her address either because why would she implicate herself if it were true?

No, it needed it to come from someone else.

An anonymous tip-off.

From someone who didn't even really exist.

It needed to come from my catfish persona, Annabella Harth, the Gmail address and Facebook profile I created at that bus stop to catch Oliver.

And so, I opened a private browser window and signed into Gmail as Annabella.

I hadn't signed into that account since I'd created it and a lot had happened since then. As it opened, all I could see was message after message with the subject line: *Annabella_Harth you have a new message.*

All the messages I'd thought had come from Oliver.

I let out a deep breath as I moved back to Brooke's emails. Slowly, methodically, I forwarded the three messages from the apps (these proved Brooke had pretended to be Oliver), the one from the lawyer (telling her to stop harassing Hornsby Private Equity) and the two from Alyssa detailing what had happened (motive). If I could piece it all together, surely the police could too. I then forwarded the spreadsheet detailing our movements. And deleted all of them out of her sent and deleted folders.

Once there was no trace of me in there, I closed down Brooke's emails and cleared her browser history. Now it was time to focus on Annabella.

I pulled up Google and found the editor's email address for the *Evening Standard* and the tip-off email address for the Met Police.

I forwarded all seven bits of evidence with the subject title

"Oliver Buchanan case" to both addresses simultaneously so they were aware the other knew too.

Then I closed down Annabella's Gmail account. I don't mean logged out. I mean, navigated to the bit where you can permanently delete it.

Finally, I went back to Instagram and changed Brooke's privacy setting to "public." Now the entire world could see that Brooke had been mourning Alyssa. That she had motive. Then I logged out of her account and cleared both browser histories.

Shutting down the computer, I wiped it for fingerprints, put it back in its case and returned it to where I'd found it.

Then, taking off my shoes, I ran to the kitchen and grabbed a rag from the sink and frantically wiped down the areas where I might have stepped, the areas the police might dust for footprints, and, covering my hand with that same cloth, I locked the window so there was no possible point of entry. I'd learnt that little trick from Brooke. No forced entry means nobody else was there.

Finally I wiped down the taps in the kitchen, keeping the rag to dispose of outside just in case.

I grabbed my shoes, slung my bag over my shoulder, made sure all my hair was tucked into Josh's baseball cap in case anybody saw me leave, checked the room once more and went to the front door. I'd done it. I was home free.

That's when my breath caught in my throat.

Because I wasn't alone.

Someone was watching me through the window.

Waving.

The postman.

Fuck. Fuck. Fuck.

I didn't know what to do, so I waved back. And a moment later *tap-tap-tap*. He was knocking on the front door. This was bad. This was very, very, very bad. Now there was a witness. But he'd seen me, so if I didn't open the door it'd look even more suspicious.

You can do this, Charlie.

And so I reached for the deadbolt, turned it and opened the door, preparing to speak.

"You almost missed me," I said in my best Scottish accent as he handed me a small, book-sized parcel.

"Lucky me," he said, holding out an electronic thing for me to sign. I wrote out the letters: *B-r-o-o-k-e*. Then I gave him a smile.

"Can I get your last name?" he asked.

"Why of course," I said, "Shaw."

And then I closed the door.

And all I could hear was *Ba-boom. Ba-boom. Ba-boom.*

There was no way around it—it was not good that he had seen me, but my hair colour was covered and my accent was strong. And with the emails I'd just sent, there should be no reason for him to be looking at mug shots.

And so, my heart banging against my chest wall, I told myself that everything was going to be okay, opened the door and finally put on my shoes.

The air was crisp and cool outside. I left the book leaning up against the door and I rushed around to the back garden. The wheelie bin was sitting there below the bathroom window, right where I'd left it. I pulled it back to its place at the front, wiped down the top with the rag, and pulled closed the cold metal latch on the wooden gate. And then, with my face angled down to the ground, I walked faster than I ever have in my life towards the Tube station, throwing the cloth into a dumpster on the way.

I was shaking.

My heart was thudding.

But I'd done it.

And now I had to do something even harder.

—

11.06 AM

So how do you walk into a police station knowing they want to arrest you for murder? You do it the same way you walk on stage, the same way you jump into a freezing-cold ocean: You don't think about it. You stay in the moment. You just jump.

I was in a small room, all alone. The woman at the front desk had taken me there as soon as she'd heard my name: a dark wood door, white walls, a white massage-type table against one wall and cabinets full of plastic jars and tubes with white and yellow lids. I suspected the door was locked.

I'd done some research on the way over and I knew they could hold me for a maximum of ninety-six hours before they charged me. That was long enough for whoever went through the police emails to realise Brooke was a suspect and pass the information on to DCI Holland. Until then, while she was still out there, I figured a police station was probably the safest place for me.

Tap-tap-tap.

"Come in," I said, my voice feeble. It felt weird, like I was at a doctor's surgery, but what else was I going to say?

The door opened and a man came inside. He had dark hair, black, square-framed glasses and was around thirty-five.

"Hi, Charlene," he said. My heart beat faster as he moved past me to the cabinet with all the jars in it. He told me his name, but I missed it. *I need to learn to listen when people tell me their names.* But I caught the next bit. "I'm going to take some swabs from you. Take a seat." He motioned to the white table by the wall.

He came over to me and I opened my mouth "ahhhh." He smiled as he reached a cotton bud inside my cheek and circled it around. He was close enough that I could smell him: bergamot. He turned around and put the swab in one of the longer tubes, screwing on the top and asking me to check my name on the label. Then he did the same with the other cheek. Next it was fingerprints: it took hardly any time at all. It was all electronic and portable. All I needed to do was place my fingers on the sensors.

But he was nice. Calming. And my heart rate was almost back to running at normal speed when the door opened for the second time. It sped up again the moment I saw her. Because you can feel in someone's energy if they have ill-will towards you. I knew it probably wasn't personal—she just thought I was guilty—but it *felt* personal.

DCI Holland.

The first thing I thought when I saw her was that she looked totally different to what I'd expected. She was small-boned and delicate looking with mousey ash-blonde hair a few shades darker than mine pulled back into a low ponytail and she wore a light pink polish on short nails. She was wearing navy trousers and a white shirt with a fine gold chain visible around her neck.

"Charlene?" she asked as she came inside, nodding at the man whose name I hadn't heard. Her voice sounded hurried, stressed. And her forehead was creased.

"Hi," I said, my heart beating so fast now I thought I might not be able to stand up without falling over.

"I'm so sorry I didn't come on Monday, like I said I would. It's all been such a shock."

She nodded, watching me with her hazel eyes, and directed me to follow her down a narrow hallway. We came to another door and she led me inside. "Would you like a cup of tea? Coffee?"

"Yes please, coffee," I said. *This is civilised.* And then she left me there and I heard the door click as it locked. It felt a lot *less* civilised then.

I walked over to the table and reached for the jug of water in the middle, pouring myself a glass. Then I sat down on one of the two seats on either side of the table and looked around. It was a stock-standard interview room. There was a black recording device right there beside me. The walls were dark green, the chairs were standard issue with a small amount of padding on the seat, the table was worn and lights flickered from the ceiling.

I let out a big exhale and looked down at my nail polish. It was chipped now. Much like me.

Then the door opened.

DCI Holland had been joined by another police officer. He was only around thirty but was already losing his brown hair, his scalp visible beneath the fluorescent lighting. His cheeks were pink and his light blue eyes turned down at the corners, which gave them a sense of kindness. Or was it sadness?

"Charlene," Holland said, placing my coffee in front of me. "This is Officer Kowalski."

"Hi, Charlene," he said, sitting down.

I swallowed hard. "Hi," I said, picking up my coffee and taking a sip. It was Nescafé. I remembered the taste from drama school.

"We're going to record this interview, okay?" DCI Holland asked, her hand already moving across to the recording device. I nodded and she flicked it on. A small red light began to glow.

Lights, camera, action.

She cleared her throat.

"This interview is being tape-recorded. It is eleven-twenty-six am on June thirteen, 2018. I am Detective Inspector Josephine Holland and with me is Officer Dennis Kowalski. We are at Charing Cross Police Station and we are enquiring into the events of Sunday the tenth of June and the days that followed." Her expression was sombre. Her mouth pursed. Her eyes moved to me. "Please state your full name."

"Charlene Paige Buchanan," I said, my voice coming out stronger than I expected. "But everyone calls me Charlie."

"Can you confirm your date of birth for me, Charlie?" she asked.

"March sixth, 1985."

"Thank you. Now, Charlie, I'm just going to read out a caution to you."

I nodded. I'd been expecting this. Everybody knows how this bit goes. I could have recited it along with her.

"You do not have to say anything. But it may harm your defence if you do not mention when questioned something that you later rely on in court. Anything you say may be given in evidence. Do you understand?" Her eyes were on mine and my chest panged. I felt a wave of panic spread through me—recognition of what was happening—and my head grew light.

"Yes." I nodded again. My eyes burned with tears and my lip wobbled. "I understand."

"You are entitled to a lawyer. Would you like to call one?"

I shook my head. *Not yet.* A lawyer would look like I had something to hide and I'd already run from them for over forty-eight hours.

"Please note that the interviewee is shaking her head 'No,' " Holland said for the benefit of the tape. Kowalski sat silently, watching me.

"Charlie, let's start with the events on the evening of Sunday the tenth of June this year. Are you married?"

"Yes," I said, Oliver's face flashing before me.

"And what is your husband's name?"

"Oliver Buchanan," I said, and then the tears started to fall as I remembered his body being wheeled out of the house, his wedding ring sparkling in the morning light. *Stop it, Charlie, stop it.* It would look like I was crying because I'd killed him. I clenched my jaw, willed the tears to stop. "I already know he's dead. I saw them taking him out of our house."

"You *saw* them?" Holland asked. She was frowning now.

Shit.

"Yes," I said. "The police. Monday morning."

"So you were there?"

"Yes," I said.

"Charlie, we spoke on the phone that day. Why didn't you come in to talk to me as we agreed?"

I shook my head and shrugged my shoulders as if to say I really don't know. But then I answered her anyway. "I was just so scared."

"Scared of what?"

"I don't know. Scared that I'd get blamed. Scared that whoever did that to him would do it to me. And I was in shock, you know. I mean, he's dead. Every time I close my eyes I see him. And we fought. The last time I saw him we fought."

DCI Holland looked down at her notepad.

"Yes, one of the neighbours heard you. Could you tell us a little more about what that fight was about?"

I nodded. "I was pretty sure he was cheating on me." Even as I said the words I felt disloyal. But I couldn't tell her that I knew it wasn't Oliver on that app now without revealing *how* I knew that. If I knew it was Brooke who faked those profiles, if I started throwing around accusations, it would open up a whole can of worms I couldn't afford to open, like: Had I sent those emails to the police? And if so, how did I get access to Brooke's email account? And then the biggie: Did that mean the information contained in those emails couldn't be trusted?

No. I needed to be patient. To wait it out and let them figure it all out on their own. And they would, wouldn't they?

"How did you discover this?" she asked, pen poised.

"I found a garter belt," I explained. "That was the first thing. But there were others." I intentionally kept it vague. I didn't want to get into the fact that I'd signed up to a dating app to catch him out in case they somehow realised the email I'd signed up with belonged to Annabella Harth.

"So can you run us through what happened on the night in question?"

I nodded. "I'd kicked him out, dumped his clothes in his car, but when I got home he was there. All his things were back in their spots. I wanted to talk to him about it but he was on the phone and he was trying to get his computer unlocked, ignoring me. And I was so angry, you know. I just lost it. I told him I was going to tell his mother about it, about the cheating, and then we were fighting and I was screaming. His hand was over my mouth and . . ."

"Go on."

"I just wanted to get away from him. I scratched him. And then I felt bad and so I ran out of the house. I wasn't planning to be out all night, but I just wanted to get away. It'd all gone so badly, so quickly. I'd always thought we were so happy, you know?"

Holland nodded.

"Then what happened?"

"Well," I said, looking down at my hands. I was picking at my nail polish. That looked guilty and so I stopped. "I thought he'd call me or come after me. Try to fix it. But he didn't. And I was upset. So I went to my friend's house."

"So you're saying Oliver was alive when you left the house?" Her eyes were boring into me and I could feel my face flush.

"Of course," I said. But I suddenly felt ill because I understood on a very deep level that I was being questioned over my husband's murder. My husband who was alive this time three days ago.

"And this friend, is this Tess Simmons?"

"Yes," I said.

"What time would you say you got to Tess?"

Why was she asking me this? She must have already asked Tess the exact same question. Was she performing her own little polygraph test? Assessing my ability to tell the truth?

"Around eight," I said. "Maybe eight-fifteen."

"And what time did you leave your home?" she asked.

"Around seven-ish I guess. I'm not sure."

"That's interesting. There wasn't any roadwork in the area that night, and it wasn't rush hour. That journey should have taken you thirty-five minutes. Forty-five, tops. So why did it take you so long to get there?"

"I went for a walk. I needed to think. I thought we might make up." Something twisted inside me because it was all true. I could feel my yearning for him as I stood on that bridge, the cold wind whipping my hair. How different things might have been if he *had* come after me. If I had gone back.

"Did you call Oliver that night? Try to make up?" she asked. And I knew from her expression she'd already checked his call log and knew that, no, I had not.

"No. He was the one who cheated on me. Not vice versa. I expected him to call. And when he didn't I was hurt but I didn't think for a moment he was in any danger."

"And then what happened, Charlie?" she asked, lips pursed as if to say: *Go on, tell us another lie.*

"And then the next morning I got a message from our neighbour saying the police were looking for me. So that's why I went home. To talk to you." I let out a deep breath, the memory of that morning—police cars, blue-and-white do-not-cross tape, an ambulance siren, me sobbing on that park bench—played in my mind.

"But when I got there, I just froze. I knew something big had happened because I could see the police in the window of our flat and I didn't know what to do. I panicked. And then I saw a body coming out of our flat and I knew. So I . . . I just left."

"You *knew* it was Oliver?" she asked.

I nodded. "I could see his hand and his wedding ring, and the sleeve of the navy jumper he'd had on the night before."

She made a note.

"You could see all this from where you were standing?"

"Yes," I said.

"So you were quite close?"

"Yes, I told you, I was planning on talking to you. Until I saw that. Then I got scared."

"And when you left, where did you go?" she asked.

"First I went to my ex's house—I still had a key—because I could see from his Instagram that he was away. Then later I saw he was coming home from the airport so I went to a friend's house." I paused for a moment. I needed her to remember the next bit. For it to stand out in her memory. "Her name is Brooke Shaw."

Oh, the relief to see her scribble that name down. To hear the sound of her pen pulling across paper.

"Charlie, would you say you have a temper?"

"No," I said, frowning. "I'd say like anyone I fight back when I'm terrified, but I don't have a temper."

Her eyes narrowed. I wasn't sure if she was talking about the thing that happened when I was sixteen—whether it was on record somewhere—or whether it was just a general question.

"I'm not stupid. I know how it looks. We fought. I am the beneficiary of his will. Then he turns up dead. Of course you think maybe it was me, but it wasn't. I know what happened: somebody set me up."

She looked at Kowalski and he looked back at her. They didn't believe me.

Charlie, just hold tight. They just need to read those emails.

"I think it was about something to do with his business," I said, pausing to take a breath. This might seem counter-intuitive, leading them down a path that wasn't Brooke, but when those emails came in I needed them to immediately discount me as a potential source. This—having them recall me suggesting an entirely different scenario—was the only way I could see to do that.

"Oliver had admitted that he worked with dangerous people sometimes. They even broke into our old flat and stole his computer. It was after that he wanted life insurance so, I don't know, I just made the assumption it might have something to do with that. Do you think I'm in danger?"

I waited for that new information to sink in. But she was looking closely at me now. Frowning. What was she thinking? Then her eyes were back on her notepad. She was making a note and saying: "Okay, well, we're in the process of gaining access to Oliver's work computer, so we'll make sure to look through for anything like that." But her voice came out a little too molasses for me to believe she was taking me seriously.

"You said whoever broke in took Oliver's laptop?" Her words came out slowly, like she was thinking it through as she spoke.

"Yes. That was *all* they took. It was weird. But the police said it was probably just some junkies looking for things that were easy to sell. I'm not so sure though. Oliver was so jumpy after that and insisted we move."

DCI Holland opened the folder sitting on the table in front of her and pulled out an image. It was of Oliver's bronze Ganesha. There was blood on it.

"Do you recognise this?"

The walls closed in on me as my mind re-created the scene.

Brooke holding that statue and hitting him with it. Blood. I clenched my eyes shut to stop the images, but that just made them more vivid. And then a realisation: my prints were on that.

She'd made sure of it.

She'd had me pick it up.

My underarms grew damp with sweat. The police were going to find my fingerprints on that weapon. And Brooke? Well, she'd have used gloves, wouldn't she?

All these thoughts zinged through my mind on the inside, but on the outside all I did was nod and say: "It's Oliver's." My voice came out broken.

Then came another picture.

It was a t-shirt. It was white, with the Rolling Stones' signature red lips on the front. And there was a dark stain at the bottom.

Blood.

My breath caught in my throat. Because that t-shirt was mine.

"Do you recognise this t-shirt?"

"Yes," I said. A bit confused. *Stay calm, Charlie.* But it was hard to stay calm when the other thoughts racing around my head were things like: *Brooke must have taken that when she was in the house planting that garter belt, when she decided Ganesha was a good weapon and she needed me to hold it . . . What else was coming?*

I needed them to see those emails.

And I needed that to be enough.

"Do you know where we found this?" She was talking about the t-shirt now.

"No," I said.

"We found it in a neighbour's rubbish bin, Charlie."

"I don't know why it was there."

DCI Holland smiled, a dark smile.

I glanced at Kowalski, watching me. He knew where this was going and my throat grew tight.

"Charlie, let me tell you what I think. I think we're going to find your fingerprints on that statue."

"Well it was in *my* house. I have held it. So yes, you might."

"And Oliver's blood was found on this t-shirt. And there was no forced entry. Yet the house was messed up to make it look like a burglary."

"Maybe someone had keys," I snapped.

"Well, *did* anyone else have keys to your home, Charlie?"

"I don't know. I lost my keys last week, but then they turned up. Someone could have copied them." I knew it sounded like I was grasping.

"Why would anyone do that?"

"Well, if they wanted to kill Oliver they would."

She frowned. Then came a meaningful exhale.

"Charlie, let me tell you what I think happened. Perhaps you and Oliver had a turbulent relationship. You might have been a bit scared of him. Might have bought a taser to protect yourself."

Dizziness overcame me as I wondered if she had already seen my search history at work: *How to know if your husband is cheating* and *Where to buy a taser in London*.

"And then one day you found out Oliver was cheating. You had an argument. It got out of hand. He hurt you, you scratched him and reached for your taser so he couldn't hurt you anymore. You used it, but badly, and he was still coming at you. And so you reached for the closest thing you could. That statue. You hit him and maybe you didn't intend to kill him. But when you realised he was dead you panicked. You knew you had to get out of there. And so you texted your friend Tess to tell her you were coming over and tried to make it look like a break-in." She paused here. "Except you're not really a criminal, are you, Charlie? And so you didn't know how to do it convincingly. You forgot to break a window. To leave footprints beneath it. To make sure the timelines match up. All the things that might have made us believe that story. Now you're trying so hard to cover your tracks—"

"*No!*" I yelled. The tears were coming again.

"My guess is *that* was why you went back to your flat the night after Oliver died. Because you'd forgotten something, hadn't you, Charlie? What was it? What were you worried we'd find? Why *did* you wipe his hard drive clean?"

I sat dead still, staring at her. This was new information and I had no idea why Brooke had done that. But Holland was staring back at me now, not even blinking. I was about to buckle under the pressure. I opened my mouth to speak, to tell her everything: about Brooke and the spreadsheet and the tracking device, but the moment before the sound formed, I stopped. I couldn't. It sounded bogus. Like an excuse. And I couldn't prove any of it. Not yet. Not until those emails came in.

DCI Holland had the Ganesha with my fingerprints on it, my t-shirt with Oliver's blood on it and a neighbour stating we'd had a screaming match on the night he died. And the only proof I had was out there, somewhere in London, at the bottom of a Longchamp bag.

—

3.39 PM

My holding cell looked just like the one I'd seen on Google, except the sliver of bed was covered in plastic fabric in a darker shade of blue. The floor was slate grey and had mop marks running over it, like someone had done a half-assed job. There was an opaque, barred window on the wall facing the door and a CCTV camera watching my every move from the upper corner of the room by the door. If I hadn't been on the verge of an anxiety attack when I walked in here and heard Kowalski shut the door closed behind me, I certainly would be now.

I sat down on the hard bed and all I could hear was my breathing. Why were they taking so long?

Had something gone wrong with the email?

Had Brooke's wifi bowed out right at the crucial moment when I pressed send? But then, if that were the case, they wouldn't have been there in her sent files when I went to delete them.

No, I had to believe that soon someone would knock on that door and tell me this was all a big mistake.

I lay on the bed and stared up at the ceiling, running the past week like a movie through my mind. The dating app. The wish bracelet. The police cars. The do-not-cross police tape, that tracking device . . .

Had Brooke planned on removing that tracker from my bag at some point? At Pilates perhaps? Or was she just going to leave it there? Allow me to show it to DCI Holland and claim someone was following me? Have DCI Holland put it down to some desperate attempt to shift the blame? Because I doubted Brooke still had that app on her phone.

But something else was bothering me about my interview with DCI Holland too. A lot of things were bothering me, actually, but this didn't make sense at all: why would Brooke have gone back to our flat to wipe his computer drive? I could understand why she might have wanted to look through it for evidence, to prove what he'd done to Alyssa, sure, but why delete everything?

I rolled over onto my side and stared at the blank wall.

There was nothing I could do but wait.

Episode 9

I woke up early, adrenaline pulsing through me, a white light coming in through the opaque window. But it was a relief to wake up: I'd been dreaming about that morning in the park. The smell of cut grass. Oliver's wedding ring winking in the morning sun. The wet park bench. The ambulance siren. My heart was thumping.

I'd been in the holding cell overnight so I was almost twenty-four hours into the maximum ninety-six they could hold me for. I sat up, reached for the bottle of water I'd been given before bed and took a sip. How had I ended up here?

Did I make all the wrong choices?

Should I have gone to the police straight away? But no, if I'd done that even *I* wouldn't know the truth. Brooke would still be just a girl I met in Pilates. And those emails wouldn't be out there somewhere, about to land on the *Evening Standard* editor's desk. Even if DCI Holland ignored them, I still had *that* to hold on to. The information wouldn't, couldn't, go unseen.

I wondered if they'd spoken to Josh. Holland had asked for his contact details around the same time she asked for Brooke's. That was just before the lovely Kowalski showed me to my new "room." I took another swig of water. Tess would be manic by now. Justin would be going ballistic—I hadn't replied to any of his texts. I thought about the day I went to meet him, of how I stood in line at the post office to buy a manila envelope just so he'd help me. *I wish I'd seen his face when he opened it and found my headshot and script inside . . .*

Wait.

Ba-boom. Ba-boom. Ba-boom.

Now I was thinking of another envelope.

An orange one.

From Easter.

The one we'd left with Mum and Dad.

Oliver's will.

What had Oliver said about it? "My will, and other things you'll need if something ever happens to me." Well, something *had* happened to him.

What if the emails I'd sent were not my only hope?

What if he'd left me something to find in there? He'd known he was in danger—the break-in, the life insurance, the will—I knew that now, so what if he'd left something to help me out if, you know, the worst thing happened? Proof. Maybe the emails Brooke had sent to Hornsby Private Equity, the ones her lawyer told her she needed to stop sending, were in there. Something to prove motive.

If he knew it was her, there was a possibility. It was slight, but it existed.

I needed to at least try. But how could I get to it?

One phone call.

I was supposed to get one phone call, right?

There was a buzzer by the door. Kowalski had explained it to me before the heavy metal clanged shut. When I pressed it a voice said, "Are you in need of assistance?"

"I'd like to make a phone call please," I said.

I needed to call my in-case-of-emergency person.

—

8.47 AM

I didn't know if Tess would find anything that would help me, but I knew that if anyone could do it, she could. I lay there in my cell, staring at the stark ceiling. No music. No Netflix. No view out the window. Just stale air to breathe, and my imagination to keep me company. The same series of thoughts on a continual loop.

First I thought of our phone call.

I'd waited until 8.30 am, when I knew she'd be at work and then called her there. Her mobile number was one of the only ones I had committed to memory, but Tess never picked up calls from unfamiliar numbers. And so, by calling her at the office I could at least leave a message with the receptionist and tell her where I was. It would be more reliable than hoping Tess listened to her voicemail.

But that day Tess picked up.

"Tessa Simmons," she'd said, in a very grown-up voice and my breath had caught at the sound of it.

"Tess," I started, my voice cracking, "it's me."

"Charlie?" her tone a few tones higher and frantic.

"Yeah, I'm—"

"Where are you?" she interrupted. "Are you okay?"

"I'm at Charing Cross Police Station. They're holding me for questioning."

Beat.

"*What?* Do you have a lawyer? Wait, I'll get someone from the office to come down. Vince can probably do it. I'll ask him."

"Tess. No. There's something I need you to do first."

"What's that?"

"Oliver left an envelope with Mum and Dad. He said it was his will, but I think there might be something in there. Can you go get it first?"

"Of course," she said. "Charlie, do not answer any more questions before Vince gets there. Do you understand?"

I nodded and said: "Yes."

But now I was wondering if Mum and Dad knew what had happened . . . "Can you tell them I'm okay," I said. "If they ask?"

"Okay, give me a few hours. Hold tight. And I mean it: refuse to answer any questions alone."

"Done."

And then we'd hung up.

As I was escorted back to my holding cell, I imagined her pulling up outside my childhood home in an Uber. Dad would look out the window, peering from behind a light yellow curtain, the way he always did when he heard someone pull up, and announce to Mum that it was Tess. After multiple offers of cups of tea were politely declined and Tess finally got that envelope in her hands, when she opened it and flicked through the pages, what would she find?

12.13 PM

I was halfway through a really suspect, white bread sandwich when I heard the door unbolt. Kowalski. My pulse sped up: that meant one thing. Tess was back. Or Vince had arrived. And whoever it was probably had the envelope with them. I dropped my sandwich, blinking hard. What was in the envelope?

Please be something.

"DCI Holland wanted to ask a few more questions, Charlie," he said. When I stood up I felt dizzy. I must have moved too fast or hadn't eaten enough or the last week was finally taking its toll. I leaned against the wall until it passed.

"Are you okay?" Kowalski asked.

I nodded. I just wanted this over with. I'd been preparing myself up until I finally fell asleep, getting ready to answer questions about Annabella Harth when her emails finally landed on Holland's desk.

"I'm fine," I said, following him through the open door and hearing it close satisfyingly behind us. It was good to be on this side of it. We moved down the hallway, through a couple of doors and another hallway, eventually arriving back at the same room I'd been questioned in.

DCI Holland was already sitting at the same table with a notepad and a couple of printouts on the table in front of her. Next to her lay my phone. But no Tess. No Vince. No orange envelope.

Shit.

"Take a seat," she said. I sat down across from her and Kowalski returned to his place beside her. We were back to the exact formation we'd been in the day before. She flicked the switch on the device beside her, ran through the obligatory script—day, time (12.22) and who was present—and I just sat there, thinking: *Tess told me not to talk to them without her guy, but what if they've got the emails? It'll look bad if I refuse to say anything. I just won't say anything incriminating . . .*

"Charlie," Holland began, reaching for the papers in front of her, her eyes on mine.

That was when the fear hit: *What if that's a report from their tech team? What if they've gone through my phone and know that I went back to Brooke's place? What if they've found my deleted dating app somehow, and know I was Annabella Harth? If that happens, I'll tell them I won't continue without my lawyer.*

"I trust you feel okay to continue?"

"Fine," I said, staring at my phone.

"Good, I'm glad to hear it," she said. All business. "Charlie, after we spoke yesterday, we got in touch with Brooke Shaw." I couldn't read her eyes. What had Brooke told her? *Shit, shit, shit.*

But I did my best to control my expression. "Great. Was she helpful?"

DCI Holland shifted in her chair and leaned forward.

"Have you ever heard the name Annabella Harth?"

Uh-oh. There it was.

This was either very good or very, very bad. I didn't know what those papers were in front of her. My next lie could go one of two ways. Should I stop?

"Who?" I asked, my throat tight.

"Annabella Harth," she repeated, her eyes narrowed. "Think hard, Charlie. Now's not the time to lie."

I frowned at her. "I'm not lying, not about any of it. I have no idea who she is."

The seconds lagged as I waited for the next instalment. But she wasn't talking. Neither was Kowalski. They were hoping I'd crack and fill the silence with truth. Fuck that.

I could play the silent game too.

But it was Holland who cracked first.

"We've received some information from her. Information about Oliver's death."

"Oh," I said, pausing for a moment. "Well, what did she say?"

"I'd like you to take a look at something." She slid her phone across the table and I glanced down at the screen. "Tell me what you see in these pictures?"

It was Brooke's Instagram account.

Fucking finally.

This was good. She, or someone else at the police, had followed the breadcrumbs and seen it. But even though it was good news, my stomach clenched as I stared down at Brooke's profile picture—big sunhat, staring off into the distance. The one I'd ruminated over back when I thought Oliver was cheating.

"Well," I said, frowning like I wasn't sure why she was asking

291

me. "That's Brooke." I shrugged, pointing to her face. My eyes scanned down through the other pictures, the ones with her sister.

"Wait, that's Alyssa, Oliver's ex-girlfriend." I looked up at Holland with one of the ingénue looks that always got me the role. "Wh-what's going on?"

Holland shifted in her seat. "How well did you know Brooke?"

I frowned again. "Not that well. I met her a couple of months ago, at Pilates."

"And did she ever meet Oliver?"

I paused, as if to think. "No. Why? Look, my husband is dead. Please just tell me what this Annabelle woman said."

"Annabella," she corrected me. She was watching me, frowning. Everything that had been so crystal clear just twenty-four hours before—her gleaming prime suspect with motive and lots of evidence—was now murky. I almost felt for her. It's shit when that happens. When the quicksand you've been building on gives way.

"The information she sent through implicated Brooke."

"Brooke?" I asked, sitting dead still.

"We brought her in this morning and have been questioning her." She trailed off at the end.

I was shaking my head as though I just couldn't believe it.

"Charlie, we found other concerning correspondence in Oliver's work emails. Brooke had been trying to get his company to look into . . . something."

"Into what? They'd never even bloody met," I said.

She let out a big breath. "Brooke *had* met Oliver." She spoke slowly, as though aware of the weight of her words. Of the fact that I might need time to take it all in. "She was Alyssa's sister. And—"

"*What!?*" I stared at her, trying to look a bit stunned, waiting for her to finish.

"Brooke claims that Oliver borrowed a large sum of money from her family under the guise of an investment. Did Oliver ever mention anything about that?"

"No," I said. "He wouldn't do something like that."

"And that Alyssa killed herself as a result."

"Oh," I said, guilt swelling in my veins. "That's awful."

Beat.

"Brooke confessed to killing Oliver an hour ago," Holland said.

I let the words wash over me, tears of relief burning in my eyes. To DCI Holland, I would have appeared in shock.

"I can't believe it," I said, a hot tear rolling down my cheek.

"It's a lot to take in," Holland continued, all business. "You're free to go." She stood up. "But we might need you to come in and answer some more questions."

I looked up at her. "Of course," I said.

Then she slid my phone across to me. "You can have this back."

I nodded, took it and slid it into my pocket, relief pulsing through me. They hadn't checked it; not properly at least. I mean they might have gone through my texts and emails, but they clearly hadn't delved into cross-referencing the exact time I finally left Brooke's house with her account of our morning—unless of course putting it on airplane mode and turning it off actually worked.

293

Officer Kowalski ushered me out. I followed him to the door and then down the hallway to collect my things.

—

12.43 PM

The cab pulled away from the kerb and I dialled Tess. I needed to tell her I was okay.

"Charlie?" she answered on the second ring.

"Hey," I said, "where are you?"

"I'm still in the Uber. Vince can get there in about an hour. Wait. You're calling from your mobile. Did they let you go?"

"Yes," I said. "They did."

"Well, praise fucking be," she said. I was so stressed.

My head felt hazy as I tried to focus on the buildings moving past the window outside. I was trying to find the words to tell her that it was Brooke. To tell her why. But she spoke before I had a chance.

"So you were right," she said. "There were things in that envelope."

"Really? What?"

"There's this company document for Lucamore Enterprises— remember the one I asked you about? It wasn't just Oliver who owned that, it was Justin too. And, babe, it looks like they were being very naughty boys."

"What were they doing?" I asked, my stomach filled with cement.

I expected her to say something about Alyssa. That they'd done similar things to other people. That they were essentially defrauding people out of their savings. One of those things you see on current affairs shows where everyone talks about how charming each of the perpetrators were and how they "never saw it coming." But instead she said: "They were taking some pretty large payments through that company, hon. A company that you, his wife, didn't even know existed. I'm not really sure what's going on here, but it doesn't look legit at all."

"Oh," I said, my mind recalibrating to take in this new information.

"And there's more. It looks like they were paying someone off through that company too."

"What? Who?"

"Someone called J. N. Machado."

I thought of the way Oliver's face had always turned the colour of tin every time Machado's name came up. What did he have over Oliver and Justin that would make them pay him off? Or what was he doing for them?

Then I thought back to Justin. Were these the documents he was looking for? No wonder he was so insistent. If they fell into the wrong hands, it sounded like he'd go to prison.

"Since when?" I asked. Had it started during our marriage or was it already happening when I met him? How had I slept beside Oliver for all those months and never known so much about him?

"November 2016," she said. "So a while."

I let out a small gasp and the cab driver's eyes darted to the rearview mirror, like he was worried I might puke in his cab. I caught his gaze and he quickly looked away. But all I could think about in that moment was the email from Alyssa in Brooke's inbox in that same month begging Oliver to give her parents back their money. That was dated November too.

I'd been right. Oliver hadn't lost her money in a bad investment. He hadn't lost it at all. Because he'd never invested it.

No, he needed it to pay off Machado.

But Justin was just as much a part of it as Oliver. Why hadn't Brooke targeted him too? Why just us?

"I'll be home in about an hour," Tess said, interrupting my thoughts. "We can look at it together then."

"Okay," I said, a bit dazed.

"Oh, and your mum and dad didn't know anything, hon, so I left it. But you should probably call them."

A pang of guilt. "Thanks, I will. See you soon."

And then we hung up.

—

1.27 PM

Forty minutes later I arrived at Tess's flat. My limbs felt like lead and I just wanted to go to bed.

My reflection was distorted in the metal doors of the lift. I looked a bit like those images in crazy mirrors at a fun fair. It was apt because that's exactly how I felt right at that moment. Like everything was distorted, my entire life was built on quicksand and it was hard to tell reality from illusion.

The doors closed, I pressed the number 5 for her floor, and watched as each number lit up. In that moment, I could see Oliver there, his green eyes smiling back at me from the pillow. I could still smell the ylang-ylang scent that always lingered on his skin. I still loved him. But I realised now that I never knew him. Not really. He was so many different people all at once.

The lift doors pinged and slid open. As I approached Tess's door I was thinking about how I'd have a shower and then put my-self to bed. I slid the key into the lock and the door swung open. Suddenly the little hairs on the back of my neck stood on end and my breath caught in my throat.

I stood there paralysed, taking in the chaos. Everything was everywhere. The sofa cushions had been torn apart, the stuffing removed. The contents of Tess's bookshelf and drawers were all over the floor. And through the bedroom door I could see that her closets had been emptied onto the floor. My ears roared with blood. What was happening? Tess certainly hadn't mentioned a break-in so it must have happened that morning.

What if they were still inside?

I held my breath and tiptoed back out into the hallway, closed the door quietly behind me and pressed the down button on the lift. I needed to get far away from here. Now.

How did they get in?

The lift came and I leapt inside. My hairline was damp from

sweat and I was breathing hard. The doors closed and it started to move. This was the second break-in I'd been confronted with. It was highly unlikely they were unrelated.

It couldn't have been Brooke—she was in custody.

Whoever it was knew about Tess. They knew we were close and I'd been there recently. And they knew where she lived.

And from the state of her apartment they were desperate to find something, probably the same documents they were looking for when they broke into our flat after Oliver died. The same sort of evidence they wiped from Oliver's hard drive. The same evidence that Tess had found with Oliver's will.

It had to be Justin.

Or Machado. Or both of them.

It had to be someone who was worried that Oliver had left loose ends and their little business might be exposed.

What if Tess had been there? What if they'd hurt her?

I would never have forgiven myself.

Ping.

As the elevator doors opened I pressed the big green exit button and rushed outside onto the main road. Witnesses. If anything happened, I wanted witnesses.

I pulled up my Uber app and ordered a car back to Charing Cross. Not the police station, mind you. I'm not stupid—no driver would choose to pick up *that* ride. The train station. I'd walk the final leg.

And then I called Tess to tell her not to go home.

2.33 PM

I was in DCI Holland's office, her on one side of the desk and me on the other. It was messy: papers, three coffee cups—one read: *Not my monkeys, not my circus*—and a screen that had fallen into sleep mode. The orange envelope was lying on her desk and she was working her way through its contents.

I could see her frowning down at the Lucamore company document. There were two signatures: Oliver Buchanan and Justin Langley. Next she laid three pages of transactions down in front of her, tracing through them with her pointer finger and pausing at each yellow line.

Every few lines was one highlighted in yellow.

Those were transfers to a certain Machado.

The others were suspect hefty deposits *into* the account, not out.

I knew all this because I'd had time to inspect those same documents with Tess in the waiting room.

"Hon, the scariest thing is that he left these for you to find, that he'd risk that. Like he wanted there to be some trail. Some proof of what had been going on. Something you'd only find if you opened his will. Was he scared of someone?" Tess said.

I thought back to last Easter. Oliver in that mustard jumper I'd picked out for him. The way he squeezed my hand at my parents' front door on the day we dropped off that envelope. Him promising me it would be okay, that he was there with me.

Tess was right of course: Oliver was scared of someone.

I wasn't sure if it was Justin or Machado, or both, but the only way Justin knew those documents existed, the only reason he was so keen to find them before someone else did, was because Oliver had *told* him they existed. And the only reason he'd have done that was to keep us safe.

It was a warning: if anything happens to me, you'll be going down too. I thought back to the way Oliver had always changed in Justin's presence: how he always pandered to him. His hand squeezing my shoulder, signalling to me not to make trouble. It all made so much sense now. He was scared. He was protecting me. Us.

And that made me scared too. Even more so after seeing what had happened to Tess's flat. I didn't have any evidence, but there were only two people still alive with something to lose via the contents of that envelope, so it was one, or both, of them.

"Do you know who this is?—J. N. Machado?" DCI Holland asked, her finger still on his name.

I nodded. "It's someone Oliver did business with. He used to get pretty stressed every time his name came up. Was Machado blackmailing them?"

"It's hard to say for certain," she said. "But it does appear so. And these other transactions do paint a rather damning picture of their business, Charlie. This is a lot of money to be flowing into a company that doesn't actually do anything. Especially this quickly. Do you know why Oliver would have left this for you to find?"

I thought of Tess's words. "I think he was scared and he was

300

trying to protect himself. If they knew those documents were out there somewhere and might get found if something happened to Oliver, it was less likely that they'd harm him, right?"

She looked up from the page, her hazel eyes meeting mine. She nodded.

But I wasn't there to surmise. I was there to get Justin and Machado arrested so they couldn't hurt me or Tess. That was why I'd handed that envelope over to DCI Holland and not tried to negotiate with Justin myself.

But DCI Holland was taking a really long time to make whatever call she needed to make that happen, and it was making my blood pump too fast.

"It all makes sense now, right? It was Justin or Machado who broke into our flat after Oliver died. They were searching for those," I said, nodding again at the pages in front of her.

"And *of course* they deleted his hard drive—they would have panicked when Oliver died, and wanted to delete any incriminating evidence. And Justin knew where Tess lived, how close we were, and that I'd been there recently; I told him. That explains the break-in this morning. Also, like you said, that's all clearly illegal, right?" I said, nodding to the documents in front of her. "All that money flowing in?" I swallowed hard. "When do you think you'll be able to arrest them?"

"Not yet," Holland said slowly.

As she said those words my pulse sped up further. Because that was a real problem. I'd asked Justin too many questions: Machado,

Alyssa, Lucamore. A flash of Tess's flat. What would happen to me if he told Machado; if they thought I was on the verge of piecing things together? If they thought I might find these documents and show the police?

"Well, when?" I asked.

"Investigations like these take a while to pull together," she said. "But we have Oliver's killer—that's a win, Charlie. It doesn't always go that way. It's been a good day." She gave me a small smile.

"They broke into a crime scene. And into Tess's flat this morning," I said, trying my best to appear rational. "You should have seen the place. I'm scared."

"We don't know for sure that it was Justin or this man Machado," she replied, her tone measured. But I could tell from the expression in her eye that she knew I was right. It's just that she had a procedural manual she knew she had to follow. "We will investigate."

"And what about me in the meantime? If they think I know any of this, do you really think they'll just leave me alone?"

"Has anyone ever threatened you? If they do, come straight to us."

"No," I said. But something inside me knew I was in danger. My mind scrambled for a solution; I needed something, anything, to spur her into action. "But what about what Brooke said? About her sister. Have you looked at the timeline?" I said, pointing to the list of transactions beneath her finger.

"The first payment to Machado happened in November. When did you say Alyssa lost her money?" Like I said before, I already knew the answer to this question. I'd seen the email in Brooke's in-box when it all went down.

She reached for her notepad, flipped through a few pages and then looked up at me: "November."

"Exactly. Doesn't that seem like a big bloody coincidence to you? Brooke might be telling the truth about what Oliver and Justin did to Alyssa. This might be why they took her money. And if they did something like that, shouldn't we do something about it?"

Now, please don't get me wrong, I *did* care about what happened to Alyssa, really I did, but I cared even more about what might happen to me. Or to Tess. If Oliver was scared of them, we should be too.

"We can't just rush in and arrest people, Charlie. We need something solid first."

"Then let me give that to you."

"How are you going to do that?"

I reached for the paper in front of her, the one with the yellow highlights, and took a picture.

"Charlie, what are you doing?" she asked.

Then I sent it to Justin with the text: *I think I've found what you're looking for.*

I did it before I'd really thought it through. And then we both stared at my phone as I thought, *Shit.*

A moment later my phone beeped.

Brilliant, Charlie, thanks. I need those urgently. Can you swing by my flat or should I come to you? 8?

My pulse sped up. I handed my phone to DCI Holland. "See? And now I really will be in danger if you don't help me. Now he knows I've seen this."

From the look on her face I could tell this was not in her manual.

She looked down at the screen. "That was so irresponsible!" she said, glaring at me. She looked at her watch, exhaled loudly and rushed to the door. "Wait here."

She banged the door shut behind her and, a moment later, in came another text from Justin: *???*

Fuck. What had I done?

—

5.03 PM

When DCI Holland first asked me to wear a wire, I thought I was going to be sick. I had visions of her taping something to my chest, something that could be found if Justin thought to look, something that could get me hurt.

But it's not like that in real life.

Holland was holding a device that looked just like the USB stick I'd copied all of Oliver's information onto. Except this one was black, not silver. There were no red lights flashing. No wires. Nothing to give me away. According to Holland, even if Justin suspected something and plugged it into a computer, it would just come up as an empty flash drive that required formatting.

"I'm going to put it in like this," she said, pushing the device into the front pocket of my handbag. "You don't need to do anything except try not to bump it. The mic is facing up so we'll hear everything."

I nodded and swallowed hard as she handed my bag to me. It felt hot now. Heavy. Scary.

"We'll be right outside the door. The moment we hear anything off we'll come in. Just remember, you're going over there to give him what he wants and have a chat. But you don't have to do this."

The truth was I wanted to do it. I needed to do it. I needed to know the truth about what had happened.

So that was my job.

Under the guise of dropping off the documents Justin had been looking for, I had to get him to incriminate himself. It didn't really matter what I got on him—admitting he'd broken into our flat, or Tess's flat, looking for those documents; that he'd wiped Oliver's hard drive clean; or ideally, something to do with Lucamore and Machado—just *something* DCI Holland could call him about. Something that put him in the cross hairs. I'd be safe if they knew they were being watched and it would be a breakthrough in the investigation. So it was worth the risk. But even so, my hand was trembling when I followed Holland's instructions to text him back to say: *Great, see you then. I'll come to your place.*

That was strategic: DCI Holland said he was far more likely to speak freely in his own surroundings where he felt safe. There was likely to be less ambient noise there too. Then we constructed a loose script; a way for me to steer the conversation. And I got ready to play the most important role of my life.

—

8.02 PM

Justin buzzed me into his apartment building a split second after I rang the bell. I'd only been there once before and that was when Oliver and I had just started dating. I moved towards the elevator, pressed the button and waited. My stomach was a swarm of wasps.

Ping.

The doors slid open and I pressed "8."

As I stared at my reflection in the mirrored walls, I reminded myself that I was there to strike a deal that would benefit us both. Justin was my friend.

The hallway leading to flat 817 was carpeted in a beige-green swirl, no doubt to complement the avocado shade of the walls, which were lit by a series of small circular lights. The walls were covered in abstract art that fitted the colour scheme—in fact, they looked like they had been chosen entirely for colour not content.

Tap. Tap. Tap.

Footsteps sounded from the other side of the apartment door and Justin's voice called out: "Coming." Then the gold handle moved, the door opened and there he was.

My pulse sped up.

He was wearing a light pink shirt with silver cufflinks, the top button had been undone and if he had been wearing a tie when he arrived home it was gone now. His trousers were a dark beige and matched the room beyond him. Yes, you notice *everything* when you're scared.

"Hi," I said, and he moved aside to let me pass. I could feel his eyes on me and then the sound of that heavy door shutting echoing through the room.

I took long, confident strides into the room. It was all beige, green and black, as if the same designer of the hallways had been at work here too. I remembered it from last time. And he hadn't changed a thing. It was still sparse. Empty. A single orchid sat on the big marble kitchen island. A brass fruit bowl full of oranges. A large free-standing metal lamp I wasn't sure I'd be able to lift. Those were the only potential weapons in this room if he tried to hurt me.

I took a seat on one of the sofas, resting my bag beside me.

As he poured a glass of wine for me and a Scotch for himself, I could see the twinkling lights of London through the floor-to-ceiling windows. I took care with my posture—I needed to seem perfectly at ease—as Justin came towards me, his strawberry-blond hair flopping over one light blue eye as he handed me a glass. He looked at my bag.

"Thanks." I smiled, taking a sip. Then I put my glass down on the black coffee table, zipped open my bag and pulled out the orange envelope.

"Here it all is," I said, laying the envelope beside me.

"That's great," Justin said, reaching out his hand in a well-give-it-to-me-then gesture. But there was something in his eyes. Something questioning. Like he was trying to figure out if I knew what it was I was handing over. The relevance. Was I a threat?

I stuck to the script, picked up the envelope and handed it to him. He opened it and looked inside.

"Thanks, Charlie," he said. "This is so helpful."

I nodded and he sat down on the chair opposite me, pulling out the documents and leafing through them. The sound of flicking pages filled the room.

Beat.

It was my line. I knew what it was. But I had stage fright: dry mouth, tight throat, wild heart. But I needed to say it. *Say it, Charlie.*

"I know what those are," I said.

His eyes moved up. Quickly. Snake-like. Now they were on mine.

"Yes, they're to do with a company we have interests in," he said. "Oliver should never have taken this information out of the office. But you know Ollie, he always *was* a bit of a cowboy."

I swallowed and nodded.

"Justin, I know it's not normal to pay those sorts of sums to a man like Machado. I know he was blackmailing you." Smile. "He still is."

A small frown. Barely discernible. If I hadn't known what was most likely taking place in his mind I might have missed it.

"Oh god, Charlie, do we have to go through all this nonsense again? I already told you the other day—" His voice took on that authoritative tone it did sometimes. But I cut him off anyway.

"I *know*, Justin."

A silence hung in the room. We'd both stopped breathing.

"You know *what*, precisely?"

I let out a big sigh. Like I was about to say something he should already have guessed. "Oliver told me a lot more than you think he did. So you really don't need to lie to me. Like I *know* it was you who broke into our place and deleted all his files. I also know *why*. That's not exactly the only damning evidence out there, is it?" I said, nodding to the envelope in his hands.

"I did no such thing!" he said, his voice rising an octave with indignation.

"Oh really?" I laughed contemptuously like he was a silly, silly boy. I knew that would rile him.

"Justin, I *know* it was you because I know what needed deleting." I stopped laughing, my face serious. "Of course, you could have just asked me to do it. It's not like I have anything to be gained by anyone finding out what Ollie was doing. I do want an inheritance, you know. And I would have done it properly." Quick. Confident. I needed to act like I had every base covered.

"What do you mean?"

"I wouldn't have missed anything." Shrug.

Beat.

He was watching me. Wary.

"I *didn't* miss anything."

There it was. Our confession.

I raised my eyebrows in a you-are-dead-wrong expression. "Maybe not on that computer."

"Are there other copies somewhere? Is that what you're saying?"

I paused for dramatic effect here, giving a little smile. "I don't know, is that what I'm saying?" There's a confidence that comes with knowing the police are right there, that they have your back. It'll make you cocky.

He exhaled loudly. "It is vital that I know this." He spoke through his teeth like I was trying his patience. "Are. There. Copies?"

I raised my eyebrows. Took my time. I needed to annoy him so he was distracted and off his guard. So he said things he'd regret. "Yes, but that doesn't need to be a problem for you. Nobody is going to find them—unless I hand them over."

A silence clung to the air. I glanced again at my bag. At the recorder.

"Do you want something from me?" he asked, taking a sip of his Scotch.

"That I do."

He was watching me with a newfound respect and if I hadn't known better I might have been flattered. "Well, spit it out. What is it?"

"Money."

"How much?"

"A lot."

"How much, Charlie?" he snapped.

"Well, you need to understand that I know more than about Machado. I also know about Alyssa. About what happened there. And that drives the price up."

The air was dead with silence and he was watching me closely now. This had deviated far, far away from what he had expected.

"Oliver told me," I continued, answering his unspoken question. "Pretty low, Justin. Not the sort of thing you'd want coming out, is it?"

His gaze snapped back to mine. "How much do you want, Charlie?"

Surely that was a confession?

I let a moment pass.

"Five hundred thousand."

His eyebrows raised. "Wow. Starting high." His expression was almost impressed.

"Oh please, Justin, I've seen what's in that envelope. I know you can afford it."

Beat.

"Okay," he replied.

I glanced at my open bag: were they hearing all this?

"And then another one hundred thousand every year after that."

His eyes grew wide. "Jesus, have you been getting tips from Machado?"

There it was: strike two. I could leave now. I had what I came for. But I was good at this. And I knew DCI Holland was out there listening. I knew I was safe. And I was so close to getting something that might truly screw him over. So instead of leaving right then, I took a chance. "Can I ask you something, Justin?"

"Do I have a choice?" he replied, downing his Scotch.

I gave a small smile. "*Why* is he blackmailing you?"

His eyes narrowed. He put his glass down on the coffee table. "I thought you said Oliver told you?"

Shit.

"I said he told me more than you realised," I said. Calm. "I said I knew what was in that envelope. And . . . I may have done some extra snooping." I smiled and crinkled my nose. "But that doesn't mean I know *everything*. I think I can guess though. But explain to me how these things play out in the real world," I said, crossing my legs and leaning forward slightly.

He watched me, cautious. I could almost see the two sides of him fighting it out behind his eyes: the macho know-it-all who wanted to share how clever he was and his instinct for self-preservation.

"How do I know you won't take the money and blow the whistle anyway?"

Ba-boom. Ba-boom. Ba-boom.

"Because I'm not sure I'd be safe if I did that," I said. Truth.

"That's a fair assessment, Charlie. Best not to forget it." His eyes bored into me, but his tone was matter-of-fact. "All you need to know is Machado was a rookie error, but he's here to stay, unfortunately. Still, it's not like he hasn't been useful."

"Yes, but I'm curious, what actually *happened* to cause that error?" I asked. "It's not like you to fuck up, Justin."

I watched his eyes flash. There we go—his ego has been ignited.

"Simple. We tried to extort money from him and it went wrong." He drummed his fingers on the side of his chair. "Honestly, it was a stupid mistake, but it was right at the beginning of our operation. I would never make a mistake like that now."

"If you were extorting money from him, why are you the one doing the paying?" I asked. And I was surprised by how willing he was to tell me; that right there should have been my cue to run.

"Well, in simple terms," he started, dumbing things down for me as per usual. "The deal was that if he paid us what we asked for into our offshore business account, we'd provide fabricated financials to Hornsby Equity and they'd invest in his shoddy company with no issues, the same way we have for many other happy customers since then. But bloody Machado recorded us, didn't he?" He gave a small smile and my blood sped up. "You need to be careful who you trust in this world."

I thought of the recording device in my bag. What if Justin searched it? If he figured out what was going on? How long would it take the police to get in here?

"So the fucker blackmailed us," Justin continued. "*That's* why we've been paying him. You see, we aren't bad people, Charlie. But it was right at the beginning and we needed to get the money from somewhere to pay Machado off, otherwise he would have blown the

313

whistle and we would have lost everything. Neither of us would have come back from that."

"So you made up an investment scheme and Alyssa just gave you her money? Why her? And how could she be so stupid?" I asked. My tone was intentionally acidic and it made me cringe to hear my voice say the words. But I needed him to believe I was entirely on his side for him to open up.

"She wasn't stupid," he said. It was the first nice thing I'd ever heard him say about her. It caught me off guard. Maybe he *did* have some remorse. "We were just smarter. And she trusted Oliver. He put the deal to her." And there he was: the Justin I so loathed. "We were desperate and we knew her family had the money to invest. So Oliver gave her fabricated financials and convinced her it was a sure thing. Anyone would have fallen for it. But that was our business. There's always collateral damage with these things. And it's not like we had a choice. We had a deadline and we didn't have enough in the pot back then."

He paused for a moment. "And, it wasn't all bad. You enjoyed the fruits of Oliver's labour, didn't you?"

I swallowed hard. What was I doing? I'd got what I came here for, now I wanted to leave.

"When will you get it to me?" I asked.

"When will I get the copies of Oliver's files?"

"I can get them to you tomorrow."

"Where are they? You didn't leave them lying around, did you?"

"Of course not," I said. DCI Holland and I had already

constructed this lie together. "They're in a safety deposit box at the bank. Old school."

"Good," he said, standing up and coming over to sit down beside me on the sofa. I didn't like having him that close to me. I could feel the heat pulsing off his skin. His breath reeked of Scotch and his skin of some sort of patchouli cologne. I needed to leave. I stood up.

"Where are you going?" he asked, grabbing onto my wrist. It wasn't a violent grab, but there was something in his eyes, something I instinctively knew was bad.

"I'm meeting a friend," I said with a small smile. A stiff, toothless, fake smile. I expected him to let go then. But he didn't. He pulled hard. My breath caught and suddenly I was being pulled back onto the sofa. I was tumbling. Burning my knees on the carpet. Bumping my chin. My vision went white and his hands reached for my throat. His thumbs were on my windpipe and all I was thinking was: *Where the fuck are the police?* But maybe they couldn't hear anything bad was happening. I hadn't screamed. It'd all happened so fast. I reached for my glass of wine, I could hit him with that, but I couldn't get to it. I tried to bang the recording device. I needed them to know something was wrong. I couldn't breathe. I gasped for breath. My arms thrashed around as both his hands tightened around my neck.

They weren't coming. I was all alone. I reached blindly again for my bag, pulled at the handle and it fell down onto the floor beside me. That was when I remembered. My audition. My hairspray. I reached inside, pulled it out, feeling desperately for the direction of the nozzle and sprayed it into Justin's eyes.

"*Fuck!*" he yelled, pulling back.

I gasped for air. I was heaving. As I tried to push myself up from the floor he was fumbling towards me again, his hands trying to clean out his eyes. This was when I tried to scream. But he'd done something to my voice box with his hands and nothing came out. It was a nightmare. And he was crawling towards me now.

Standing up.

He could see.

He was moving, lurching towards me.

I didn't really think, it was instinct, years of planning a defence strategy, of looking for weapons and paying attention to exits. I reached for the lamp, which was luckily lighter than it looked, and swung it at him. It hit him on the side of the head and he fell.

Ba-boom.

Then he was lying there, blood pooling by his head. So much blood. It was just me and him and the lamp in my hands. All I could hear was my breath: short and sharp. And I had this moment: I could hit him again. I could make sure he was dead. Then I wouldn't need to be scared anymore. I held my breath. I went to swing.

And then I didn't.

Instead I dropped the lamp, a metallic clang bounced off the walls, and then I just stood there. Watching him for movement. Waiting for the police to finally come. To help me. And the blood, it just kept coming. I was watching it, dazed, bile rising in my throat, shaking with adrenaline, when the police finally rushed in.

In my memory of that night, I don't hear them enter. One moment I was standing there staring at Justin, and the next there were hands on my arms, holding me up. Only then came the noise. The dizziness.

Three policemen were gathered around Justin. One was putting handcuffs on him. One was yelling for someone to call an ambulance. And then a blanket was put around my shoulders by the third one and I was taken back out into the beige-green and avocado hallway. Then out into the summer night air.

It was the next morning in bed that I first read the newspaper's version of the story. I was back at Tess's flat by then and she was in the shower.

The headline read: OH, THE TANGLED WEB WE WEAVE.

Why the newspapers always try to wax poetic is beyond me.

Below the headline were two pictures.

The picture of Brooke was terrible—she looked the epitome of evil—but the one of Justin annoyingly good. That right there exemplifies all that is unjust in the world.

And the article read:

Brooke Shaw (pictured above left) was charged yesterday with the murder of Oliver Buchanan last Sunday night. Mr Buchanan was killed in his home. It is believed Ms Shaw had been stalking both Mr Buchanan and his wife for months, planning the attack . . .

My eyes scanned down for the bit about Justin.

Justin Langley (pictured above right), Mr Buchanan's business partner, has been arrested. He is currently in critical condition in hospital. No further details are available as to the circumstances of his arrest.

That's what a good lawyer will buy you: privacy.

I let out a sigh and put my phone down. I was scared to get out of bed. What else might be waiting for me?

The bathroom door opened and Tess emerged wrapped in a blue dressing gown, a cloud of steam behind her.

"Hey." She smiled at me.

"Hey," was all I could manage. I stared up at the crack in Tess's ceiling, the same one I'd been staring at the morning I found out Oliver was dead. And as I lay there, I couldn't quite believe that all that had happened was real.

Tess went through to the kitchen and flicked on the kettle: "Coffee?"

"Thanks," I called back. And I remember that it struck me how even after everything, some things stayed the same. Tess was still making coffee. Grace would be flipping through the papers at Boulevard later that morning. All the most mundane details of everyday life remained the same.

But other things were not the same and every time I allowed my mind to drift to things like the timbre of Oliver's voice, hot tears would roll down my cheeks.

The kettle whistled in the distance and I twisted my head to glance outside: blue skies. Blue. Fucking. Skies. A moment later I could smell coffee and Tess was coming into the bedroom and putting a cup on the bedside table.

"Thanks," I said. Tess sat down on the bed beside me, blowing on her coffee, watching me. I clenched my eyes shut and then the sobs I'd held inside the night before started.

"Oh, hon," she said, putting down her cup as she lay down beside me. "It's okay," she soothed, stroking my arm as the whole room filled with my guttural, ugly sobs. The kind that wouldn't make it to film. He was gone and he was never coming back.

"I know it doesn't feel like it, but it will be okay. Eventually."

I nodded and sniffed. Because she was right, it *didn't* feel like it. And it wouldn't for a long time.

—

The first few weeks were inky black. Twenty-four hours lasted ten times as long as usual. Every time I saw "DCI Holland" flash up on my phone screen, my entire body would clench as I readied myself to learn something else about Oliver I didn't want to know.

It was two weeks after it all happened when she told me Justin was out of the hospital. He'd been charged with tampering with evidence and assault.

The next time she called was to tell me Brooke's trial had been set. I had to go—she had murdered my husband. But how could I look at her, at her parents, knowing they were victims in a way too?

But I did go. And I listened. And I wept.

The more extensive charges against Justin took a lot longer to substantiate—though they were helped along at least in part by the silver hard drive Brooke had taken from me and since relinquished. Still, the truth of that situation was worth the wait. It was like watching a true crime documentary unfolding before me.

It was Machado who cracked first. He was eager to cut a deal. And so he provided the police with the audio file he had of Justin and Oliver trying to extort money from him in the first place. Them telling him the deal: you pay us, we'll get Hornsby Private Equity to invest in you.

That was what Lucamore was for, you see: collecting payments like this from a multitude of companies. Machado was their only real expense and had become a mandatory partner. But not an entirely useless one; not for Justin at least.

Because then Machado confessed to organising to have Alyssa killed, on Justin's order.

Alyssa had been threatening legal action, and Justin decided it was the only way to keep her quiet and preserve their thriving "business interests."

He told the police that Oliver had met with Machado privately to make sure Justin wasn't going to do anything rash, but by then it was too late. In Machado's words, "Justin said it needed to be done."

So yes, Alyssa *had* lapsed into a depression. She *had* suffered terribly. But she *hadn't*, it turned out, killed herself.

I thought back to the tangible sadness that had clung to Oliver for those few weeks after I followed him to the Mandarin Oriental hotel. Now it made sense: he knew what had happened to Alyssa. He was mourning. It had nothing to do with me.

But he'd also discovered what Justin and Machado were capable of. Especially Justin.

So when Brooke started doing things like breaking into the flat and stealing his computer, he took out life insurance. But when she started drawing attention to him and Justin by emailing Hornsby

Private Equity, Oliver got scared. He couldn't afford to be seen as a liability by Justin because he'd seen how that played out. And so he took precautions.

He left that damning evidence with his will in a place he knew Justin would never find it. And then he told Justin it existed. It seemed like a clever way to stay safe—from one sort of danger, at least.

Of course when Oliver died, Justin was desperate to find it. Hence his messages to me and the break-ins.

I wondered for a long time why Brooke had targeted us and not Justin, and the answer to that finally came during Brooke's trial. She had no idea Justin was involved. Nada. He'd kept himself at a safe distance. Oliver had presented the investment opportunity as a secret; something Justin didn't know about. My money says that was Justin's suggestion, as he knew Alyssa would trust Oliver implicitly. So when Brooke went looking for the culprit, her sights landed on Oliver, on me—on us—not on the puppeteer himself.

And so, when Justin was sentenced, a huge wave of relief came over me.

But with Brooke it was different. I cried. To anyone looking on they would seem like tears of relief, but the truth was more complicated. Because, even though she had murdered Oliver, I understood that, as much as she had hated me, and tried to frame me, Brooke was a victim too; she was tired of feeling helpless. I knew what that was. And when I thought of that moment standing over Justin, of how my arm twitched and I almost swung again, I understood her in a way that made me question myself.

So, no, recovery wasn't going to be easy. During those first few months, I spent a lot of time staring at the wall, smoking Marlboro Lights, unsure I'd ever get through it.

But here's the thing with life: You have to get through it. There's no choice. Eventually, even in real life, the heroine *has* to win out in the end.

And all that happened almost a year and a half ago.

I still think of Oliver every night before I go to sleep. I don't think of the man who betrayed Alyssa the way he did. I think of the Oliver I knew him to be, the one who tied that wish bracelet around my wrist, the one who made me feel safe. My stomach still turns at the thought of Justin. And I still wish more than anything that things had gone differently for Brooke. That she'd chosen differently at that final moment. But, here's the thing: I understand why she didn't.

So I intend to treat her character kindly. Justin . . . less so.

Because there is one good thing that came out of all of this.

It was about five months after everything happened—Justin and Brooke were still making appearances in the paper and London was twinkling with Christmas lights, the airwaves filled with "Rudolph the Red-Nosed Reindeer" by then. It was around 3.30 in the afternoon and getting dark, and I was fiddling with the tree in our window display and trying to make a set of fairy lights behave. Grace was over at her desk sipping tea and flipping through the paper. She'd just told me some news about the Royals and I was thinking about Tess. I was meeting her that night for a drink. She and Zach, the guy she met that night at the art gallery, are all #couplegoals now. But at the time it was still relatively new and ill-defined and I was wondering how long it would last. That's when the call came in.

It was *my* phone that was ringing.

I turned my head to see it flashing white from my desk.

I put down the wooden rocking horse ornament I was about to place on the tree and fumbled out of the window display towards it. It was probably DCI Holland.

But it wasn't. The name flashing back from the screen was: *Clarence.*

I picked it up. "Hello?" I hadn't heard much from Clarence since the last audition that went pear-shaped and I hadn't had the energy to chase him.

"Darling," he said, "I have news."

I thought it would be about an audition. I should have learned I couldn't predict what was coming next by then.

Because Netflix had been in touch. They wanted to make a series based on my story. They wanted me to consult.

And so began negotiations: Clarence and I insisted on me being an executive producer, so that's what I am. I mean, I needed something good to do with all that insurance and inheritance money paid out after Oliver's death. It was all too sad otherwise.

If you want to watch it, it's going to be called *The Strangers We Know*.

So my acting career might have never taken off, but this just might give me a sense of purpose, a reason to have gone through everything I have. A way to bring someone else hope that no matter how bad things get, or how fucked up they feel inside, things can always get better. I'm going to tell this story exactly as it happened (minus, of course, the bit about breaking into Brooke's place and using Annabella Harth's email address to tip off the police. I'm pretty sure that was illegal, so that bit I'll claim as fictionalisation . . . *Shhh*). But aside from that, I'm not going to try to portray myself as anything other than what I am. There will be no token-blonde wife here. Just me. Still standing. And coming soon to a Netflix screen (and maybe a dating app) near you.

So yes, I stand by what I said at the beginning of this story. We like to believe we're in control of our lives; that if we buy insurance, think positive thoughts and pay our bills, we'll be safe. Everything will be okay. But the truth is that sometimes it's not okay. Sometimes all it takes is one plot twist to realise nobody is who you think they are and everything you know to be true is actually false.

But here's what I didn't say, what I myself am proof of: sometimes the converse is also true. If we hold on long enough, hard enough, and refuse to give up, every now and then those plot twists . . . well, they go the other way too.

Acknowledgements

Thank you to my publisher, Fiona Henderson, not only for publishing me and having faith in me, but for all our creative problem-solving chats. To Dan Ruffino, for always making me feel like part of the Simon & Schuster Australia family. To my editors, Deonie Fiford, Siobhan Cantrill and Michelle Swainson, for your attention to detail and general brilliance. To Nita Pronovost and Adrienne Kerr—thank you for bringing my work to Canada! To Rob Sternitzky, for your eagle eye. And to Mollie Glick, my agent, thank you for always being in my corner.

Thank you to the sales team for your tireless work, enthusiasm and support, to Tina Quinn and Jamie Criswell in Marketing for shouting about me from the rooftops, and to all the bookstagrammers, bloggers, booksellers, foreign publishers and press who got behind me and my work. Without all of you, nobody would even know my books existed. Thank you!

To my parents, sister and closest friends for picking me up when things were impossibly hard and for never pulling me back down when they weren't. To all the friends who've patiently answered intricate midnight text message questions while I was still trying to figure out the plot. And to Ben Evans for your thoughts on the earliest of drafts and your assurances that I could, in fact, do this.

Finally, to Life: for the plot twists I never see coming. Thank you for keeping things exciting . . .

About the Author

Pip Drysdale is a bestselling author, musician, and actor. She grew up in Africa, Canada, and Australia, became an adult in New York and London, and lives on a steady diet of coffee, dreams, and literature. She has written four bestselling novels including *The Paris Affair* and *The Next Girl*. Her debut, *The Sunday Girl*, has been published in five countries. *The Strangers We Know* was shortlisted for the Ned Kelly Award and is being developed for television.

To find out more about Pip head to:

pipdrysdale.com

Facebook.com/pipdrysdale

Instagram @pipdrysdale

Turn the page for a preview of

Pip Drysdale's

THE PARIS AFFAIR

Chapitre un

I met Thomas three days ago in the laundromat. Romantic, I know. I was bored, I saw him checking me out, I liked the look of him, and so I asked him a question in my broken, shitty French. But he's not French. He's British. He has big, rough fingers, and right now those fingers are interlaced with mine.

We're lying in his bed, on the border of the 7th arrondissement and the air smells of candle wax and his cologne. My gaze is on an oil painting circa 1750: a man in a high, frilly neckline. He has no chin and a stern expression on his face. It's valuable. I know quite a lot about art, so I can tell these things from the subject, the craquelure and the grandiose gold frame. But even without all that, I could guess. Nobody keeps an ugly painting like that unless money is involved.

"My parents are in town this weekend," I whisper, my eyes now on our clasped hands.

"Already?" he says. "That's nice."

By "already" he's referring to the fact that I only moved to Paris five weeks ago.

I look over my shoulder at him, my blonde hair catching the light. He has blond hair too, but his is caramel and has a deep side part. It's the exact same colour as the tan on his forearms that hasn't faded from the summer yet. His eyes are that kind of brown that flecks orange in the right sort of light, his eyelashes are long and pale at the tips, and his body is lean and healthy looking.

"Yeah, they want to meet you," I say with a small, coy smile. And then I watch for his reaction.

Is that a minute clench of the jaw I see? A bob of the Adam's apple? The usual signs of panic? He's wondering how I went from cool girl to stage-five clinger so quickly. Now he's thinking, *It's the sex. That's what did it to her. The sex was clearly* that *good.*

I let a moment pass. Let the anxiety settle in nicely.

"You don't have to," I say, breaking eye contact and looking back at the man on the wall. Guy on the wall does not approve of the stunt I'm pulling at all. He can see straight through my little game. But guy on the wall was from another era. He wouldn't understand. "I just know Mum would love to meet you," I add. "She thinks you're super handsome."

His muscles tense up. I can almost feel his heartbeat accelerate. I swear to god the heat pulsing off him under the covers just went up a couple of degrees.

"What? How does she know what I look like?"

"I sent her a photo. Why?"

Now Thomas is thinking, *Shit, it's only been three days and her mother already has a photograph of me? Wow. I'm the man. The MAN. But I need to escape. ESCAPE.*

This is the exact reaction I'm hoping for.

Because he needs to think us ending things is a good thing. That it's his idea. Things get messy when a man's ego gets hurt.

"I'd like to." His voice comes out a pitch or two higher now. "But I have plans this weekend."

Thomas is fibbing. He *doesn't* have plans. I know this because we spoke about perhaps seeing each other on Saturday night or Sunday afternoon via text this morning and his exact words were: "I'm all yours this weekend. Wide open." That was when I knew I had to end things. That, and he liked three of my Instagram pictures in a row.

But I expect now that he's told the lie, now that those syllables are hanging in the air, that text is floating back to him. He's thinking, *Shit, shit, shit.*

Poor Thomas.

This is why dating is stressful.

This is why I avoid it.

Well, one of the reasons.

I pull away and sit up. The air is cool on my skin. Goosebumps form as I look around for my clothes. They're lying in a pile on the floor by the bed, right by the condom wrapper. I loop my arms through my bra straps and fasten it behind my back as I scan the titles on his bookshelf. They're mainly photography books—Henri Cartier-Bresson, Man Ray, Robert Doisneau—and a couple on positivity-slash-manifestation. I pull my white T-shirt over my head and can feel his eyes on me as I stand up, reach for my short black skirt and put it on.

"Are you leaving?" he asks. And there's an edge to his voice but I can't tell if it's panic or relief and I'm intentionally not looking at him so I can't read his expression.

"Yes," I say as I do up my boots. *Ziiippp.* The sound echoes in the silence between us.

"Why?" he asks. Small.

I turn to face him and try to match the sour expression of the man in the ugly, expensive painting. "This isn't going to work," I say.

My bag and jacket are lying on the brown leather sofa. I move over to it, pick them up and head for the door. And without even saying goodbye I open it, move out into the hallway and let it bang behind me.

I rush down the three flights of stairs—the same wooden staircase I came up just two hours ago—as quickly as I can. I pull open the security door and head out into the mauve dusk light, go right, past the red and white lights of a *tabac* and disappear around the corner.

And that, ladies and gentlemen, is how it's done. That's how you lose a guy in less than three minutes.

~

There's a main road ahead of me and as I walk towards the hum of traffic, a rubber band flicks something deep within my chest.

Because I'm not some psychopath (I know this for certain because I've done an online quiz). I don't fuck with people's feelings for fun. And I liked Thomas; really, I did.

Which is precisely why I needed to pull my bunny-boiler routine now, before things went any further. Because I could tell from the way he looked at me, from how he held my hand so tight after sex, that if I didn't do something soon he'd get attached. And he needs to find a normal girl who'll want normal things. Someone who listens to "How to keep your man" podcasts and doesn't sabotage things the moment a guy wants more than a casual hook-up. Someone looking for a white dress, a set of his-and-hers towels, a dum-dum-da-dum-dum and a couple of offspring.

And that's not me.

Not anymore.

And not just because I tried love once and it didn't do what it said on the box, not just because I'm pretty sure the whole thing is bullshit. But because every time I open the newspaper a new continent is on fire, World War III is about to erupt, a big corporation is screwing over the vulnerable or some expert or another is talking about how sooner or later water will cost more than gold. It's depressing. So, what? I'm supposed to ignore all that, pretend that Orwell isn't the new Nostradamus, couple up, invest in white goods, pop out a baby and then leave it here in this shitstorm?

No thanks.

I prefer my life clean. Simple. My weekends free to write.

So this is best for both of us.

I look around as I weave between taxis, motorcycles and bicycles and cross the street. There's an H&M sign glowing in the distance, lots of cursive, neon restaurant signage, one of those bottle-green Parisian newsstands with postcards on racks, and a homeless man sleeping beneath a pile of cloth in a doorway across from it. I get to the other side and am about to walk the short distance home when "Hot in Herre" starts playing from my handbag. That's Camilla's ringtone—she's my best friend. Who am I kidding? Camilla is my *only* friend but that's entirely by choice; I don't really like that many people. They're fake and try to make me fake too and it's tiring pretending I don't see it.

I reach for my phone and move out of the pedestrian traffic, past the rows of postcards into the newsstand to talk.

"Hey sexy," I say, pushing a finger into my free ear so I can hear her beyond the hum of traffic and chatter of pedestrians. I can still smell Thomas's cologne on my fingertips and I have a flash of memory. His breath on my ear. Goosebumps.

"So, I have news," she says in a sing-song happy voice.

"You got the job?" I ask, hopeful. She's still back in London, works in corporate communications at an investment bank, hates her boss, hates her job, and has been waiting for word on a new one just like it for weeks.

"No. But almost as good," she replies. "I think I saw my soulmate tonight."

~

didn't believe in it, but this was it, he was going to propose. Everything was finally working out.

His exact words were: "Harper, you know what John Lennon said about how life is what happens to you when you're busy making other plans? Well, that's what happened to me, baby. You were my plan. *She* just happened. Don't be angry."

But I *was* angry.

And not just because he was leaving me for Melody, his keyboardist. I'd given up on my own dreams in favour of his, I'd lost eight years of my life—that's 70,128 hours, I checked—and here I was with no degree, no writing career, a credit card debt (independent tours are expensive, you know), a job in an office that I hated, and no idea who the hell I was anymore.

It took a long time for me to realise that was the day I was born.

~

"Where did you meet him?" I ask Camilla, scanning the headlines of the newspapers laid out in front of me: last night the Paris police shot dead a man in a park after a stabbing rampage, the mayor is coming under scrutiny for something I can't quite understand, and *Le Monde*'s headline translates as "No Justice for Matilde Beaumont?" She's been in the papers a lot over the last couple of weeks, so her picture looks almost familiar now as it smiles back at me: young, blonde, pretty. She could have been cast as Laura Palmer in

Twin Peaks. And as I scan her features I can't help but wonder how it happened. How does a normal girl like her end up on the front page of the newspaper?

"In the elevator at work," Camilla says, breaking my chain of thought.

"Well, what's his name? Send me his Instagram profile," I say, still staring at Matilde's picture. "I'll vet him for you."

"Oh I didn't actually talk to him," she says. "But he looks just like the sketch."

Six months ago, Camilla paid some guy on Etsy to draw a picture of her "soulmate." She provided her full name, her date of birth and her address. She says he needed that information to tap into her aura and she has been convinced ever since that she can use that sketch to find her other half. I, on the other hand, have been convinced that it's some sort of elaborate identity theft scam. The jury is still out as to which of us is correct, but that right there tells you everything you need to know about us, our respective life philosophies and the vital balancing role we play in each other's lives.

My phone beeps with a text.

"Hang on, Mills." I pull the phone away from my ear and squint down at the message.

Urgent! Need you to cover an exhibition tomorrow night at Le Voltage. 7 pm. Brand new series. Due Friday 10 am. Make sure you network! H.

That H stands for Hyacinth, my new boss. This new job is the reason I moved to Paris. I put the phone back to my ear. "Can I call you back later? I've just got to deal with a work thing."

"Okay, sure. Big love."

And then we hang up and I stand there rereading Hyacinth's message. An exhibition tomorrow night. Due Friday.

Shit.

Because tomorrow is already Thursday.

That doesn't leave me much time to write something impressive. And it *needs* to be impressive. Uber-impressive. Because this will be only my third story for *The Paris Observer*. My first was a review of a gypsy-jazz band. I thought my piece was amazing but it only got a depressing twelve likes and two shares. And my second, a walking tour of Paris's street art, is still on Hyacinth's desk awaiting the "constructive notes" she told me were coming. Mine's an entry-level position and they're easing me in slowly, but if I don't hit it out of the park soon, Hyacinth is going to start wondering why the hell she hired me. And I can't afford to screw this up. I've worked too hard to get here.

Because after Harrison left me, let's just say things got a lot worse before they got better. It didn't matter what I drank, who I fucked or what colour I dyed my hair, every time my lungs moved they hit my newly returned and wounded heart. It wasn't so much losing Harrison that haunted me; it was losing myself. I'd let this happen to me. I'd ignored everything I'd seen happen to my mother and let him in anyway. And he'd done exactly what I was scared of: taken what he could get from me and left.

In short, I'd betrayed myself.

And then, one very ordinary day that wasn't marked by anything I can recall now, I was sitting at my desk, pretending to put together a pamphlet for work, when something truly miraculous happened.

I started to write instead.

I hadn't written anything other than marketing copy in eight long years. But as I typed out the first line—*Why I hate John Lennon*—a light flicked on inside of me. And I knew: this was it. This was how I could make things right. Yes, I had given up my own dreams in favour of his, but I was only twenty-eight and I could still become a writer. And so every night that's what I did: I wrote. I wrote rave reviews about the music Harrison hated. I wrote about the art I now knew so much about thanks to his tours. I wrote about fitness trends, movies, intermittent fasting, music, sex, mascara and had a recurring micro-column inspired by my love of true crime podcasts called: "How not to get murdered." I even wrote about tax time once. Basically, I'd write about anything and everything as long as it added to my portfolio and took me one step closer to my dreams. And I did it largely for free.

Then one day, after about two years of that, Camilla sent me an advert for a journalism job in Paris with the note: "What's the worst that can happen?" It asked for one year of fulltime experience and a portfolio. I only had the latter, but I applied anyway.

There was a call, a Skype interview, a Eurostar trip, an offer and now we're in October and here I am.

They pay me a (meagre) salary and I can put "Journalist" on forms beside: "Occupation."

Yes, as of three weeks ago, Harper Brown (that's me) officially works for *The Paris Observer* online magazine. It's *so* official that my voicemail now says: "Hi, you've called Harper Brown at *The Paris Observer*. Leave a message and I'll get right back to you." I'm their newest art and culture writer. That makes two of us now: me and glum Wesley.

I mean, no, I'm not writing hard-hitting pieces that end human trafficking or expose white collar crimes, but it's a cool job in a cool area—Bastille—and I'm thrilled to have it. It's a stepping stone to my dreams. Which is why it really matters that everything I submit to Hyacinth is impressive. So that, one day, when an opportunity in news comes up she'll think of me. But how the hell am I supposed to put together something "impressive" between Thursday night and Friday at 10 am?

Unless . . .

There's a small fridge full of Evian and soft drinks in front of me, and I check my reflection in the glass: dark roots that fade into crème blonde at the ends and eyes that are either green or hazel depending on the weather. But right now, those eyes are sex-smudged with mascara. *Shit.* I use my fingers to try to wipe them clean.

Because I was planning on going home right now, but we all know what John Lennon said about life and plans . . .